W9-ACJ-878

Fay Weldon

was born in England and raised in New Zealand. She took degrees in Economics and Psychology at the University of St Andrews in Scotland and after a decade of odd jobs and hard times began writing fiction. She is now well known as novelist, screenwriter and cultural journalist. Her novels include *The Life and Loves of a She-Devil* (a major movie starring Meryl Streep and Roseanne Barr), *Puffball*, *The Cloning of Joanna May*, *Affliction* and *Worst Fears*. *Big Women*, a dramatised history of feminism, was screen by Channel 4, and she has several collections of short stories to her name: her latest being *A Hard Time To Be a Father*. *Rhode Island Blues* is her new novel. Fay Weldon lives in London.

Also by Fay Weldon

Fiction

The Fat Woman's Joke
Down Among the Women
Female Friends
Remember Me
Little Sisters
Praxis
Puffball
The President's Child
The Life and Loves of a She-Devil
The Shrapnel Academy
The Heart of the Country
The Hearts and Lives of Men
The Rules of Life
Leader of the Band
The Cloning of Joanna May
Darcy's Utopia
Growing Rich
Life Force
Affliction
Splitting
Worst Fears
Big Women
Rhode Island Blues

Children's Books

Wolf the Mechanical Dog
Party Puddle
Nobody Likes Me

Short Story Collections

Watching Me, Watching You
Polaris
Moon Over Minneapolis
Wicked Women
A Hard Time To Be a Father

Non-fiction

Letters to Alice
Rebecca West
Sacred Cows

FAY WELDON

Godless in Eden

A book of essays

Flamingo
An Imprint of HarperCollins*Publishers*

Flamingo
An Imprint of HarperCollins*Publishers*
77–85 Fulham Palace Road,
Hammersmith, London W6 8JB

Flamingo® is a registered trade mark of
HarperCollins*Publishers* Ltd

www.**fireandwater**.com

Published by Flamingo 2000
9 8 7 6 5 4 3 2 1

First published in Great Britain by
Flamingo 1999

ISBN 0 00 655164 5

Set in PostScript Linotype Galliard
Typeset by Rowland Phototypesetting Ltd,
Bury St Edmunds, Suffolk

Printed and bound in Great Britain by
Clays Ltd, St Ives plc

Contents

The Way We Live Now

A new Britain indeed: a Third Way, a great sea change in how we see ourselves. Fifty-eight million people, in fact, in profound culture shock. To determine how we live now, first determine how we lived then.

From *The Scotsman* Millennium Lecture, delivered at the Edinburgh Book Festival, summer, 1998.

Pity a Poor Government

Adam and Eve and Tony Blair. The beginning and the end: or at any rate as far as we've got at the close of the fourth millennium since the Garden of Eden, when we all began, and the second since Jesus, when we started counting.

But these things may be circular; the end may yet turn into a new beginning. We now have a New Adam and a New Eve (if the same old Cain and Abel kids). God is no longer seen to exist, to bar the door with flaming sword. The bearded patriarch has been replaced by Mother-Goddess Nature. The happy couple walk again in paradise. The Garden, mind you, is pretty battered these days, it lacks its ozone layer, it is buffeted by the storms of global warming and so on. But at least the serpents of hunger, poverty and ignorance have slid off into the undergrowth, driven out over the centuries by marauding parties of the Great and Good.

Pity any poor government as it tries to keep up with unprecedented social change and the collapse of the old ways of living, dealing as it has to with an electorate still immersed in the old myths of what we are and how we hope to be, obliged to piddle about with Ministries for Women when what we need is a Ministry for Human Happiness. Changes in the female condition, however welcome, have had their effect on men and children too. Takes two to make the next one – and our evolution as a species, over too many millennia to count, suggests to us most forcibly that we are all inextricably interlinked, and if we try too hard to escape our conditioning, fly too obstinately in the face of our human and gender nature, we will be very miserable indeed. But what are we, if we don't try? Let government admit a paradox, and help us all pursue our happiness, not just some of us our rights.

The young couple, the New Adam, the New Eve – he beginning to feel the effect of the lack of a rib, she taking over the gardening: their life expectancy now in the late seventies (him) and the early eighties (her) – have in returning to the Garden been returned to innocence: they walk about its glories in a daze. Innocence may not be enough if they are to remain, this time round, in the state of grace we want for them. Let them have some information.

I can't cover a thousand years of gender politics but I can just about manage the last hundred years. The great advantage of being no longer young is that what to many people is dead history to me is living history, if I add in my mother, that is, who is alive and well and thinking and ninety-one. Since she was there for the decades I was not, between us we can set ourselves up as experts on the century.

I spent my early years in New Zealand, where the education was based upon 'the Scottish system'. By which is meant that the young are not trusted with independent judgement, and no-one asks 'what are your feelings about this?' because your feelings are irrelevant. We learned what others older and wiser than ourselves had to say. We quoted authority if we wanted to prove a point. (In those pre-television days it was possible to take authority seriously. Put Locke, Berkeley and Hume on a late night chat show and you'd soon lose respect for them.) In 1946, my family, mother, grandmother, sister and myself, took the first boat 'home' after the war, and I went to a girls' grammar school in London which expected its pupils to join the great and the good and work for the betterment of mankind. Many of us did. And later I went to the University of St Andrews, where I developed the art of rhetoric. Thus: you make your case, overstating it dramatically. Your opponent does the same. In response you reduce your argument a little: so does he. Thus a consensus, or at any rate a moderation of extreme views can be reached. Except of course if you're arguing with someone who doesn't understand the rules of engagement, and they usually don't down South, you're in trouble. Others conclude you're hopelessly argumentative, given to rash overstatement, and would be well advised to stick to writing fiction, which as everyone knows, and as my mother pointed out to me long ago, is all lies and exaggeration anyway. You make a statement: they leave the room.

It was my Professor in moral philosophy at St Andrews who, when obliged by new university directives to accept females into his class – there were three of us – declined to mark our essays or acknowledge our presence, other than from time to time to remark, with a toss of the bald head, that females were not capable of moral decision or rational judgement. The only conclusion we could come to was that we were not female. That was in the early fifties, of course, and in those days to be denied 'moral decision' and 'rational judgement' was meant as an insult. Today a young person might well interpret the remark as a compliment. Feeling takes such precedence over morality and judgement, emotional response is declared to remain so much the woman's prerogative, that it is the young men in the class who would be the ones to feel inadequate, and long to be women, just as we then longed to be men, to be allowed out after our begrudged education into the great wide world of adventure, excitement, earning, and freedom. Not into the domesticity which seemed to be our fate, both as natural born women and because it was so difficult for a woman to earn anything other than pin money. And today's young man might well find himself the solitary male in a Gender Studies Class expected to stay quiet when the female lecturer tells the class that all men are potential rapists.

When my mother observes, as she did the other day, that when she was a girl only working women wore blouses and skirts, and that a lady would be horrified to be seen in anything but a dress, and equally horrified if a working woman turned up wearing something in one piece, you realise how profoundly and invisibly and silently things can change, and how easy it is to forget the kind of society we once were, as we try to make sense of the one we have now. You understand why the office liked you always to wear a suit to work, and wearing a dress made them, and you, feel uneasy, and why the BBC got so upset in the sixties if you wore trousers to a meeting.

Why, I asked my mother, if there are only six million more people in this country than there were in 1950, and this is only a ten percent increase in the total population, is it so difficult to get along Oxford Street for the crowds? And why is it that the simple purchase of a pair of shoes these days takes so long and requires a lengthy session with a crashing computer? To which she replied 'Because once upon a time everyone used to stay home, you silly girl. They were poor. Their one pair of shoes was wet and they couldn't go out until they were dry. They didn't even aim to have two pairs. No-one ate in restaurants, bread and cheese was the staple diet and you got them from the corner shop and paid cash, and if you didn't have cash you went without. And that was in the fifties – things were twice as quiet when I was a child.'

My mother's parents, at the turn of the century, ran to a cook and a maid who lived in, and had one half-day off a week. They were certainly not out littering the streets, buying shoes or overcrowding public transport.

In the East End of London, before bombs razed so much of it during two world wars, and the planners got busy with their theories, nearly everyone lived within walking distance of work. And how they worked! In 1901, we had 75,000 boys under fourteen in the factory workforce, and nearly as many girls. The school leaving age was thirteen and child labour was common in spite of it, and it was normal for women to work before they had families. But not after, if they could help it. In the civil service and in teaching, what was called the Marriage Bar meant a woman had to give up her employment – in blouse and skirt, of course – when she got married. Otherwise who would run the nation's homes? A whole lot of women just got married secretly, of course, and failed to tell their employers.

Halfway through the century, by the time I was being taught by Professor Knox, though the Marriage Bar was gone, it was certainly assumed that an educated girl chose between a personal life and a career. Now it is assumed that somehow, what with the washing machine, the microwave, the vacuum cleaner, and this strange thing called childcare, which is another woman looking after her child for less than the mother earns, she will be able to manage both. And she can, just about, and often wants to, and often has to. And it can be hard. We have paid a heavy price for our emancipation, but more of that later.

And when I say people worked hard then, believe me they work harder now. My mother views with horror today's average working week of forty-eight hours – and middle management works sometimes sixty or seventy, plus the journey to and from work – saying that even before World War II the attempt was to get the figure down to thirty-five. And that when in the late fifties she worked as a porter on London's Underground – the winters were cold and staff were issued with heavy greatcoats, for which she was thankful – even then the staff worked only a forty-hour week. What happened? And as for part-time work – the kind women with children so often do – this is usually an employer's definition and doesn't necessarily mean shorter hours, just that the employee works without holiday or sick pay and has no statutory rights. I know 'part-time' college lecturers who work longer hours than the full-time staff, but for less money, and are still grateful. It's that or nothing.

Of course things have improved. They must have. Our life expectancy is greatly increased. My mother's life expectancy when she was born was fifty-two years. My father's was forty-seven. A girl child born today can expect to get to eighty-one, a boy child seventy-six. The gender gap in this respect has neither closed nor narrowed. Women are born to live longer on average than men, in the human species as in most others. At the beginning of the century one hundred and sixty males per million did away with themselves: the figure for women was forty-eight. Now it's down to one hundred and four males and thirty females. Woman is not so given to despair, it seems, as Man, and though the totals drop, thank God, they stay pretty much in the same gender proportion, three times fewer women than men. We both mostly do away with ourselves when we're old and lonely. We were not bred for loneliness, though the contemporary world forces too many of us into it. The government plans to build 4.4 million new housing units, to house those expected to live alone in the next decade, and that figure rises steadily. As Patricia Morgan at the Institute of Economic Affairs points out, in a booklet on the fragmentation of the family, men's disengagement from families is of immense and fundamental significance for public order and economic productivity. This is something which is only just beginning to be acknowledged – as we blithely head for a situation in which, by the year 2016, fifty-four percent of men between thirty and thirty-four will be on their own.

So pity the poor male as well as pity the poor government. One's anxiety on their behalf has less to do with girls doing so much better at school exams than boys, which they so famously do, but with changes in society which make it difficult for us all to do what comes naturally. That is, to fall in love, marry, and live happily ever after in domestic tranquillity, even though we prefer now to do this serially. The late twentieth century is wreaking havoc with our aspirations to life, liberty and the pursuit of happiness. May we please have our Ministry for Human Happiness? Or if the government really wants to be useful, and preserve the marriage tie and so forth, thus saving itself large chunks of the £800 thousand million annual benefit budget spent mopping up the mayhem left by divorce, it could institute official stigma-free dating agencies, and set about arranging sensible marriages. The self-help system seems to be breaking down. And the steadiest citizen is the married citizen, and the one most pleasing to the State, tied down and sobered by kids and mortgage obligations.

My mother and I, of course, both have to thank the twentieth century for our continued existence. Let me rephrase that. Were it not for medical advances we would neither have seen so much of it. I would have been dead twice, once for lack of antibiotics, once for lack of plausible surgery. So would she. I would have three surviving children, not four. One would not have survived birth. Mind you, were it not for the advent of contraception, I might have ended up having ten. When Marie Stopes worked in London's East End at the beginning of the century there were women around who had survived twenty children or more: but the normal fate of the married woman was to die young from repeated childbirth, contraception being both illegal and seen as immoral. For every child she carried, Stopes estimated, a woman's chance of dying in childbirth increased by fifty percent. If the marriage rate then was a mere one in three I am not surprised. Marriage might have meant status and children, and even, in George Bernard Shaw's phrase, been a meal ticket for life for women, but was still too often a death sentence, especially amongst the poor. Things are better now: infant and maternal mortality is way, way down to almost nothing – from over one in ten in 1900 to less that four per thousand now – but with improved health, prosperity, the advent of contraception and women's control of her own fertility, comes a new set of problems. So it goes.

My mother at the age of five, when first required to go to the little Montessori school around the corner, set up such a wail that my grandfather, a novelist, came down the stairs in his silk dressing gown, waving his ivory cigarette holder and said what can be the matter with little Margaret? To which the reply came she doesn't want to go to school. 'Do you want to go to school, Margaret?' he asked, and my mother replied no, though she knew even then, she told me, that it was a life decision and she'd made the wrong one. My grandfather said, 'Don't send her then,' and went upstairs again, and they didn't. She stayed at home and read books and by the age of twenty was writing novels with her father.

Education for my mother and myself was for its own sake. It was not training, as it is now, for the adult world of work. The motive behind the education acts of the nineteenth century, which made school compulsory, was not by any means purely philanthropic: rather it was to accustom the children of an agrarian society to industrial ways, so by the time they left school they'd have got into the habit of turning up at the factory even when it was raining and cold, they felt poorly, or their shoes were wet and it was Monday morning. Monday was always a bad day for turning up at work. And the truant officers of the new compulsory schools, the morning and afternoon register, and the sick note required to prove illness, did indeed quickly train the new generation to daily work in the factories, bother reading and writing.

Likewise today we train our children, through longer and longer years, from their first day at the creche or the playgroup, to their last day at college, to turn up, to be there, to answer the register, to compete in exams as later they will for jobs, computer fodder in the new technological society, as once they were factory fodder. It is the effective use of computers we care about, just as once we cared about getting a return on our new industrial machinery: alas, machinery works day and night and doesn't tire, as humans will.

Our children, training for their future, in which there will always be too many workers and not too few, and so a permanent level of anxiety to keep everyone striving, end up living in an examination culture: they are tested and tried on entry to playgroup, they have SATS at 7, 11 and 14, GCSE's, A-levels, secret personality records and all. What price the old hated eleven-plus now? That exam was as nothing. Who wanted to go to the grammar school, anyway, it separated you out from your friends. Passing it was the problem, not failing it.

Life for the child mid-century was comparative heaven. No over-trained teachers, no national curriculum, and very little truancy, why should there be? School was where you went to meet your friends: education was a by-product: they were small, quiet places. Holidays were longer, the years spent in schools were fewer, educational standards were higher. And even so, my mother didn't want to go.

Mid-century I was lucky. I got the best of perhaps any education system the world has had to offer. Under Mr Attlee, the last of the great disruptive wars behind us, having got off the boat from New Zealand in 1946, a small family of female refugees, without possessions, into the confusion and turmoil of that grey, pock-marked, war-torn city, London, with its rationed food and its icy cold, all of us living in one room with only a glimmer of gas to light and warm it, the State plied me with orange juice and cod-liver oil. It not just sent me to a 'maintained' grammar school, but paid for me to go, bought me my clothes, gave me free meals, sent me to university when I was seventeen to study Economics and Psychology and become part of the future. What you have in me is what the Attlee government made of me. I got a student's grant of £167 a year plus tuition, paid for me by the London County Council, which seemed to me to be unbelievable riches, and which indeed, if you worked in the coffee shop in the evenings, was enough to keep you and indeed even buy you a second pair of shoes. And in the summers you hitched South: the world after the war seemed a safe and gentle place: it had got its violence out of its system. Now the violence is in the tent, not out of it. Forget hitch-hiking, we feel we can't even let our children walk to school alone in safety. Lacking an outside enemy, the attack from Mars or a meteor from outer space, I fear it may well stay like that.

Conflict at the turn of the century, and indeed up to the middle of it, was solved by war, male antlers locking, carnage on the battlefront. War, at least in the mind, if not so much of course by those compelled to participate in it, was to do with courage, chivalry, sacrifice, nobility, prowess, endurance, patriotism. Traditional male virtues, now much despised. These days in our female way we negotiate, cajole, tempt, explain, forgive, apologise, touchy-feel our way to world peace, while small savage macho wars, mini-skirmishes, little spasms of ethnic cleansing, break out here and there.

The International Monetary Fund bales out the Japanese, the Russians: we look after our economic relatives: old enmities are forgotten. And of course this is preferable to war. But without our external enemies we turn inwards: societies and individuals go on self-destruct benders. Crime, drugs, the break-up of the family, the abandonment of children, the loneliness of the individual, the alienation of the young, the pause button so often on the sadistic act of violence on the TV: are all features of today's peaceful, caring society. And perhaps they are all inevitable. Jung would talk about a process called enantiodromia, when all the currents of belief that have been running one way suddenly turn and run the other, in the same way a river zig-zags rather than flows steadily down a hill, reversing its direction when too much pressure mounts. The more smoothly the confining, caring, peaceful society seeks to conduct itself, the more likely some of its members are furiously to run in the wrong direction, lost to all responsibility and decent feeling, vandalising and tearing everything to bits as they go. It wasn't what they wanted: it was never what they wanted. What they wanted – because the source of the trouble is mostly male – was to be allowed to be men in a society which so disapproves of maleness.

Signs of maleness – interpreted as aggression, selfishness, sexual addiction – are treated by the therapists and counsellors, who take the place of the old patriarchal priesthood: they are the new pardoners, forgiving our sins for the payment of money, releasing us from personal guilt. Women are confirmed in their traditional self-absorption: seek the authenticity of your own feelings, they cry. Go it alone! You know you can! Assert yourself, your right to dignity, to personal fulfilment! Never settle for second best.

And of course they are right, except, in the face of such stirring advice, and because in the new Garden of Eden men and women *can*, when once men and women couldn't, marriages and relationships crumble and collapse. According to a recent poll in the women's magazine, *Bella*, more than fifty percent of young women think a man isn't necessary in the rearing of a child, and seventy-five percent think that if she wants to conceive a child when she doesn't have a partner it's better to go to a sperm bank than have a one-night stand. Seventy-five percent. Back at the turn of the century sex was something women put up with in return for a wedding ring and all that went with it, not something they were meant to enjoy. So what changes, in spite of what a lot of other women's magazines have had to say on the joys of sex in between?

I am not lamenting the past. We live a whole lot longer than we did; that must prove something. Though quite how we keep our Zimmer frames polished I don't know, as both the birth rate and the marriage rate falls. Many of today's young will grow up to live alone and not with families: friends and colleagues will have to look after us, the New Adam and the New Eve, when we grow old, or break a leg, or are made redundant, or go mad or whatever. What price independence and self-assertion then? The State is increasingly determined not to look after us, and if our families are fragmented, how can we look after ourselves?

We are all so much weaker than we believe, than the myth of the strong man, even the new one of the strong woman, allows us to be. We need all the support we can have. And as for our financial arrangements! Good Lord, you can't trust them. Banks collapse, as do whole national economies, nothing is secure, not even your Insurance Company, not even your PEPs. It's understandable, I take the view. I belong to the robbed generation. I started work at the Foreign Office in 1953 – earning £6 a week as a temporary assistant clerk; I worked for some fifteen years, here or there, before I became self-employed, on PAYE, paying out a vast proportion of my weekly pay packet, or so it seemed to me at the time, for my Social Security stamp. Now I get the old age pension they promised me and it's 44p a week. Robbed! And what about all those who having no savings, no longer able to earn, endure the indignity of having to ask for income support? Their mistake, having been told they were providing well enough for their futures, was to believe what they were told. Successive governments simply did a Maxwell with the pension funds, and didn't even have the grace to acknowledge it, let alone jump overboard.

The State is increasingly cavalier with its dependants. I know of a man with two artificial legs who because he can walk across a room – just – doesn't get incapacity benefit any more. It was withdrawn in the last so-called fraud purge, a few months back, when everyone on incapacity benefit was called to a fifteen minute interview with a non-specialist doctor and the lists cut across the board by some ten percent. Just like that. Sure you can appeal but if you do you lose a whole set of other benefits while you wait, and then how do you eat? Is so much misery worth so small a saving to the State?

The matter of the burden to the tax-payer of the benefit bill preoccupies government to an absurd degree. States with any spare money tend to go to war, and then we pay for that. Look at the books. Total government receipts, 1998, £309 thousand million. Total government expenditure £320 thousand million. We borrowed £11 thousand million from ourselves to balance the books. (You can get all these figures from the back of your *Economist* Desk Diary. Take off a few noughts from the sums and it's no different from adding up your own cheque stubs.) Out of that £320 thousand million, Social Security costs us a mere £79 thousand million. I suspect one way or another we'd go on paying the same taxes even if we stopped spending on our poor relations altogether, and allowed the unemployed, the undertrained, the sick, the weak and the inadequate, the helpless in our highly complex society, to starve to death on the streets. And what kind of family would we be if we did this? How would we live with ourselves?

One of the phenomena of the late twentieth century has been the growth of political correctness, of self-censorship, a quite false belief that we have reached the pinnacle of proper understanding, and a fear of saying what we think in case we offend our friends. It becomes important that we all think the same: and indeed, the rise of emotional correctness requires that we all *feel* the same. We allow ourselves as little freedom of thought as if we were Marxist-Leninists, even though there's no-one around to put us in prison. Sexism, it is held, contrary to the evidence of the eyes and the ears, can flow only one way, from man to woman, just as racism can flow only from white to black. That both are now two-way streets we find difficult to accept.

Sometimes it seems to me that with the fall of the Berlin wall freedom fled East and control fled West. Jung's enantiodromia at it again. Turn, and run the other way down the tramlines. In Russia now see the worst excesses of venture capitalism and personal freedom, wealth which breaks all sumptuary laws brushing up against extreme poverty, an abundance of crime, coercion and murder, and the flight of altruism. While here in the West we have the creeping Sovietisation of our culture: the advent of a dirigiste government: we are controlled, surveyed, looked after, nannied, bureaucratised. We live amongst secrets: our news is manipulated. We all know it, but don't much care. We have direction of labour. What else is Welfare to Work? If you can't get your own job, take the one we give you. On which I notice the government spent £200 million last year, and did get a few actually back to work, but for the most part only temporarily. And for every person who got a job there must be another one put out of work – how can it be otherwise, when we still have a seven and a half percent unemployment rate. Wouldn't it have been cheaper to just go on paying out benefits and saved everyone a lot of aggravation, humiliation, cold calling and letter writing? Or better still created work for people to do? But that would interfere with the Bank of England's belief that there is a 'natural' rate of unemployment – defined by them as the lowest rate compatible with stable inflation. They like it pretty much as is – not too high to cause rioting in the streets. High enough to keep workers in a state of anxiety and doing what they're told. In the light of such official or semi-official policy, Welfare to Work projects look oddly like window dressing. Or, less cynically, the thinking goes like this. True, we need a calculable pool of people standing around doing nothing, to cool an overheating economy – but it's just so irritating when they stand around. Let them at least be seen to be working at not-working, which is what the new Jobseekers' Allowance amounts to.

Since the unemployed appear to be burnt offerings to the stability of our economy, martyrs in the cause of the low inflation and the high interest rates which keep the City happy, I think they should be treated with vast respect and allowed to live in peace, dignity and the utmost comfort.

As for the employed, the conviction seems to be that if only everyone works longer and harder, women alongside men, we'll all be better off. But better off how? Where's our Five-Year Plan? What exactly is all this effort *for*? And has no-one noticed that in spite of having the longest working hours in Europe we have the lowest productivity? Of course we do. We're exhausted.

And we're certainly no longer working for the children: they poor things are Kibbutzised, taken away from their parents and returned to them only at nights, so the parents are free to work to make the desert bloom. Which is all very well, but there's no desert outside the window when the children look, and no drastic emergency, just a whole lot of new cars and new roads and new buildings and shoe shops and the Millennium dome.

We live now under Ergonarchy. By Ergonarchy I mean rule by the work ethic. Forget Patriarchy, rule by the father, it's Ergonarchy which is woman's current enemy, now that she's joined the workforce. While she was doing battle with Patriarchy, Ergonarchy sneaked in under cover of darkness and ambushed her. Ergonarchy insists women work but goes on paying them less. This isn't because Ergonarchy is male – Ergonarchy's an automated accountant, neuter and blind and unable to tell one gender from another – but simply because women, if they have children, can't give their bosses the time and attention they require, and so end up contributing less and getting paid less. Ergonarchy's best friend being Market Forces.

And thus it will continue until society gets Ergonarchy under control, by the drastic measure of accepting that men are fathers too, and inviting them on board as equal parents. On the day when the problem of the working father is talked about as often as is the problem of the working mother, we will be getting somewhere. All children have two parents, though you'd never think it.

I am not suggesting, you must understand, that mothers should stay home and look after the children. I don't want them forced back into the kitchen, heaven forfend, for this is just another kind of loneliness, albeit temporary. I want my Ministry for Human Happiness to ensure mothers are out there doing half as many hours for twice as much money.

Evidence of continuing male prejudice against women comes from the fact that the female wage is persistently lower than the male wage: though in Britain the gap is smaller than in the rest of Europe. But it is not on the whole the villainy and prejudice of men that leads to this undoubted inequity: it is the fact that the majority of women end up with children, and choose to give them more attention than they do their jobs. Even when partnered, many back off when the time comes for promotion, deciding that time for a personal and emotional life is more valuable than earning more money. The part-time nurse does not take the job as full-time ward sister, the TV researcher turns down the job as producer, because if they move up the ladder, when would they ever get to see the kids. The piece-worker in the home stitches shoes at 50p a pair because she has an ill child and is open to exploitation – not because she is a woman but because she is human being with a baby, and has no other options open to her. The earning capacity of the lone father (a fast growing group), falls as drastically as does that of the mother, when loneness strikes. While every working woman who has a small child pays another woman less than her own market value to look after the child – and she must, or she can't afford the job – how can equality of wages be achieved? What meaning does 'equal opportunities' have, other than for the childless woman? If the statistics which told us about our comparative earnings made a distinction not just between men and women, but between men, childed women and unchilded women, we would begin to get somewhere – but they don't. All women come under one heading. The fact that we do so well in the European league table suggests to me not that we're moving towards gender equality, but that we have too many tired and overworked women with children amongst us.

We are barking up a dangerous and creaky old-fashioned seventies tree, when we go on struggling for equal wages, with the ardent encouragement of the government, when we would be better occupied turning men into resident and supporting fathers, instead of dismissing them from the case and saying, 'Which way to the sperm bank?' or, 'How dare you treat me like this,' or, 'Oh I can manage alone and anyway there's always the CSA, not to mention benefits. What makes you think I need a man?'

These days we tend to call our employment our 'career' and not our 'job'. A career is something in which you compete with your colleagues for promotion, must be sharper and faster and harder working than they are, and put in longer hours. Thus we are divided and ruled, by big bosses so well hidden in the bureaucratic undergrowth it is next to impossible to fight them, let alone detect them.

There is no-one around these days to protect the employee – except now perhaps legislation out of Europe, for which God, male or female, be thanked. In the big State organisations – health, education, local government – accountants rule. Their duty is to cut costs and save the tax-payer's money. So for the employee it's all downgrading and re-writing of contracts, and here's your redundancy money if you argue. The big companies look after the interests of share-holders first, customers second and employees last if at all. And the individual employer profits out of your skill and labour and always has but at least he's around to meet your eye.

This Garden of Eden of ours is still open to Marxist interpretation, even in this the Age of Therapy.

Adam and Eve and pinch me
Went down to the river to bathe,
Adam and Eve were drowned,
And who do you think was saved?

Pinch Me, says the innocent child, and everyone runs round the playground screaming. Well, that's how it used to be. The New Adam and the New Eve know better than to drown in the river, and the children's playgrounds no longer ring with traditional rhymes: playtimes get shorter, and holidays too, as the schools adjust their working hours to the offices and not the other way round. The New Adam and the New Eve, victim of the Ergonarchy, have no time left to go down to the river and stand and stare, and contemplate the marvel of creation.

The New Adam, I say, and the New Eve. We are not what we were. Our instincts may lead us in the same old direction: our rational understanding leads us in another. Four things happened in the middle of the twentieth century to change our gender relationships profoundly and for ever, so that our nature and our nurture are no longer at peace. We're just not used to it. The first two events are to do with medicine, the third to do with that powerful revolutionary idea, feminism, and the fourth to do with our new technological society. These are converging dynamics: you can't have one without the other, like love and marriage back in the fifties. That was when we managed a marriage rate of nearly ninety percent, and the majority of those marriages were permanent. It can be managed.

The first event was female access to contraception. At the beginning of the century, as I say, contraception was illegal: it offended the Church – the flow of souls to God had to be maintained: it offended the State – whose need was for labour in time of peace and cannon-fodder in time of war. The convenience of authority sheltered, as ever, under the cloak of morality. From the sixties on, with the advent of the pill, gruesome in its early workings as it was, men no longer controlled female fertility. Sex was no longer intricately bound up with procreation: it could, and did, become recreational. A world outbreak of permissiveness, as we called it, with some relish. To have sex, in the New Age, you didn't have to be married. And to be married, you didn't have to have babies. Though it took a decade or so for people to get used to the idea, and the change to show through in the family-fragmentation statistics. But almost overnight men lost their traditional role, creator and protector of the family. The majority of men had lived up to their former responsibility very well. By and large, pre the nineteen-sixties, if you made a girl pregnant, you married her, and you looked after her and the child. Abortion was illegal, the world wasn't set up for women to support themselves, and there were no State Benefits: other than that the State provided orphanages for abandoned children. Oddly enough, the moral censure thrown at the lone mother is greater today than it was back in the fifties, or that at least was my experience. Rash you may have been: lovelorn or deceived you probably were, and the consequences were dire enough without others feeling they had to join in, in condemnation.

The second great change is this. For the first time in history we have a preponderance of young men in our population. Young women are, believe it or not, in short supply. More men are always born than women – in this country it's about one hundred and four males to every hundred females. But once upon a time illness, war and accident so sharply cut down the numbers of young men they were outnumbered by young women and so had a buyer's market amongst them. It was they who picked and chose and women who did their best to attract. But young male life is safer now, thanks to medical care, the unfashionableness of war, and the trauma wards – and these days in all age groups up to forty-five men increasingly outnumber women: after that age the genders level-step until sixty or so, and with advancing age and man's shorter lifespan, women once again begin to predominate. Today's young woman does the sexual picking and choosing: she has the power to reject and uses it no better than the young man ever did. Women discover the gender triumphalism that once was the male's preserve. See it in the ads. One for Peugeot at the moment: a brisk, beautiful, powerful young woman, followed by her droopy husband. She's saying to the salesman, 'It moves faster and it drinks less! Can they do the same for husbands?' Try role-reversing that one! Does it matter? I suspect it does. It deprives men of their dignity: we all grow into what we are expected to be: this is the process of socialisation. Once women were indeed the little squeaky helpless domestic creatures the culture expected them to be. If we expect men to be laddish and appalling, that is how they will turn out. Where once it was the female fear that she might be left on the shelf, now, as young women get so picky, it is the man's. We see the arrival of the men's magazine: in which are discussed the arts of laddishness, flirtation, temptation, seduction: higher up the scale of sophistication, man as father, man as victim, man as sexual partner, man as cook. The way to a career woman's heart is through her need for someone to do the child-care and the housework. Men are from Mars and women are from Venus but the space ships still need to flit between. Of course we are confused: courtship rituals are reversed. We have no traditions to fall back upon because tradition no longer applies. Poor us.

The third great change came with the seventies wave of feminism, when the personal became the political. In the course of writing a novel '*Big*' *Women* (as opposed to '*Little*' *Women*), in which I charted in fictional form the course of the feminist revolution, its causes, its progress, and its results. I came to realise the extent of the change we have lived through: to understand how difficult it is to see the wood for the trees.

The novel opens with two young women putting up a poster. *A woman needs a man like a fish needs a bicycle.* Outrageous and baffling at the time, it turned out to be true. That is to say, she didn't need one at all. The world has changed, the laws have changed; our young woman is out into the world. She may be lonely at night sometimes but she has her freedom and her financial independence. She can earn, she can spend, she can party. She can choose her sexual partners, but is not likely to stick with them: somehow she outranks them. And she knows well enough that if she has a baby all this will end. And so, increasingly, she chooses not to. The fertility rate, 3:5 in 1901, is now down to 1:8 and falling, below replacement level. Which may be okay for the future of the universe, but isn't good news for the nation. We lose our brightest and best.

And the fourth thing that happened was that in the last fifty years we stopped being an industrial nation and turned into a service economy, and male muscle became irrelevant. I remember the days when they said women would never work on camera crews because of the weight of the equipment. Now there's the digital Sony camcorder. Put it in the palm of your hand, your tiny hand, no longer frozen. Anyone can use it.

Adam and Eve and Tony Blair, we all have a lot to cope with. And Pinch Me's always hiding just around the corner, of course, waiting to spring: changing his form all the time, like the Greek god Proteus, to avoid having to tell us the future.

On being asked by the Features Editor of *The Daily Telegraph* to write a piece, in the wake of the Countryside March, in the early spring of 1998, to defend the city against the country.

Behind the Rural Myth

The countryside is pretty.
It's pretty because there are so few people in it. There are so few people in it because there are so few jobs in it. And that's the nub of the matter.

Yes, you can have a mobile office. Anyone can work from home in these the days of the computer, e-mail, fax, phone and scanner. Who needs the soap-opera of office life? Who wouldn't want green trees not concrete the other side of the window. So move out. Except it's insanity, isn't it? For aloneness, read loneliness. And the blinds stay down to keep the sun off the computer screen. And when the crunch comes you're the first to go. If the boss has never seen your face why should he bother about the look on it? And try getting the dole in the country: it's so personal. They don't just dosh it out like they do in the city: no, they read every word you've written on the form you've just filled in, and compare last week's answers, and look everything up in the book – they've got time – and say no. And you don't *belong*.

The countryside is relaxing.
Yes. You can tell from the clothes of the people who come up on the Countryside March. They don't have many full-length mirrors in the country; countryfolk being either too haughty and grand to need them or else the ceilings are too low to fit them in. That must be it. The

countryside's not for the vain – heels sink into the mud, like the heels of little Gerda's pretty red shoes in the Hans Christian Anderson story. Down and down they pulled her, 'til she stood in the Hall of the Mud King. The countryside's all practical woolly mufflers and crooked hems and garments it would be a wicked waste to throw out. The country's full of good worthy people. A good girl in the city is a bad girl in the country. In the country the hairstylists like to turn you out looking like their mother. Well, they do that anywhere in the world, but you get the feeling in the country that they don't like their mothers very much. Not that it matters; go out for the evening and the place is hardly jumping with film crews and flashbulbs. Who's to see you?

The countryside is healthy.
No. It isn't. But it's unkind to go into that one. Let's just say, organophosphates have made fools of us all. What goes onto the crops and what goes into the soil? We moved to the country once – kept a tranquil flock of rare-breed sheep which roamed our fields, in the most natural of natural ways. We fed them sheep nuts by hand. What was in the sheep nuts? Ground-up protein from more than one animal of origin. 'Dip them!' said the government. We built a trough and pushed the startled, innocent animals in, one by one, dripping and shaking and spluttering, nerve poison all over the place. Oh, thanks!

Pollution drifts over the countryside from the cities, lingers over the valleys. And the pollen count! Good Lord. Just listen to the countryside sneezing and wheezing. The cottage hospital closes. The trauma ward's an hour away. People live longer in the cities.

And yet, and yet! I know. The warm glow of the setting sun on the old barn walls. The brilliant acid green of early spring. The blackness of night, the great vault of the firmament. The sense of a benign and fecund nature, of being part of the wheeling universe.

But what's weakness, irrationality. Let's get back to the brisk facts of the matter.

The countryside is our heritage.
Fact is, it's shrinking and shrinking fast: suburbia creeps out from the towns. Forty-one percent of British marriages end in divorce, and rising. Twenty-eight percent of us live in single-person households, and rising. We have to build houses and build we do. No choice. And where are the bus services to get us to work, from our new 'countryside estates'? Not down our road, that's for sure. And work still stays in the city, so travel we must, and travel we do, and use the car, and know every radio presenter by heart. The countryside becomes somewhere to go, not somewhere to be. A car park here, a car park there: this way the castle, that way the old oak tree, and a fast-food snack as you go! Oh, goodbye, countryside. What rats we are, to leave the sinking ship!

You're not cut off when you move to the country. Friends will visit.
Well . . . the friends from the city who came down at first don't seem to come any more. For a time they overlooked the fact that you'd deserted them, ran out on them, which is what you did, come to think of it. Nobody likes that. looked down your nose at their way of life and left them. So soon the inconvenience gets to them: the overnight bag, the traffic, and the hours that stand between you and them, your strange new friends with straw in their hair wearing long strands of New Age beads, and no proper signal for the mobile, and you've been nowhere and seen nothing except the back of the Aga. They settle you in, and their duty done, abandon you. Serves you right.

And the friends who do persist just seem to want a free weekend (well of course they do: what did you expect?) with you cooking and washing up because now you're in the country that's the kind of thing you do, isn't it? Back to nature, back to the sink, and what, no home-made bread? Friends who seemed perfectly civilised for the length of a dinner, reveal over a weekend all kind of gross personal traits. Eat breakfast in their pyjamas, or smoke dope in front of the children, or complain about no dry towels, and quarrel with your neighbours, knowing you're stuck with them and they can leave.

Let's compromise. Let's try a country cottage.
That one used to work, and very well, when husbands had nine-to-five jobs and wives stayed home and looked after the kids. But that's in the past. Then there was time and energy to work out the logistics of transporting a family, its goods, its bedding, its games and toiletries, to a place some scores of miles away on Friday nights and the reverse process on Sunday evening. Plus guests. And it was lovely, if you were skilled at logistics, that is. Log-fires and cheerful talk and mild drunkenness and happy flirtations and country walks and pink cheeks and a ploughman's lunch at the pub and no-one worried about drink-and-drive. Oh paradise.

But nine-to-five drifts to eight-to-eight. And Saturday mornings too, and women are working, and the mobile phone and the laptop turns Sundays into Mondays, and the traffic's worse, and they've tarmacked the track and lopped the trees and it's sensible, but the romance has gone. There's a strong steel fence where you used to nip under the wire, and the badger set's been cleared for fear of TB, and what's that smoke on the horizon – surely not a funeral pyre for the poor dead cows? Or else the Right-to-Roamers have found a footpath through your garden, past your very own back window.

When change comes in the countryside, it's seldom for the better. And the village store has closed. Okay so you never went in it – if you did they always said, pointedly, 'Haven't seen *you* for a long time' – so it got embarrassing; but you like it to be *there*. Say no to the country cottage; it isn't what it was!

The countryside's good for the children.
Yes. But you wouldn't think it to listen to them. They don't sound all that appreciative. They look at TV a lot. They miss McDonald's

and the corner shop. There's a strange-looking man lurking in the playing fields, and you see drugs behind every hedge. There's nothing for the kids to *do*. Mother turns into a taxi-service, unpaid. They've got to see their friends, learn to ride, remedial speech, whatever. Mother's gloomy and bored. Father's commuting, now the home-office idea has collapsed, and becomes part of the divorce statistics. He met someone cheerful on the train. Someone who, like him, longs for a loft apartment in Islington – and if both country houses were sold and each took their half, and mother kept the children – well, they are her life – why then the move back to the city could just about be managed. For him. What's good for the children is not necessarily good for the marriage.

But who's listening? 'We're moving out,' friends say, thrilled to the gills. 'It will be different for us.' And so it may be, and so I hope it will be. Humankind cannot live by reason alone, nor should they try to. And it is the spring, after all. And the mud's drying out. And the early sun catches the hill-tops, and the wheat field's sprouting green and strong, and lambs bounce in the fields, and what's so good about *here* anyway?

The entrance to the Garden of Eden may no longer be barred by a flaying sword, but Mother has to get back to the baby. No way she can enter.

Mothers, Who Needs 'Em?

Not employers, certainly. Mothers demand equal wages but have their minds on things other than their employer's interests. Sick babies, for example, toddlers with chickenpox, sudden calls to the school, child-care. Mothers can't be asked to stay late, won't do overtime, use the phone a lot, won't relocate, demand maternity leave. And they don't look so good in the front office either.

ERRATUM: sweatshop employers rather like mothers. Desperation means mothers will put up with anything. No-one else will do the job, anyway.

Fathers, on the other hand are much like anyone else. Sometimes they take an afternoon off for the Christmas play, or for a session with Relate, and insist on having their holidays in August, but otherwise who notices?

ERRATUM: lone fathers of course count as mothers. Same problem. Who needs 'em?

You can't blame employers. They're not philanthropists. The rational aim of the individual employer is to make a profit out of the worker's time and labour. If the employer is a company it must put the profit of the shareholder before the interests of the worker (let alone the customer). If the employer is the State – a shrinking section of the new economy – managers and accountants take the place of the old-fashioned boss. Their object is to save money, not make money. Which puts the employee in exactly the same situation: the pressure is on for longer hours and lower wages.

The working class can kiss my arse,
I've got the charge-hand's job at last.

– as they used to sing in the old Marxist days. Thank you, Mr Blair.

Not that anyone admits to being working class any more. Who wants the Union to fight for their rights? It's an indignity. Except we all go on working and earning, especially mothers, harder and longer than ever. Forget lone mothers, one average pay-packet is scarcely enough to keep even a family with a father in Pot Noodles, petrol for the car and Nikes for the kids. So out she goes to work, which is fine in one way because being with small children alone in a house can drive you crackers, but not in another because cramming stiff unwilling arms into coat sleeves on a winter's morning in order to be at the nursery by eight and work by nine is no fun. When you and the child are half asleep.

It's no use the self-righteous (usually the childless, who can afford to be minimalist) telling you you're being 'greedy' or 'materialistic': you should magically do without the extra money. You have to have a new car because the old one breaks down on the way to work, and where's the public transport? And you have to have a microwave because there's no time for 'proper' cooking. It's a vicious circle. Since the introduction of the poll tax no-one has been able to live cheaply.

Mothers, who wants 'em? Stay at home (if you're lucky) and be told you're boring and unaspirational. Go out to work and be told you're breeding delinquents.

Mothers, who wants 'em? Not the State. Mothers are a drain on the national purse. They're either lone or divorced and on benefit or claiming low income family supplement, or kicking up a fuss because their child didn't get to the school of its choice, or failing to teach it its times-tables before it gets to school or irresponsibly going out to work so it ends up delinquent.

Mothers, who wants 'em? Not even children. The crèche, the nursery, the school, the after-hours homework club takes the place of home. As the traditional family turns into a unit with two breadwinners and no parent, children learn to do without mothers very fast. (Even grandmother's out at work.) The teacher, the peer group, television and youth culture become more important in their lives, are a greater cultural influence. Watch the four-year-olds dancing to the Spice Girls. And that can be even if you don't go out to work.

What's to be done? This is not a happy situation for mothers. Everyone wants to be needed. Feminism has been the only movement in recent times to turn its attention to matters of social justice, personal dignity and the quality of our lives. Let the New Feminists attend to these rather than the gap between male and female wages. Let them stop congratulating themselves on how happy they are to wear lipstick and what a good thing Mrs Thatcher was, and extend their remit. Let them start by diving the world into four separate categories, not two, and looking at what is really going on. Men, Women, Mothers, Fathers, not just Male and Female. Let them bring about a society in which there is parity of parenting. So 'the problem of the working father' is as much talked about as 'the problem of the working mother'. Younger men, trained by earlier feminists to have full and loving relationships with their children, will co-operate. Apart from a few emotional dinosaurs. We might all even end up working less hard, having fuller lives, and happier relationships with our children.

As for Mrs Thatcher, it was she, remember, who in repealing the Shops Act took away the right of the shop assistant to have a chair.

As written for *Harpers Bazaar*, New York, to celebrate the New Year, 1998, and a New Age, in which New Eve rules in the Garden of Eden, and New Adam feels weaker for the loss of a rib.

The Feminisation of Politics

Back in the seventies the feminists argued that the personal should become the political. So it did. The word *sexism* was coined, men (in this scheme of the universe) could no longer operate by dividing and ruling; a woman might be a victim by virtue of her gender, but she no longer cried into her pillow alone. Her woes, politicised, became the stuff of legislation and social disapproval.

Time and the process rolled inexorably on and lo! one day we woke up (some say the morning after Princess Diana's death) to find that the political had become the personal, and that person was a woman. Not perhaps the nicest woman in the world, perhaps now the archetype of the wicked stepmother (sweeping out everything that went before); not lisping like a fairy princess, but certainly speaking in a womanly tongue. Here in Britain, Tony Blair's New Labour Party presents itself as female, using the language of compassion, forgiveness, apology, understanding and nurturing – qualities conventionally attributed to women.

The Conservative Party, who ruled the country for the greater part of a hundred years, is to all intents and purposes no more; the old male values – so epitomised in John Major's grey-suited self – of *gravitas*, responsibility, self-discipline, the Protestant work-ethic, stiff upper-lippedness, the appeal to reason and intellect – have vanished in the sudden wind of gender change. They try to learn the new language fast: the old philanderer Parkinson talks of love; the hard case Portillo, once scourge of the immigrant, talks of caring and compassion; William Hague, the new Tory leader, takes off his tie and undoes his top button, and wears his baseball cap back to front, but it's all too late, too late. They were too old and too male too long to be credible now. This is the Age of the Anima. Male voters searched for it in themselves and found it.

This stuff may be catching. Does not President Clinton eschew penetrative sex, does not his nation forgive him his waywardness on this account? The otherwise strange behaviour of the feminists in failing to condemn in this analysis becomes explicable. A sweet smile, a confiding air, as he sets about nurturing. What price masculinity now? Let American spin doctors keep an eye on what happens in Britain. The symptoms of social change tend to surface here first, erupt in spots, if only because we began first. First to abandon the feudal system, to endure agricultural and industrial revolutions, to fight Germany; Thatcherite monetarism started here. Flu may spread from Asia, and economic confusion, but for the infectious mechanics of cultural change, the converging dynamics of religion, politics and feminism, watch this space.

One way or another along the path, the gender switch was thrown, the male-female polarities were reversed. Even God has become female. He is no longer the single bearded patriarch in the sky, Lord of Guilt and Retribution, to whom one kneels, but She of the multiple personality, Mother Nature, creator and healer of all, Goddess of victims and therapees everywhere. Princess Diana dies. Gay Sir Elton John sings the lullaby, the new women priests nod and smile, Tony Blair takes the Queen's arm, daughter-like, the candles flicker in the wind and the ceremony is complete. The bearded patriarch slips out the Great West Door at Westminster Abbey, and dissolves in the scent of a million, million, tearful roses.

Politics, in this new gender theory of the universe, ceases to be a matter of right or left, Conservative or Labour, Republican or Democrat. Confrontation is de-moded. The old language no longer applies. It is not the rulers against the people, management against labour, the rich against the poor, the strong against the weak – all that fell with the Berlin Wall – rather it is the animus fighting a losing battle against the anima. Even the old Freudian concept of the superego, like the Conservative Party, has vanished in the wind of change: the id now acts without restraint or overview. The old complain that the young are de-politicised, but where are they to go? Where are the young to find their resentments, other than in themselves? What price revolution now, since the enemy is within? The harm was done by an unkind mother, an abusing father, a cold spouse, not by any grievous social arrangement. Let us change ourselves, not change the world. The government may rule in peace.

Sure, in today's Britain people of all parties still unite. They will raise their banners to save the noble tree and the poor hunted fox: the Rights of Man is extended now to the Rights of all Sentient Creatures above the Ranks of Roaches, and anyone who saw the film *Men in Black* will know that even that last barrier begins to fall. The Humanitarian Society of America, so we are told, in case you think it's only in Britain, counted in four hundred roaches a day onto the set and checked them back out at night, to make sure not a single one had been harmed in the making of that film. Nor were they. The ones who got crushed by a human boot were made of plastic with yellow slime filling. It was only after a day's filming that the fumigators were sent in to control the native inhabitants. We are beset by an excess of empathy: how we feel for others, even insects! Men and women both, we are thoroughly female, in the traditional, not the power-dressed, sense.

I am reminded of the joke about a certain conjurer, entertainer on the *Titanic*. Every afternoon he'd make his parrot disappear. 'Where'd it go, where'd it go?' his delighted audience would yell. The ship sinks. Parrot and conjurer barely escape with their lives. For days they float upon a raft. The parrot keeps silent. The conjurer assumes it's traumatised. But after three days the parrot speaks. 'All right, all right, I give in. Where'd the bloody ship go?'

We were only playing feminism. Now where's the bloody opposition gone? Down the gender divide, that's where. I write, you must understand, more of patterns of thinking and speaking than of anything so vulgar and simple as generative parts. If women can wear trousers and still be female, men can wear trousers and be women in spirit. (The English language hampers us by defining only men and women as male and female: the French, with their '*le*' and their '*la*' do it to the whole world, including abstract notions, and a very fine thing that is.) In New Britain see woman-think and woman-speak. The marginalisation of the intellect is registered under the heading 'seeking a feeling society'; a pathological fear of elitism as 'fairness to others'; the brushing aside of civil liberties as 'sensitivity to the people's needs'. The frightening descent into populism becomes merely a 'responsiveness to the voters' wants'. New Labour is to put lone mothers and the disabled on harsh Welfare to Work schemes – 'tough choices, long-term compassion'. And all this is brought about by men in open-necked shirts, not necessarily heterosexual, on first name terms, speaking the deceptively gentle language of the victor.

The personal became the political, the political personal, and lo! that woman was a female, and victorious. The gender switch was thrown and women turned into the oppressors of men, and men, as victims will, retaliate by taking on the role of those who oppress them. The first step that women took in their emancipation was to adopt traditional male roles: to insist on their right to wear trousers, not to placate, not to smile, not to be decorative. The first step men have taken in their self-defence is to adopt the language of Therapism; a profoundly female notion this: that all things can be cured by *talk*. (By Therapism I mean the extension of what goes on in the psychotherapist's consulting room into the social, political and cultural world – but more of that later.)

Now it is no easy thing to suggest to women that men have become their victims. That, as Ibsen remarked in *An Enemy of the People*, give or take twenty years and the truth turns into a lie. That what was true for the nineteen-seventies – that women had a truly dreadful time by virtue of their gender – had ceased to be true by the nineteen-nineties. For murmuring some such thing recently in *The Guardian*, I was described in the *Sunday Telegraph* as the Winnie Mandela of the feminist world. I will survive.

Perhaps, I suggested, feminism in Britain goes too far. I know it's hardly even begun to move in many parts of the world, but here at home perhaps the pendulum of change has stuck and needs nudging back to a more moderate position? I used as evidence the fact that in middle-class London mothers long for baby girls and have to bite back disappointment if they have boys. Girls are seen as having a better life ahead of them. Girls do better at school – even in traditionally male subjects as maths and the sciences – gain better qualifications, are more cooperative about the house, find it easier to get jobs, make up a smaller proportion of the unemployed, and in the younger age groups already break through the old 'glass ceiling' into the top income brackets. Women are better able to live without men than men are to live without women. Married men live longer than unmarried ones: the position is reversed for women. Sons are more likely to be born Down's syndrome, autistic or criminal and not to survive beyond the age of twenty-five. (Dare-devil activities carry off many a lad.) Daughters will provide their own dowries, and look after you in your old age. Who wants boys? Girl power triumphs. Women have won the revolution.

Roundly I am chastised for such heretical views. The perception remains that women are the victims, that men are the beasts. Women are the organising soft-centred socialists, the nice people, the sugar and spice lot, identifying with the poor and humble: men are slugs and snails and puppy-dog tails and rampant, selfish, greedy capitalists. No wonder conservative and puritanical politicians, for such ours are, adopt female masks. It's the boys who these days suffer from low self-esteem, don't speak in class, lack motivation, hang around street corners, depressed and loutish. It is the men, not the women, who complain of being slighted, condemned by virtue of gender to casual and automatic insult. 'Oh men!' say the women, disparagingly. Males hear it all the time, in the workplace and in the home, at the bus stop and over the dinner-table, and suffer from it. No tactful concessions are made to male presence. Men, the current female wisdom has it, are all selfish bastards; hit-and-run fathers; potential abusers/rapists/paedophiles; all think only with their dicks, and they'd better realise it. So men shrink, shrivel and under-perform, just as women once did. So where'd the bloody men go?

'Serves the men right,' I hear the women say. 'We're glad if they suffer a bit, after all those centuries! Give them a taste of their own medicine.' Except, except! Feminism was never after vengeance; simply justice. And it is hard to argue these days that women are still victims in a patriarchal world. In the new technological society, their smaller size does not handicap them: machines do the heavy labouring. Female fingers are nimbler on the computer. Women are economically independent of men: they control their own fertility, and need have children only if they want to. They fill the universities, and the restaurants. True, they have menstrual cycles and tend to swap, weep and drop things from time to time, but this is no handicap any more, just fashionable: men are to be pitied for their month-in, month-out sameness. Dull. And Nurofen cures the headache. Exercise eases the need for sex. If women are victims it is from choice not necessity: an agreeable whiff of recurrent erotic masochism.

Meanwhile young nineties men grow restless under the scourge of insult. They offer the same excuses for their passivity as once women used to. 'A masculinist movement? Don't be absurd. Men will never get together against female oppression,' they say. 'Individual men don't want to offend individual women. They're too competitive with other men ever to pull together, except for a few religious nuts who want to put women back in the home.'

But I remember women saying exactly the same thing of themselves, back in the seventies, before the truth became the lie. 'Feminism will never work,' pessimists said. 'Women are too catty, too bitchy – a function of competition for the male – ever to get together.' It just wasn't true. Sufficiently oppressed, women acted, and brought about a new world.

Now it's the men who complain of being used as sex objects, thrown out of the bed and the home after a one-night stand, waiting by phones for the call. If they make sexual overtures they are accused of harassment. Males must ask before they touch, and impotence lies in the asking. If a man wants a child he must search for a woman prepared to give him one. If he succeeds, if the woman doesn't change her mind and have a termination, he is expected to bond with the baby and do his share of minding and loving. And yet the baby can still be snatched away; if the relationship goes wrong he has no rights. Fathers can find themselves driven from the home with no warning, the locks changed, a new lover in the bed they once occupied, minimum visitation rights to the children, and alimony to pay. They suffer.

Yes, yes, I tell my critics, I know that for every one male horror story there are probably ten that are female, but ten wrongs don't make a right. And since the men seem too terrified to speak, or are too extremist to be taken seriously, someone has to speak for them.

Look, I say, don't get me wrong. Women shouldn't be complacent. The price of female liberation is eternal vigilance. Men could revert to type easily enough. (See, the in-built assumption that there's something wrong with the male 'type'!) Maintaining a just society in an unjust world is no easy matter. This is still the age of the Taleban. In Afghanistan women who were once engineers, teachers, writers, social workers, earners of all kinds, have been driven back indoors and shrouded in black by fanatical young men who live by principle however odd that principle may seem to us.

It is not likely to happen here, I say, but nasty surprises can still occur. Supposing Tony Blair isn't just a wicked stepmother putting her house in order, throwing out the poor relations and hangers on, supposing she's just a man in drag after all and a woman-hater?

Let no-one forget that Hitler solved Germany's high unemployment problems at one fell swoop, by simply banning women from most of its workplaces. One wage earner per family please, and that wage earner the man. And Hitler, like Blair, spent the early populist years, just like any other politician, having his picture taken with dogs and children. Women are right to be fearful.

The Blairs fall down rather on the dumb animal front, as it happens. Cherie failed to love the Downing Street cat, Humphrey, sufficiently for public taste. Indeed, it was rumoured that she'd had the poor, mangy, incontinent old thing put down. But the murmurings of the people quickly produced pictures of Humphrey safe and sound if looking surprisingly young, retired, 'living quietly' in a distant suburb, away from the hurly-burly of No 10. No-one quite believed it. And then Tony's offer to 'ban hunting' and save the poor fox somehow seemed to hang fire – the foxes still flee, the hounds still run, the horns still sound over the green English countryside.

The electorate worries about this, more than it does about the projected abolition of the House of Lords, the new government's habit of issuing edicts and by-passing Parliament, the strange programmed zombification of hitherto lively and intelligent politicians as dull-eyed and brain-washed they spout the party line. If I were the Blairs I'd quickly get a dog – preferably not a beagle lest anyone forgets and holds it up by its ears. No, a corgi would be better: one of the palace puppies perhaps – to restore the first family's animal-loving credentials.

In 'women' I do not, by the way, include the category 'mother'. Mothers remain a separate case. The feminist movement does not know what to do with them and never has. The child cries, the mother hurts and runs home and no amount of conditioning seems to cure it. The 'problem of the working mother' seems insoluble; 'the problem of the working father' is never referred to by either employers or government, though paying proper attention to it, I do believe, would pretty soon solve the technological society's overlong, over-exhausting work schedules. Paradoxical that the more automated the society, the harder and longer everyone seems to have to work. But all that's another story.

See feminism and politics as a converging dynamic: see another one creeping up on the outside, a softly implacable, bendy-rubber force, that of Therapism, surging alongside the others into the Parisian tunnel, into that solid concrete wall, to meet the sleek, phallic Mercedes which was to make a martyr of Diana. (Ah Di, poor Di, what you are responsible for!)

Therapism is the 'therapy' we are all familiar with entered into public life: a belief structure edging in to take the place of Christianity, Science, Marxism – all overlapping, none coinciding – as those three fade away in a miasmic cloud into the past. Therapism gives us a new idea of what people *are*, why we are here; one which denies God, denies morality, is 'value-free', which rejects the doctrine of original sin – the notion that we were born flawed but must struggle for improvement and replaces it with the certainty that we were all born happy, bright and good and would be able to stay this way if only it weren't for harsh circumstances or faulty parenting. It is a cheerful idea espoused by the nicest and kindest of people, which is why it's so hard to refute. It is also dangerous.

This being the Age of Therapism we turn our attention, like Princess Diana in the famous BBC interview, to our anorexic and bulimic selves, not to the state of the nation. We see ourselves as wronged, not wronging, victims not persecutors; we ally ourselves with the underdog. We 'felt' our way to a Blair victory, didn't 'think' it. When it comes to a decision about joining the common European currency, abandoning the Pound Sterling for the obnoxious new Euro, it's the people's intuition which is to decide the issue, not their judgement. A referendum's to be held; let the people emote their way to the truth, since even the nation's economists are defeated by the complexities of the matter.

This being the Age of Therapism, my local school, which has a leaking roof and no pens or pencils for the children, recently enjoyed a visit by a team of forty counsellors. They stayed for two weeks. Talk and listen, talk and listen. Adapt the child to its circumstances: reality is only in the head.

This being the Age of Therapism, the NSPCC, which knows how to wring hearts and raise funds, now focuses its ads along the lines, 'Just £15 will provide counselling for a child.' Forget hunger, poverty, wretchedness. Talk and listen, talk and listen. All will be cured.

Therapism absolves us of personal blame. The universe is essentially good! The fat aren't greedy, or genetically doomed: no, their unaesthetic shape is caused by abusive fathers. (All switch! In Mother Nature's new creation the old man is the villain of the piece, as in Father God's it was the female witch.) As in *Erewhon*, our criminals are mentally ill, poor things, and the ill (as in AIDS) are the criminals. They didn't eat right. All things are mendable; the paedophile and the rapist can be cured by talk and investigation of the past; the police, unlikely to catch the robber, can put the robbed in touch with their Victims' Support Group. All will be well, and all will be well. Once Christianity was the opium of the people: now its sleeping draught is Therapism.

Poor suffering wretches that we remain, but now without sin, without guilt, and so without possibility of redemption, searching for a contentment which remains elusive. Though at least we cry 'Love, Love, Love,' not 'Kill, Kill, Kill'. We strew flowers in St Diana's royal parks, where'ere she trod, and try not to sew land mines.

Therapism demands an emotional correctness from us – we must prefer peace to war, tranquillity to stress, express our anger so it can be mollified, share our woes, love our children (though not necessarily our parents) and sacrifice our contentment to theirs, ban guns, not smoke, give voice to our low opinion of men (if we are women), and refrain from giving voice to our low opinion of women (if we are men), and agree that at any rate we were all born happy, bright, beautiful and free, and what is more, equal. This latter makes educational policy difficult: Mr Blair, little Mother of the Nation, loves us all the same: we must all strive for academic achievement and when we grow up must all work from nine to five, or eight to six or seven; not because work pays the rent, but because work makes you free.

'Take up thy bed and work' as *The Daily Telegraph* recently subheaded a rather extraordinary article in which a bold new Social Security Secretary of State declared that the disabled must not be condemned to a life of dependence on State Benefits. This government has the opportunity and the mandate – a familiar phrase from ministerial lips since the Blair Government swept into power – to reform the Welfare State so that it provides proper help and support in order to allow those people who can work to do so, while helping those who cannot work to live independently and with dignity. Disability grants, in other words, are to be cut. And indeed, and in fairness to the government in its new stepmother mode, she certainly finds her house cluttered up by unfortunate poor relations she truly cannot afford to keep. If only at the same time she didn't throw quite so many good parties. (£7 million worth, they say, at Downing Street alone, since the election was won, attended by pop stars and flibbertygibbets.) If only, ancient mutton dressed as lamb, stepmother didn't keep claiming to be so cool and young and new; miniskirting those old blue-veined legs.

Everything's being re-logoed. British Airways loses its flag and crown and becomes a flying gallery for 'new, young' artists – those two adjectives apparently being sufficient recommendation for excellence. (I won't fly BA any more: the tail-fins bring out the critic in me.) The retiring head of the British Council in Madrid – the BC is the cultural arm of the Foreign Office – told me sadly the other day that its logo is to change too: from admittedly mysterious but at least recognisable rows of orange dots to something that demonstrates the Council is 'all about people'. 'But it isn't about people,' I protested. 'It's about civilisation, culture, ideas, the arts.' Said he, sadly, 'I wish you'd been at the meeting.' Claim that anything is 'about people', magic words, and all opposition melts away. Diana reigns!

Stepmother doesn't like other women much. Doesn't want rivals. She gives them hot potatoes to hold and sniggers when they drop them. Clare Short of International Development, Mo Mowlam of Northern Ireland, and Harriet Harman of Social Security were all too powerful and popular not to be given office when the transition from old to New Labour was made. Clare Short is manoeuvred into taking the rap for Foreign Office bungling over the evacuation of Montserrat when the volcano erupted: Mo Mowlam is held personally responsible for failing to solve a two-hundred-year-old Irish problem within the year: sweet, pretty Harriet Harman, taking the rap for doing no more than mouth Treasury policy, is now universally disliked as cold and cruel. Oh, stepmother's a smooth operator, all right.

When Diana died, when the black Mercedes crumpled, when the gender switch was finally thrown, when the male-female polarities reversed, when we all took to weeping in the streets and laying flowers, there was, let it be said, an ugly moment or so. That was when Monarchy, male in essence, headed by a head-scarved Queen, refused to show itself as emotionally correct. The Queen wouldn't lower the royal flag to half-mast: the Prince declined to share his grief with his people. (Nor was that grief allowed to be in the least ambivalent: it was as if the divorce and the infidelities had never happened.) For an hour or so the milling crowd outside Buckingham Palace took on a dangerous mien. The people were angry. For once they wanted not bread, or circuses, not even justice – just an overflowing female response to tragedy. Forget all that dignified 'private-grief' stiff upper lip stuff. The crowd got their way. The flag was hauled down. The Prince shared his grief.

Since then the Palace too has shown a female face. Prince Charles is photographed with the Spice Girls, is seen tie-less with his arms around his boys, turns up somewhere in Africa to apologise for Britain's behaviour in the past and has never been so popular. Even Prince

Philip, that dinosaur out of the old patriarchal era, turned up on the occasion of the Royal Golden Wedding Anniversary to apologise to his wife. 'She's had a lot to put up with.' The Queen glittered terrifically in a gorgeous outfit and looked pretty and smiled. Tony Blair escorted her once again as might an affectionate and indulgent daughter.

Women win.

Taking the plough to the Garden. The earth's so stony: nothing blooms any more without effort. Written for the *New Statesman* as New Labour prepared its manifesto, preparatory to taking over the reins of government.

What This Country Needs Is:

– So vast and profound a re-organisation of its manners and customs it's hardly worth even dreaming of.

– But given the dream; a world in which utopianism ceases to be a dirty word: and a vision arises of a human society which echoes actual human needs; in which it's recognised that daily nine-to-five work (if you're lucky) is inappropriate in a prosperous technological society in which machines and computers do the donkey-work, and was never much cop anyway. (People wake and sleep in rhythm – sixteen hours on, eight hours off, roughly – but endeavour tends to come in bursts – weeks on, weeks off: how can nine-to-five be anything but a tedious pain?) In which over-manning is seen as desirable, and inflation is not a devil to be feared and loathed. In which everyone can walk to work. In which every child is a planned and wanted child and parenthood a matter of a joint opting in, not a failure to opt out, and compulsory parental leave (both parents) extends for six years (that would soon cut the birth rate): thirty million is probably a good workable level for the nation. In which school is not compulsory, but in which TV and film fiction is banned by order of the censor general: too much fiction is bad for you. So boredom, not the law, drives the young to school. In which people have enough confidence to see that the cloning of people is a perfectly possible route for humanity's future. If nature creates the Taleban can human ingenuity do so much worse? Courage, courage!

Okay, I'm joking.

Failing all this, I'd settle for one little simple change in the law. That someone who leaves their employment because they're expected to do something immoral or disgusting isn't then declared to be wilfully unemployed and ineligible for unemployment or housing benefit. Employees once had the courage to blow whistles: now it is too difficult. It's a pity. Societies are self-righting, given just half a chance.

'Oh well, business as usual,' was my mother's sighing response to news of NATO's bombing of Serbia. 'How the menfolk love a war.'

Take the Toys from the Boys

Look at the pictures coming out of the Kosovo war. What do you see? Men with blood lust. Men in uniforms, waving guns like phalluses: men in iron tanks, pounding and crushing. The men have got war fever again. Men launching cruise missiles, smart bombs; men having a great time with the toys of death, all the hard metal technology of killing and destruction. Older men back home proving they're still virile and brave, spouting noble sentiments, sending young men to their deaths. *This village must be destroyed to save it!* Slobodan Milosevic, the old Stalinist hardman, happy to face death rather than dishonour. Into the bunker like Hitler, while the nation collapses into rubble around him. No-one's going to give in, no-one's going to back down, males antlers are locked.

What else do you see in the pictures out of Kosovo? Women and children suffering, of course, the natural female sacrifice to the God of War. What fun the men have, stampeding them from their homes. Not just ethnic cleansing, domestic cleansing, atavistic, of the pitiable and pitiful, the too young or too old to breed.

Couldn't we perhaps get a gender perspective on what's going on? This is the War of Lewinsky's Mouth, of Tony proving his virility. All the electorate-friendly girlie touchy-feeling sentiments gone like a flash: let's show some muscle here! Let's forget about the Euro, about the collapsing Peace Accord, about education, education, education, every

Scottish school a computer, the composition of the Second House; all that domestic stuff's so boring, let's be men, let's bring Milosevic to heel.

It's enough to turn you back into a feminist, holding hands around the US cruise missile site at Greenham, chanting *take the toys from the boys*: that was when the wimmin were fed up with living in the terror of nuclear threat.

> *'Take the toys from the boys*
> *Take their hands off the guns,*
> *Take their fingers from the trigger,*
> *Take the toys from the boys.'*

But that was then and this is now. The trouble with the gender perspective at the turn of the millennium is that the sex divide is not so clear. Women are men too. They wear trousers, join the Army, beam blondely from tanks: Madeleine Allbright initiates the hard line: Clare Short declares pacifists to be fascists, Blair's Babes bay for blood. White feathers are back in fashion. And our reconditioned, therapised men have discovered their anima. They run the Aid agencies, care and share, fund raise for refugees, train the army to keep the peace and not to kill (SAS excepted), pick up the pieces while others make the mess.

But that's in the NATO countries. In the former Yugoslavia men stay men and women stay women. The God of War found his opening in the gap between the cultures, alighted laughing with his uranium tipped, incendiary wings, fanned the flames of discontent, cried havoc! and that was it.

Once unleashed the dogs of war are hard to recall, no matter what mantra you chant as you let them go. '*In the name of humanity.*' '*An ethical war.*' '*They deserve it!*' If you're one of the women and children, does the nationality of the bomb that kills you bother you? Whether it was meant or accidental, justified or not, or who apologises? It's the end for you.

Once we send in the ground troops, albeit on the side of good, will the uprooted and dispossessed ever be able to return to Kosovo? The favoured weapons of destruction today are tipped with depleted uranium, the metal that's left over when the radioactive element has been extracted to make even more fearful weapons. Depleted uranium (DU to its friends) is cheap and plentiful and safe, just so dense that when fired with enormous speed, as it is, it pulverises itself and the first thing it meets, without the bother of explosives. A mist of heavy metal rises and falls, permanently poisoning the earth. Such missiles are already being launched over Kosovo. When a shell meets the metal of a tank that turns to dust as well, and falls in a pinkish mist, mixed as it is with human blood. Depleted uranium was used in Southern Iraq in the Gulf War: the level of leukaemia in the children who live there is now, they say, equal to that of Hiroshima. Already, in the heart of Europe, the Danube is polluted, oil and toxic waste runs free.

What form exactly does the 'unconditional surrender' we now require take? Are we dogs, that one has to roll over on its back with its legs in the air, to stop the other biting? Wars are not for 'winning' any more. The victor has to clear up the mess, pay the costs of the conquered too. Serbia may be punished for electing the wrong man, just as Germany once was, but Serbians can't be left to starvation and epidemic, any more than can the Kosovan refugees. Massive aid will be required to get the country on its feet again, under the ruler we impose. (Democracy being what we say it is, not what you thought it was.)

NATO, having destroyed Serbia's infrastructure from the air, and poisoned Kosovo on the ground, will have to follow through its humanitarian gesture by itself taking in the dispossessed, in that same proportion as its members contributed to the war. We can do no less. And the 850,000 Serbian refugees still on the Bosnian border, whom no doubt Milosevic meant to resettle in Kosovo, will have to be dispersed and settled too, with us. We are as responsible, one by one, for the actions of NATO as the Serbians are for those of Milosevic, and we too must put up with the consequences.

But can it really be thought that Milosevic as an individual is to blame for the war, and not the sour dynamics of ethnic and religious antagonisms, cultural incompatibilities, and the legacies of Stalinism, which our bombs can only acerbate? The long-term way through, oddly enough, may lie with gender politics. The way our own macho-war-speak collapses at the drop of a hat into head-girl-speak sounds absurd but may be healthy.

Question: Why did we bomb the cigarette factory?
Answer: They may have been making arms and anyway we don't approve of smoking.

Let the new Kosovo and Serbia Protectorates stand firm on equal opportunities, equal pay, and emotional and sexual correctness, until the politics of testosterone wither away. In the meantime let Blair and Clinton put their mouths where there bombs are and call a summit meeting with Milosevic, since he's taken to playing Stalin, the greatest ethnic disperser of them all. Blair as Churchill. Clinton as Roosevelt. Yalta worked okay, didn't it?

The Way We Live As Women

Two years, 1996–8, spent writing the novel and screenplay of *Big Women* – a fictionalised account of the course of feminism over twenty-five years – and an increasing awareness of just how difficult it is to chart the course of revolution, produced a spin-off in the form of articles and lectures.

Somewhere along the way the gender polarities reversed. Men, being suddenly disadvantaged, notice it. Women, advantaged, tend not to. Why should they?

Girls on Top

Something fairly earth-shattering has occurred. In the face of the old-age worldwide tradition that a boy baby is more valuable than a girl, Birth Clinics here in Britain report that the majority of parents now want girls, not boys. And why not? Everything has changed. Feminism happened. Girls are expected to have better lives than boys, to be better able to care for aged parents, to have better characters. Girls do better at school than boys, get higher qualifications, are better able to find jobs (albeit as cheaper labour), have higher self-esteem, are less likely to destroy themselves with drugs, go to prison, or take their own lives.

In many parts of the world, at worst, girl babies are still aborted, exposed after birth, fed less than their brothers: at best, parental faces fall at, 'Sorry, it's a girl.' Here, all of a sudden, it's different. Girls earn, girls control their own fertility, girls can do without boys. Girls are on top.

'And high time too,' as many a feminist would say. 'Let the men see what it feels like for a change,' – but tit for tat is no way to human progress. The danger is that the oppression of women will, little by little, be replaced by the oppression of men. It is true that in the top echelons of society, dinosaur men still rule the roost; run the government, the banks, the corporations, the institutions, and can command vast salaries, but do so more and more as figureheads. Women have the knowledge, the confidence, run the back office. If they don't yet get full credit for it, they're working on it.

It is also true that outside our metropolitan areas, our sophisticated cities, things tend to go on as they always have: men stay on top. Wash my shirt, woman! In places where Andy Capp still rules, and in our traditional ethnic communities, girls on top may sound far-fetched: but look round the corner and see it coming.

A gender switch has operated. Twenty-five years ago men gave women a hard time: now women give men a hard time. Hear it in our language; once the terms of abuse for women were plentiful – slag, slut, hysteric, castrator, shrill (if she opened her mouth in public), cackling harridan (if she laughed), and terms of opprobrium for men were almost non-existent. But now we have nerd, wet, wanker, macho, wimp, snam (Sensitive New Age Man), and the list is growing. Okay – evening out the balance, but careful! Better men as equals than inferiors. Moaning men are no fun.

In the last twenty-five years women have taught men tenderness and now deride them for it. Women have learned toughness from men, call it assertiveness and turn into bullies on the male model. Women lump men together as macho beasts. Women taught men how to love their children, and now are the ones who initiate divorce and snatch them away. Everyone dutifully talks about the problem of the working mother, but who mentions the problems of the working father? But for every mother there's a father too.

Where does this leave the boys now growing up in a woman's world, lumped together, as women once were, as the inferior gender? Having a hard time of it, confused and failing at school, struggling for self-esteem, wondering what exactly men are *for*. Unemployable, unmarriageable, and hoping for the love of a good woman to save them. For men are no longer a scarce resource. In age groups under forty there are now more men than women. Medical care keep the boys – the weaker sex – alive. So girls become the sexual pickers and choosers. If you have acne forget it. If you want to be my lover, you'd better get on with my friends. God help you!

If a girl wants a man at all, that is – nasty, uncouth, ugly things! She can get sexual pleasure from a pill. She can get herself pregnant at a clinic. She can get the State to take over the traditional paternal role – though a grim and grisly Victorian-style provider the State increasingly turns out to be. If she doesn't want to be a mother – and now it's the men who yearn to be fathers, and the women put it off, and off – she uses the man as a sexual object, a status symbol down the rave. The tables turned.

Our very society is now wholly feminised: we have turned our back on militarism, on toughness, on discipline: the aim now is to care and nurture. Even the old stern patriarch God is gone: rather we worship tender Mother Nature.

Male sexuality becomes a problem. Follow your natural instincts, and find them construed as sexual harassment. What you thought was sex turns out to be an abuse of power. A girl invites you into her bed for the night, then complains to the police that you did what (to you) comes naturally. So train yourself out of it! Which may lead to a problem. How are you doing, lad, potency-wise? Probably not too well. Tarred with the brush of the rapist one day, jeered at for bad performance the next? There is no brotherhood, as women have a sisterhood (in the last twenty-five years women have learned to be friends, not competitors for male favours, as once was the case) to show you a path out of your confusion. The therapists are on the whole female, and out of sympathy in sexual matters. Turn on the TV and see female comedians jeering at men, as husbands and lovers, as no male comedian would dare jeer at women, and cower. Every drama, every novel, shows woman as victim, men as villain. Never were so many male egos so regularly deflated. What price self-esteem now?

Sure, it's men's turn, but the aim of feminism was not to win, not to put men down, but to achieve equality: to be allowed to be a person first and of a certain gender second. These rights are now encapsulated in law. But how about the rights of a teenage boy in a working-class area? Girls jeer at you, police harass you, teachers (mostly female) give up on you. School inspectors shake their heads over you. Ofsted maintains that the underachievement of boys, particularly white, working-class boys, is one of the most significant problems that schools face today. Parents find you impossible. Old ladies cross the street to avoid you. What do you look forward to? Insecurity is the name of the male game. Thirty percent of all our unemployed are under twenty-five; and of that thirty, twenty are male, ten are female. Twice as many. Male unemployment goes up, female unemployment goes down. One in three men have suffered at least one period of unemployment in the last five years. Once a man could look forward to starting a family and the *gravitas* and dignity that came from being the family provider. Forget it. At best as a man you're decorative and look after the kids, and earn a bit sometimes, at worst you're a write-off. Women are elbowing the men out. The boys get anxious, the girls swagger. The male suicide rate goes up, female down.

Twenty-eight percent of us now live in single person households – a lonely and unnatural state – and most of the twenty-eight percent consists of young single men. It is strange that it is left to a woman to suggest in the normal nurturing way that men start some kind of movement to promote their gender's status and self-esteem – call it masculinism, homoism, brotherism, machoism, what you want – and some mark of the success of the feminist movement, that it needs to be done.

The Fish and the Bicycle

Back in the seventies feminists slapped up a poster which announced to a startled and disbelieving public: '*A woman needs a man like a fish needs a bicycle.*' That is to say, she didn't need one at all. Time, for good or bad, has proved that once unlikely poster right. The world changed: the laws changed: and any young woman these days can live without a man. She may not want to, but she can. It may feel unnatural, she may be lonely at night, but she has her freedom and her financial independence. She can earn, she can spend, she can party. She can find casual sex if she wants to and there's contraception to ward off babies. (Because what she can't have, if she values her freedom and independence, is a baby.)

If a woman is young, bright, educated, able-bodied, attractive, childless and in the professions she can live very happily indeed. And just as well, because this seems to be the kind of woman – like poor, nervy Ally McBeal: poor all-over-the-place Bridget Jones – who these days *has* to do without a man. 'No wonder,' observes my mother, who is ninety-one. 'She's too proud and picky for her own good. She wants someone she can look up to, and where's she going to find him?' New Woman, claims my mother, shocks potential partners to the core by demanding sex and refusing love (just as men once used to) so he's off and away by morning. 'And if they're not shocking him they're insulting him,' says my mother. 'So who can blame him?'

Sexism becomes something more directed towards men by women than from men towards women. Women can speak about men as men can no longer speak about women (at least in company). To do so becomes so much a cultural knee-jerk women don't even notice they're doing it. It is commonplace to hear the entire male gender written off as selfish, obtuse and bullying; rapists in spirit if not in deed. '*Men, who wants them? Who needs them?*' And men laugh uneasily but, astonishingly, collude in this description of themselves. Men are portrayed as braying, despicable fools in cartoons, books, plays and advertisements. Male journalists and TV interviewers, talking to me on 'pity the poor men' themes, are even more scathing than traditional feminists. 'But we're crass fools,' they say, in effect, 'How can you have a good word to say for us?' They behave like hostages who have fallen in love with their captors; with the colonised who admire the colonisers: I am perpetually amazed. Try writing a film these days about a woman who isn't 'strong and independent'. It won't get made. You can be as insulting as you like about men.

When girl-babies are born – certainly in my part of London – there's rejoicing: if it's a boy, it's, *Oh well, better luck next time.* Because it's girls who on the whole look adorable, who don't bang and crash about, who pass exams, take fewer drugs, don't crash cars or go to prison, who get the jobs as school-leavers and satisfy today's definition of what a good citizen is: a responsible, caring, sharing, nurturing, hard-working, mortgage-paying, not over-intellectual person, without too much aggression and not inclined to rock the boat: someone who makes a good employee. A woman, in fact. This is the age of oestrogen, not testosterone. Men begin to have a low self-image that women once had. The suicide rate for young males grows at an alarming rate, for outstripping that of young women. So yes, pity the poor men, whose maleness has become unfashionable. Even the male models are all gay, everyone knows. Pretty boys.

What, pity those football hooligans, pity those lads? Is it possible? Phwooaring as they do, leering and lurching round the streets, cracking foul sexist jokes, refusing to grow up? Pity? 'Oh yes,' says my mother firmly, 'It's not their fault. The new young men respond to the new young women by turning laddish. It's the only defence they have against rejection.' While the men are watching football, the wives and girlfriends – should the lads be lucky enough to have them – are back home sneering, deriding the men behind their backs, or off down the club cheering on the male stripper, making lewd comparisons. 'If the women behaved more like proper women,' says my mother, 'even the most laddish lout might discover the protective gene deep within himself, grow up, and develop the kind of nobility and *gravitas* a woman likes to see in a man, and which makes a decent husband and father of him. It's a chicken and egg situation, you can't have one without the other.'

If laddishness is a response to humiliation and indignity, so too I suspect is the *girl-power! girl-power!* female triumphalism which echoes through the land – even in the school-playground by poppety-tots scarcely old enough to tie their own shoelaces. To go into girl-power mode is New Young Woman's defence against the possibility of male rejection, and the humiliations that go with it. All those old phrases still echoing in the race memory of the female – *spinster, left-on-the-shelf, old maid!* So get in first: who wants a man? Who needs one? Can't we earn, spend, party perfectly well without them? All men are (rapists) (paedophiles) (bastards) (selfish) (impossible) (the same) – the vehemence of expression depending upon the degree of anxiety – so why do we bother with them?

As to babies, the women begin to say to one another, *well, we'll just have to do without them, and make a virtue of it, or if we fail to sit out the broodiness, choose a passing sperm donor. Real men only get in the way, tell you what to do, you can't trust them with the children, paedophiles all! So come on everyone, down to the sperm bank! And then what have you got to look forward to? All those childcare problems, all that anxiety and expense? On second thoughts, forget it!*

All over Europe the birth rate falls, as working women decide they can't afford time or energy for children. A family with more than three children, once a commonplace, becomes a rarity. In Spain and Italy the birth rate is now below replacement level, as women flee from the traditional life and the religion that once tied them so firmly to the home. Which is all very well if it's a matter of choice, but too often it's a matter of necessity: money has to be earned. How can one income, in our taxed and technological world, keep a family in comfort? Both husband and wife must go out to work. And older women (and men too) look around in despair and wonder whatever happened to the grandchildren? *What have our lives been all about? Are we not to hand the good things on?*

Men, encouraged by women to look inwards and discover their anima, have done so with a vengeance. Once grown out of laddishness they long for fatherhood. But how is it to be achieved? The world of work scarcely allows it. 'The problem of the working father' gets hardly a mention; the working mother gets all the attention. The government focuses on 'getting mothers back to work' as if fathers didn't exist. Employers demand long hours and full attention and if a man doesn't offer it, there's a long queue behind him who will. In the world of high unemployment workers, men and women, dance to the employers' tune. It is true enough that some men are only too pleased to get off the hook of fatherhood, and probably more of them percent-age wise than there are mothers doing the same, but there's still a whole lot of would-be good fathers out there who can't do their share of parenting but long to. Mothers resent the father's absence, everyone's exhausted, the baby cries, relationships split: one in four children are now tossed into the world of visiting uncles, passer-by aunts and the traumatic acquiring of new step-parents and siblings.

At the turn of the century the children of erring mothers stayed with their fathers. Current divorce laws now favour mothers, and just as unfairly. Men begin to complain. This being the day of the 'no fault' divorce the judge now looks to the best interest of the child, and decides that East-West, mother's best. So mother ends up with home, child and maintenance, though it may well have been mother who took a lover and threw father out, for no better reason than that she was bored and fed up. Lover moves into father's bed and gives the child its cornflakes when morning comes; father suffers atrociously, and still has to pay up.

It's no good saying, as women will, 'Oh well, it's men's turn to suffer now, serve them right, look what they once did to us.' Revenge was never the purpose of the women's movement, merely justice. What are we, *tricoteuses*? Sitting round the guillotine, watching the heads roll, gloating?

Both men and women suffer with the death of love, but children suffer most of all. And the cry of today's splitting parents, 'Remember we both love you very much,' must ring pathetically false to the child's ears. Obviously both parents love themselves most: what are they talking about? The very word 'love' loses meaning.

This century has seen such profound changes in the way we live, and marry, and bring up our young, it's amazing we're doing as well as we are. A hundred years ago only one in three women married and had children. It may be that this is a more appropriate rate, being better fitted to our natures, than the ninety percent we'd managed by the fifties, a level now falling fast, and that it is to this one in three proportion we are fast returning: a population in which only the most maternally (or paternally) inclined amongst us marry and have children. The rest will work, as the majority of women did a hundred years ago – though not as servants, or in the fields, factories or laundries, but at the computer, as managers, in the service industries, the professions, or of course as child minders for other women.

As matters stand today, in the absence of shared parenting, the solution for most mothers who work must be to hand over their children to another woman who gets paid less than they do. This being the case, how can there not be a gap between the male and the female wage? Though one less to do with gender discrimination than the fact that it's women who give birth, and are left, willy-nilly, holding the baby.

A hundred years ago, contraception was illegal and immoral. Sex and babies went together – the law insisted, and the Church. Since the advent of the pill mid-century, for the first time in human history, women have controlled their own fertility. Once this was the man's job, and for the most part he took his responsibility seriously: and if he didn't there was hell to pay. Yet another traditional role is lost to him. Sex was, obviously, a graver, more sacramental, less impulsive matter than it is today: now for good or bad it's all feeling and emotion, feminised.

A hundred years ago, adding to the trauma of social change, there were more women than men. Now there are more men than women. Some one hundred and four male babies are conceived in this country to every one hundred females (don't ask me why: or why the rate should vary from nation to nation, climate to climate: actually rising to one hundred and nineteen to one hundred in the Gambia). Improved medical care means that the great majority of male babies (born more delicate than girl babies – and if that makes you cheer, that's sexism) live to maturity. So far as girls go, and for the first time in human history, they enjoy a seller's market. The girls are the ones who do the picking, choosing, and rejecting. Evolution pulls us one way: suggesting to girls that they must flirt and charm and compete for boys: and to boys that all they have to do to get the girl is swagger and impress. The practicalities and realities of our new altered world pull us the other way, making nonsense of our traditions.

The upheaval is tremendous: social and demographic change came on us unawares: there will be further surprises yet. Feminism must stop fighting old wars: the battleground has altogether changed. If women are oppressed, it is no longer by men, but by the society which feminism has helped bring about. Patriarchy – rule by the father – is no longer the enemy: rather it is the ergonarch, rule by the work ethic, and by empliarchy – rule by accountant and employer. We are all in the workforce now, men, women and children, and our interests may not be identical but they more than overlap: they are insolubly linked. The feminist brief must extend to cover the rights of men, as well as the rights of women, or we are all in danger of living unhappily ever after.

New Adam finds he suffers, as Old Adam didn't.

Pity the Poor Men

'The great question' observed Freud, 'which in all my thirty years of studying the female psyche I have not been able to answer is: "What does a woman *want*?"' Men must be more transparent than women. It doesn't take thirty years of studying the male psyche for a woman to work out what it is a man wants. It's so obvious. Though please, please, pity the poor man! These days so few women are prepared to take his wants seriously. They will keep laughing.

Question: What does a young man want from his girlfriend?
Answer: What he's always wanted. Sex, love, loyalty, sex. Sex, flattery, status, sex. Different sex. Lively chatter from her about nothing in particular. Sex, admiration, adoration, sex. Style. Short skirts, big bosom, little waist, long legs and strappy shoes. Sex with freedom to drift off tomorrow without being reproached or made to feel guilty. Sex followed by 'I'll call you, don't you call me.' And no tears.

Sex, to prove manhood, virility, and effectiveness in a world which is increasingly feminised, where male values are out of fashion, and governments, to be well thought of, employ the female language of caring, sharing and apology. Where aggression is despised, technology makes male muscle-power irrelevant, and careful! careful! that touch might count as sexual harassment. A much changed world for men to live in, one in which women control their own fertility, earn their own living, and enjoy their own status, not that of their husbands or fathers. In which a woman, exhausted by a day's work, is as likely to fall asleep after sex as a man ever was – and hope to heaven he does too.

Pity the poor man, don't despise him. So much change to cope with!

Question: What does a man want from his wife?

(For wife or husband, read partner too. Not quite the same thing, mind you, because partnerships break up at a faster rate than marriages. The legal tie is the more binding tie.)

Answer: What he's always wanted. Love, loyalty, sex, contentment. Beauty. Love, acceptance, good cooking, sex. Love, adoration, sympathy, sex. Children, and her total attention as well. A kind woman, not too thin and bony. A cheerful temperament, a ready smile, compliance. A second honeymoon? More sex! To be allowed to have it all ways. Fidelity from her, but instant forgiveness should the desire for new sex lure him temporarily from the home. A wife other men envy. One who earns enough to take her share of the financial burden, but doesn't neglect the house or children. A wife to be the meaning and purpose of his days.

Today's wife finds such requirements ridiculous. She demands equality, justice, the right to argue, the right to decide what's for dinner and to expect him to cook it too, to go out to work and earn as much or more than he does. She answers back and teaches the children to do the same; she refuses to take male tantrums seriously, favours her daughters over her sons, goes on diets, demands sex, is on the mobile phone all the time, and out with her friends when he'd rather she stayed home watching TV on the sofa with him. Pity the poor man.

Pity the poor man, since most divorces these days are initiated not by men but by women. And a high proportion of these are women earning more than their husbands. Women, it seems, somewhere deep in their psyche, still want to look up to men. They marry their equals, outstrip them, divorce them.

And when the wife goes she takes the children. Or rather she and they get to stay, he goes. But wasn't he there at the birth? Didn't she train him to love their children, nurture them, invest all his caring emotions in them? And then, just like that, at her behest, is it to be goodbye? It's hard! There's more upset and misery caused by divorce than ever there used to be, in the days when men were kept out of the nursery, and the rearing of the children was seen to be the woman's province.

As to what women want, Herr Freud, I'll tell you. Please don't turn in your grave. You changed the world for us, and by and large we're grateful – apart from all that nonsense about penis envy and the merits of the vaginal orgasm. What we didn't want was to be subservient to men. We wanted our *dignity*.

Question: What does a young woman want from her boyfriend?

Answer: What she's always wanted, but more. Love, companionship, sex. Someone to care, to make her laugh, to understand her. More love. Outings. More sex. Money. Someone to teach her about food, wine, art, without noticing she needs teaching. A handsome man other girls envy, but who has eyes only for her. A good lover who can maintain sexual interest while she searches for a condom. A sensitive man who understands when the magic's gone and it's time to move on. Someone who isn't going to turn into a stalker. Someone who isn't depressed, but who lets her have her own moods; who never accuses her of premenstrual tension when it's obvious that's what's going on. A really intelligent sexy charming man who shares her interests and doesn't want her to cook dinner for him. A man her therapist approves of (she's got a hope! Even parents are easier to please) whose heart she can break but who doesn't break hers. A man who agrees with her that women are superior to men, yet *does* something when the car's clamped: who will match her tear for tear. Who will also provide a strong male shoulder to cry on. Sex, to tell her friends. More sex, so she's sure she loves him. A man who sees her as thin even when she isn't. Sex. Good sex. A multi-orgasmic her, created by him. Everything, in fact. Plus a reason for living.

A man who doesn't exist. Which is why these days you meet so many bright, beautiful, single young women with good careers, waiting to meet the right man. A few bemoan their lack of boyfriend, the rest congratulate themselves. '*We're the Singletons*,' as they say in London. They rejoice in their free, proud, independent state. '*How happy we are with our friends*,' they say. '*How fulfilled with our careers! Who wants a man?*' These are the 'New Feminists' or (as some unkindly call them) the 'Lite Feminists', the ones who in their longing to get it right and be universally loved want the word feminism to stretch to include the high-heeled and the fancy-free. And whoever thought it shouldn't? Feminism never had a party headquarters, a manifesto. Take it as you find it.

Question: What does a wife-and-mother want from a husband?

Answer: A lot. Love, help, support. An income. An identity of interests. A sharing of the shock which comes with the having of children – later in life now than it used to be, so the shock's greater. (*No sleep, no time, the loss of personal identity – drowned in the ocean of the baby's needs – exhaustion.*) Parity of parenting. He to go to the school gate as often as she does. (*If only the world were set up for it. If only!*) A husband who allows her to decide the baby's name, the style of child-rearing, but loves the baby just as much as she does, who makes enough money so she doesn't have to go back to work if she doesn't want to, who says who cares about the promotion race anyway? A husband who shares the anxiety of child-rearing as well as the joys, yet who doesn't pay more attention to the child than he does to her. A husband who'll disappear, vanish, cease to exist, should she wish to divorce him to go it alone. (*As happens in thirty percent of marriages.*) Love. Sex. Adoration. Magic. Myth. Meaning. Sharing. Caring. Husband and father, provider of happiness, centre of security. A husband who looks the other way if the yearning for adventure, for difference, gets too much, and you have the silliest of affairs. '*Sorry, darling, it didn't mean a thing. Okay?*' Love, laughter, togetherness, point and purpose. Everything.

How can a mere man provide all these things? He can't, in perpetuity.

Any more than a woman can, for him. So love, forgive, forget, excuse: the other as much as the self.

We carry our happiness within ourselves. Pointless to blame, argue, wrangle. There is no set way for anyone to be, male or female. Others ought to do this and ought to do that, of course they should. How nice it would be if men showed their feelings, how nice it would be if they were more like us. But would it? Opposites attract. If women devalue men, as they seem to be on the way to doing, denying them all expressions of their natural and useful aggression, mocking the simplicity of their desires, what sort of time will we have in bed? Not much of one. What sort of husbands and fathers will men make if they're too like us? New Men are fine in the kitchen, but who wants them in the bedroom? Go carefully, young women, if you want to go on loving and find someone worthy of your love. Look after his feelings.

After a session with the grandchildren . . .

Today's Mother – Bonded and Double-binded

Today's mother has a hard time. She may have a washer-dryer and a microwave but her duties are onerous. Not only must she look after her child's physical, cognitive and emotional welfare, but she must look after its soul as well in the short time the need to earn allows her. *Don't Steal, Don't Cheat, Don't Lie, Don't Bully, Be Nice, Be Aware of the Prime Mover*, are now all firmly in mother's court. The Church used to do some of it. The Church would take responsibility for the child's soul at the christening; it would appoint godparents, givers of bibles and bringers to heaven. No longer. The school? The school teaches Environmental Guilt and Feel-Good down the Reclamation Centre and not much else. Mother in the meanwhile, has not a single sanction to help her socialise her child. Mother must not hit, slap, harshly condemn, invoke hellfire, God's all-seeing eye, or offer gentle-Jesus-meek-and-mild as a role model. Even a maternal tear – *tread on a crack, break your mother's back* – is seen as over-manipulative. Today's mother must not withdraw love. She must lead by example and example alone, and who's looking? The kids are watching TV.

Today's mother is in a double bind. Only an unhappy child is a bad child, and whose fault is it if a child is unhappy? Mother's. She has failed in love. So the worse her child gets the more she must love. Heal all by hugs and kisses. Little children riot, flailing, breaking, abusing, marvelling at the idiocy of the adult world.

I'm not saying good or bad, merely remarking.

Childcare fashions change with the decades. Yesterday's mother saw babies born out of original sin, into sin. Imperfect as she too was, she did her best, no more could be expected of her. Today's baby is seen as a *tabla rasa*, bursting into the world bright, perfect, sinless, evolution's triumph and finishing point. Upon this slate the mother writes her child's future, and all manner of good and evil. If the baby cries it is mother's fault: she must allow it not a minute's distress: any misstep can spell both cognitive and psychological mischief, as mistakes in an earlier age could result in severe physical illness. If baby cries at night don't roll over and forget it. Up, up!

Today's mother can't rest: she must talk to her baby incessantly, develop its tactile, spacial and communicative abilities. (*Next door's baby can read at two. What have* you *been doing, mother?*) Yesterday's mother thought spacial and tactile whatnots grew by themselves, like teeth, and got more rest. Yesterday's mothers swaddled babies and bored them to sleep, occasionally sang to them to soothe them, rarely read to them. Yesterday's children learned to read fast, by themselves. How else were they to find out what went on in the world? Some of these children grew up to have Firsts in Philosophy, some didn't. Today's mothers don't dare leave a thing to fate: they'll be blamed if they do. Today's mothers are trained to be interventionist.

Mothers forever have been sensitive to reproach, passionate to get things right. They believe what they're told. Now they're told their brain shrinks by ten percent while they're pregnant. This may well be true.

On the subject of singing, if the baby gets croup in the night, call the doctor, take the baby, go to the bathroom, run the hottest steamiest bath possible, and sit there with the baby, singing to it. The baby's so astonished the choking stops. It may just be the steam, of course. But it works.

Childcare fashions change with the decades, sometimes suddenly and drastically. The educated classes, those who read childcare books, are the most sensitive to the obsessive notions of those who write them. In the thirties the advice was to rear babies at a distance, not to pick them up, to avoid physical contact whenever possible, to feed at strict four hourly intervals (three hourly for the first month, lucky baby), and to ignore their crying. These babies became the isolated young mothers of the fifties, who took to tranquillisers and alcohol, who kept their babies in prams at the bottom of the garden; part of a generation of guilty stoics. Forties babies, reared without theory, with bombs dropping from the sky and a State doling out goodies, turned into sixties radicals, flower-powery, drug-taking and disingenuous. Those fifties mothers, tranquillised, produced a grunge seventies generation of blackly glowering, pale-faced youth. Sixties mothers, their bible Benjamin Spock, were responsible for the yuppie eighties; seventies Penelope Leachites produced today's solipsistic, mumbling sharers and carers. It's the childcare 'Book of Fashion' that determines the character of the decade twenty years on. And all Mother's fault.

Well, it's a theory. I'm working on it.

Today's mother must put up with the pain of childbirth; swinging back to yesteryear, in pain and sorrow, et cetera, must she bring forth issue. Today's mother is brainwashed into believing that childbirth, being a natural process, must be painless if only she could get it right. Today's mother goes into labour. She pants, she relaxes, her husband has the video camera out – keep smiling, Mother, stop screaming, or be a failure –

Today's mother is required to 'bond', a concept which only came into existence twenty years ago. Ordinary affection and responsibility for a child will not do: something more primitive must cut in: a fiercely protective instinct which has very little to do with common sense. Here comes Nurse, marching down the maternity ward! 'Has your milk come in, Mother, have you passed water, have you bonded yet?' Bonding is a life sentence of love and irrational anxiety mixed. The bonded mother can only have a quiet mind when the child is sleeping at her breast, and God knows what the trauma of the dream can be. How can she save it from that?

Better the sabre-toothed tiger outside the cave, if you ask me, than the current ad on TV. See there, pictures of blighted mites! Did you know, your child, happy and healthy today, can be blind, deaf, dead within the week? Childhood diseases! Immunise now before disaster strikes. Measles, meningitis, whooping cough! Yet don't these jabs cause brain damage, asks the double-binded, bonded mother, handmaiden to the State. When the State says 'safe' mother knows the State means 'acceptable risk'. Acceptable to whom, exactly?

Today's mother has to trust nature to know best. Here comes the Breast Milk Lady, marching down the ward. Away with those bottles you thought would set you free! Breast-feed! (Here's a fine way to keep the fathers out. Only mothers can breast-feed.) Statistics are flung at the sore-nippled, swollen-breasted mother. Do this or damage your baby for life. You can't go home 'til suckling's established. Yesterday's mother thought breast milk was nature's minimum for a baby's survival, not the best that could be done.

As I say, I'm not saying good or bad, I'm only remarking.

Today's bonded double-binded mother is out at work anyway. One income is not enough to support today's family. Come rain, come shine, she must daily hand over her baby to another woman who earns less than she does: who has lower status. Mother can no longer guard her child from physical, cognitive, emotional and moral harm. She has to trust where no trust should be. Today's mother is exhausted. Forty-seven percent of women with children under four work part time or full time.

Today's mother, bonded or not, can keep her child only for the first four years and then must send it to school under penalty of law, into classes of thirty, forty, to the care of State-appointed strangers, where it will catch colds and infections, brush up against other religions, other customs, be perpetually 'examined', learn about sex from strangers, be bossed, bullied and humiliated. Public humiliation being the only sanction left to the unfortunate teacher. But that's another story.

Yesterday's State assumed it took care of the child from the moment it left the parental door to the moment it returned: the State undertook to keep it warm, safe, fed and clothed in the interval. Today's State remembers only its rights, not its obligations. Today's mother must escort the child to school, for fear of maniacs, serial killers and the car, cut sandwiches, buy uniforms; she'll soon have to supervise homework on penalty of a fine, the better for this child to pass exams: (what exactly *for*? So the best at exams can get the jobs? But if your child's 'best', what about your neighbour's child? Where exactly does this competition lead?)

If the recent overall figure of twelve percent of women expected to get to forty-five without having a baby has gone up to twenty percent over the last decade and is rising, who can be surprised? The figure is higher still for the professional middle classes, those most susceptible to childcare theories. They give up. Understandably.

In 'today's mother' I include 'today's father'. (In legal contracts the word 'he' is seen to include the lesser 'she'; in terms of parenting, the father, like it or not, is always seen as the lesser.) Today's bonded father, and there are many of them, has an even more complicated, more distressing time of it than the bonded mother, and that's saying something. Society is punitive towards both; the pattern of that punishment changes with the decades, but remains both ingenious and harsh. The executive sixty-hour week hardly helps. The world of work runs as if the human race did not have children.

I was speaking on a platform the other day with Ken Livingstone, Melvyn Bragg and Peter Stothard, editor of *The Times*. All the men happily acknowledged and constructively addressed 'the problem of the working mother'. No-one, nevertheless, mentioned the working father, though for every mother there's a father too. When men of power, employers, and governments recognise this simple fact, and society learns to shape itself round its members, rather than requiring its members to content themselves around society, we will be getting somewhere.

From a panel debate at the Purcell Room, Royal Festival Hall, in June 1998, with Will Hutton, editor of *The Observer*, and Melanie Phillips, writer and broadcaster. Will Hutton arrived late, to ironic clapping from an almost all-female audience and shouts of: 'It's a man's privilege to be late!' and 'We're only women, after all.'

Has Feminism Gone Too Far?

These are delicate matters to discuss. They can make people very angry. Courage is required.

Yes, I think for mothers feminism has gone too far. Or rather feminism has been used as a cloak under shelter of which women have been driven out into the workforce, and their children turned over into the nightmare called childcare. And most women turn into mother in the end. The right of a woman to work, to earn, to make her contribution to society, has been turned into the necessity for her to work at any old job if she and her child are to survive. One wage packet is not enough to keep a family in comfort and dignity; everyone knows. Takes two, these days, unless you're very lucky. Well, it would, wouldn't it? Women joined the workforce, real wages were driven down. Though I think Mr Hutton would disagree. If only one wage packet is available, let alone lone parent benefit, life's grimmer for women than it ever was.

I am not blaming feminism for what happened. Well, not feminism alone. I'm saying this is where we are now. The whole social landscape has changed. Feminism took off and flourished in the seventies, in the days of full employment. Times are different now. If feminism is to regain its credibility it must start paying attention not just to unmarried, childless, bright young things who do very well indeed in the world, thank you, but to women with children. Who are not in a position to give their full-time attention to their employers.

What has happened to even ordinary married mothers in the last twenty-five years, the changing pattern of society which makes life so difficult for them, the need to juggle the needs of the child against the needs of the employer became evident when the Blair government suggested that lone mothers on State Benefit were to be directed into work, under Welfare to Work schemes. They could not expect to be kept by the State, they were in effect to be directed into work. A return to the Soviet system of directed labour, of children compulsorily put into care. Think of it. From crèche, to nursery, to school, into jobs, seeing far less of their parents than they do of nurses, teachers, therapists, and of course more of one another. The peer group is increasingly important for the growing child, and how can it not be. It is the peer group which lays down its standards, defines its aspirations – and being young is not necessarily wise. And if we could protest on behalf of lone mothers, what about the plight of the lessalones? Work Makes You Free! I have this vision, as in those Soviet posters of the thirties, of we, the workforce, marching over the hill into the new dawn, shoulder to shoulder, men and women both, shaking off the little children as we go, but working for what? – and to no purpose, no perceived end. Not even a Stalinist Five-Year Plan to give it meaning. As if motherhood was not work. Benefit is only an indignity if those who administer to make it so. And they certainly do. Mothers demand the right to work! Well yes, staying home with the kids is a nightmare for any thinking active woman; being alone at home with the full force of a powerful mother's attention is no fun for any child. No-one wants to put the clock back. I want to see posters. *Mothers demand more money for less work!* That's what the new improved remorseful feminism, its remit extended to include mothers, should be aiming for. Having changed the world it must now start picking up a few bits.

Feminism should not just be asking for more crèches, where babies from three months old are left, by exhausted, worried mothers. This is a time in which with one hand society stresses the importance of the mother–child relationship, and with the other hand snatches away the possibility of doing anything about it. Twenty-five years ago Germaine Greer's solution to the baby problem was that babies would be left to the care of nice, motherly, peasant women, of the kind you found in Tuscany. Try finding them: rare then, none now. All are out at work. Grannies too. No-one in feminist thinking seems to have got much further than that initial non-solution ever since. *More childcare, more childcare*, comes the votive murmur, like the *Hail Mary, Hail Mary*, of yesteryear, the *market forces, market forces*, of Eastern Europe after the collapse of the wall. More and more professional women solve the real problem by just not having babies, and who can blame them?

Now to this business of glass ceilings – the shattering or otherwise of. Statistics pour out of government saying women haven't achieved equal pay, urging us on to more effort, more struggle, yet more ambition, to be more like men, to rise in the hierarchy, to have the same competitiveness as men, the same aggression as men. Paradoxical that the qualities which women affect to scorn in men, are what they are now urged to emulate. How few men break the glass ceiling, get to the top of the tree. Most are left behind in the race; that's the point of the race. If somebody wins, a hundred lose. Do women really want to compete in these strange hierarchical, antler-locking institutions? Railtrack, British Gas. It was never our ambition to be men. Was it? It's just if you have to work, I suppose, you might as well work to some advantage.

And the statistics mean nothing, say nothing about gender discrimination, or injustice, until they are divided into women without children and women with, and into age groups – which they are not. I suspect it is not gender prejudice that still works against the female, as once it did, it is the fact that females give birth to children. When it comes to the age of shattering glass ceilings, many women prefer not to, because by then they have children, and don't want falling glass to hurt the baby. They want to be there at bathtime. My feeling is that what stops women getting to top jobs is not the men any more, but the children. The new improved remorseful feminism, the NIRF. The Nirf, picking up bits, must require that the statistics which came out of government departments and quangos are properly detailed so we can come to proper conclusions. You can no longer divide the human race into two categories, male and female. Let us at least extend it to four. Men, women, mothers, fathers. Then we'll see.

Men as the enemy! I'd like, with Melanie Phillips, to call a halt to the gender wars, declared back in the seventies by feminism. Times change: enemies, as once they certainly were, turn into allies. I'd like to see a change to that cultural knee-jerk response we all have – I'm guilty too – of having an agreeable laugh at the follies of men, at the expense of men. There were three strains in seventies feminism, the separatist, the radical, the socialist. The separatist tendency still comes through the most strongly: the women who felt life was better without men, all male sex being an attack. This is the strand of feminism the new young feminists most deplore, and rightly. They don't want to be associated with all that. Believe me, the separatists were a necessary element in feminism at the time. Back in the seventies, men were indeed great coarse, predatory beasts, and the cultural knee jerks the reversal of what it is now: all women were seen as fools and idiots, silly, romantic and incompetent, and viewed like that by women as much as men. And many of us were, because that's how society defined us. We do grow into what we are expected to be. But women learned better. Men can too, and must. The inevitable consequence of feminism is that it has taken away from men their duty, to support us and our children: by so doing we have removed their *gravitas*, their purpose, and turned them into studs, as once they turned us, the non-mothers amongst us, into sex objects. The least we can do is listen to their complaints and attend to them, as once they attended to ours.

Feminism is the only movement in recent years to turn the personal into the political, to pay attention to the quality and dignity of our lives. I have been obliged by the terms of this debate to assert it's gone too far – let me rephrase that; it has gone too far in its neglect. Its neglect of the role of mother, its neglect of the role of father.

Feminism by now should have brought about a society in which 'the problem of the working father' loomed as large as 'the problem of the working mother'. Because every child has a father, takes two to make the next, and the obvious way to take the burden of being both mother and earner, is to hand half of it over to the father. And many a father would be happy to do this. But how can he: the hours and necessities of employment prevent it, and many a mother, I fear, is reluctant to see it happen: regarding men as a rather inferior and untrustworthy class of human being. Let feminism extend its remit, and express its remorse, by including the welfare of women as mothers and of men as fathers, and I will stop saying it's gone too far, just that it hasn't gone far enough. Wouldn't it be nice if we all worked to live, not lived to work. I see no reason why if we put our mind to it, it shouldn't happen.

A Royal Progress

Essays from London for Abroad.

On the announcement of the Royal Split.

Princesses and Other Myths

What are we to tell our little daughters now? When one myth sets out to destroy the other? Now Happy Ever After's gone for good, destroyed by the Fairy-Tale Princess herself?

What's left for the little girls now, all over the world, for an archetype? *Barbie? Baywatch?* Kate Moss, and the Calvin Klein ads? Really, princesses should show more responsibility to little girls in party dresses.

But I'm no myth, the Fairy-Tale Princess beseeches us – pretty as ever, if a little wan, aerobiced to the point of exhaustion – I'm no archetype. By trying to make me one you all but destroyed me. You followed me round with your cameras and judgements, and insisted I bring you happiness. but it was all I could do to look after myself. Poor me, poor little me, I was only ever little me. As for Happy Ever After, you must be joking. All I had to do was kiss the Prince, and lo, he turned into a frog.

Of course I said yes, of course I dressed up for Happy Ever After. That fabulous satin train, those solemn rites, the vaulted Abbey. Wouldn't you? I was fed the myth as well as you. Truly I tried. I brought life and love into the Grey Kingdom: I glittered and glowed for it: I sat on the beds of the most despised of the land and earned their love, and the people's too. That was easy. But you try earning the love of a Prince! It was Beauty and the Beast and the Prince turned really beastly, and now see what he's done to me! See. And as for my mother-in-law, you've no idea! What was the reality, the other side of myth? A postnatal depression, a flurry of bulimia, an episode of self-mutilation, let me tell you all about it, when all I ever wanted was his arms around me, and he wouldn't. Why not blame him for the loss of your archetype? Takes two to tango, two to make Happy Ever After. And there was only one of us trying.

Tell you what, if the little girls are still suffering, I'll give them another archetype. How about the She-Devil? The woman scorned? The one who won't let go? Who craves justice, takes revenge? She's pretty popular these days, now that women work, and can do without men well enough: just use them for status, appreciate them as decoration. These days men insult women at their peril.

Won't that do for an archetype for your daughters? A transformation myth? Princess turned Empress, with absolute power: or at any rate enough to destroy Kingdoms? Good Lord! She-Devil, Powerful Mother, Woman Who Won't Forget, High Priestess, Prime-Time Therapee? Take your pick. What are you complaining of? Time your little girls grew up, turned from sweet little things twirling in front of mirrors in party dresses with their heads full of nonsense and got a clear view of the new world. Fairy-Tale Princess was a pretty stupid idea anyway.

When the Duchess of York slims in the run-up to Christmas, 1995, but still does not get a good press.

Three Cheers for the Duchess of York!

– for Her Royal Highness, hoorah! As for her detractors, let them be despatched to icy Siberia, deprived for life of food, sex and fun. Her detractors are, I notice, mostly female. Men tend to like impetuous pretty women who smile a lot, no matter whether they're size twenty or a size ten, and if she gets from one to the other in the space of a year, as the Duchess of York has just done, merely shrug and say, 'Well, if that's what you want – ' (Not that the good opinion of men is meant to *matter* much, these days, but even so, for a sensuous women it can be agreeable.)

It's the women who are now gritting their well-flossed teeth and talking about body-fascism, orgies of self-mutilation, and what a bad example the Duchess is setting the young – encouraging the anorexic in their anorexia – and so forth. To be fat remains a sin: it's to suffer from low-esteem, to be unhappy, to be a 'comfort-eater': to have no self-control. And now all of a sudden to *want* to be thin is a sin as well – let alone *get* thin. Then it's all nyah-nyah, ni-na-na, you'll only put it all on again; don't you think you've achieved a thing! You're still fat in your head, poor old you, no matter how you look.

Any plump dieter knows how skinny friends keep trying to put them off. 'You look just fine as you are.' What they mean is, we don't want the competition. You just stay as you are, with your elasticated waistband.

These days the only merit seems to be to have been born lucky, that's to say with a steady metabolism, not one that's all over the place. The scales rioting up and down: first fat, then thin, then fat again. Disgracefully inconsistent.

What's more, Royal detractors get it all wrong. Born-thin people know nothing about fatness. They think unhappiness makes you fat. My own experience is that fat equals content: thin equals discontent. Content, you live in the present and eat and grow fat. Discontent, you live in the future and don't eat and grow thin. Fat women have more frequent and more intense orgasms than thin women. Statistics prove it. (Mind you, statistics can prove anything.) For a Duchess skinniness is an obvious mission: you take better photographs thin: your subjects don't snigger, your tiara suits you: other women envy you – what, she's got everything and not even *fat*! – and it's quite pleasant to be envied, and, until hindered by matrimony, normal and natural to be competitive with other women, Duchess or not.

'Fergie wants to be thinner than the Princess of Wales,' they say, 'that's all it is; that's her ambition. Look at her! Ridiculous.' They can't wait to bring her down a peg or two. Off with their heads, say I. Treason.

Because good heavens, these Royal detractors are bold. Time was when they'd not only get sent to convents in Siberia for the slightest anti-Duchess murmur, they'd get sent with their tongues cut out. That's what the Empress Elizabeth of Russia (who didn't believe in capital punishment) tended to do with any woman at court who spoke ill of her and was prettier than she. And that was only a couple of hundred years ago. Just as well that today's Elizabeth, Queen of England, doesn't have absolute powers. What a sudden dearth of journalists there'd be!

Elizabeth of Russia's niece-in-law became Catherine the Great. Catherine started as a lovely, Sloaney, bouncy girl, minor German nobility, not so different from Sarah Ferguson, now Elizabeth of England's daughter-in-law. Catherine was married off to the horrible, dribbly Peter, boy Prince of all the Russias, when she was fifteen. They managed one son and then she was off and away on the road to success. By the simple process of being *nice* to everyone, never saying an unkind word, always bribing, never punishing, being *liked*, she ended up on the throne – her husband, the Czar, poisoned by her lover, as it happened, but behind her back, and not before she'd elegantly deposed that impossible husband-monarch, and without bloodshed too.

Catherine was the most absolute of all absolute monarchs, loved by everyone. She could have offed everyone's heads, but she didn't. She was bright, mind you: she was the French philosopher Voltaire's favourite pen friend and a patron of the arts and ever so pretty. Most notably, of course, and scandalously, she was in the habit of choosing her lovers from amongst the Imperial Guards. 'I'll have that one over there, I think; looks good to me . . .' and before he knew where he was he'd be named her official Personal Aide-de-Camp.

Catherine reigned for fifty years; she died at sixty-seven, the subject of scandal and speculation, but greatly loved and immensely wealthy, having expanded the boundaries of her great nation, winning campaign after campaign against the Turks, the Poles, the Swedes, and appropriating large chunks of the Church's immense wealth into her own coffers. Though some complained that by the end of her reign she'd reduced ninety percent of her subjects to serfdom, few carped. When she died her Personal Aide-de-Camp was young Plato Zubov, aged twenty-two, and he was devastated by her death. Detractors say that was just because he'd made so many enemies he was frightened for his future, but I think he just loved her.

So three cheers for the enigmatic and beautiful Empress of Russia, three cheers for the Duchess of York, but perhaps thank our lucky stars that the efforts of anti-Royalists and republicans (in the original sense) over the last couple of hundred years, have ensured that monarchs no longer have power of life and death. I could vouch for the Duchess of York's temperament but I'm not sure about her mother-in-law's. Just think of life at the Court of Elizabeth II. Snap! 'Off with your head, Mrs Thatcher, you're far too ambitious!' 'Di, off to Siberia!' 'Into exile, Charles, we'll have no more talking to trees.' 'What was that you said, Mr Major? I don't agree with you! Out with your tongue!' I like to think that Sarah, Duchess of York, who married the most handsome and most easy-natured of all the young English Princes, Andrew, would never be like that. She'd take more after kindly Catherine the Great and rule by carrot not stick, just by being nice.

Give Fergie absolute power, what would she do? She'd probably forbid the use of the word 'Fergie' as a start. That belongs to the old chalet-girl, ski resort days. The penalty for publishing an unflattering photograph would be a mere banishment to the boondocks and nature photography for life: those who insulted her would have to eat their own adjectives. Nothing worse.

Catherine was extremely good to her lovers. Discarding them, she treated them rather as racehorse owners treat their favourite steeds once past their prime. When they ceased to enthral she'd put them out to green pastures, with as many estates, titles, serfs and as much money as they could possibly wish. (These were the men who created Russia's later aristocracy, just as a hundred years earlier, the sons of Charles II by the prettiest girls in the kingdom founded the English aristocracy of today, from which our Sarah emerges.) But woe betide Catherine's official lover if he was away from Court or ill for more than a couple of days. He'd find himself out on his ear, supplanted; Catherine's lovely eye would have lighted on someone new. (Catherine too was a weight-swinger – sometimes thin, sometimes fat. Someone needs to do some research on the connection between weight-swings and excessive sexuality.) She'd have her lady-in-waiting check out the background of the new contender; his family, morals, reliability, potency and so forth: the royal physician would give him a quick once-over, and if all went perfectly he'd be introduced at Court next morning as the new Royal lover, and all honour, respect and courtesy would be granted him. The other Courts of Europe found themselves both fascinated and appalled, but soon got used to it. The Personal

Aide-de-Camp would quickly get over any initial embarrassment: as for Catherine, she seemed to feel none. He would have the suite of rooms next to hers; a private staircase connected to them. He could expect tenure for a couple of years or so.

Catherine was *so* pretty, *so* bright, so nice, so straightforward about her sexual desires, so competent, so good at running an army and a nation – and offered the other royals of Europe such lavish and excellent hospitality – who could really object? Had not male monarchs always behaved in much the same way? Don't men and women of power, energy and wealth today do pretty much the same – calling it serial marriage, or playing the game of 'meet my mistress'? Power is its own aphrodisiac: gender gets to be of less and less importance as women take the reins of our society. Sex and love between men and women remain, for most of us, our overwhelming obsessions, but are not meant to interfere with our careers.

I met Sarah Ferguson once, at a Charity Do: I had expected a great big bouncing girl and found an agreeably large-eyed, fragile young woman, slim, pale and haunted. If I were her I'd take back the Royal card fate dealt me and replay it. I'd make it up with nice, bluff Andrew, and start plotting now to end up on the throne. Stranger things have happened. Anyone who can lose four stone in a year is determined and self-disciplined enough to achieve anything. Three cheers for the Duchess of York, Czarina of All Europe!

Odd, looking at the latest set of press cuttings relating to the new-style skinny Duchess, the epithets that get applied to women. All of a sudden she's gaunt, is out of date (curves are back), is cravenly manipulated by dress-size: she cares more for herself than her children, is trying to please men. (Oh, wicked!) If she doesn't bother but eats what she likes, why then she's depressed, spurned, unhappy; she's grotesque, not fit to be seen out in public. The worst thing of all, I suspect, is to change from one state to the other; it means our preconceptions have to change along with her waistline. We can hardly remember the source of our original disapproval. Too bad, too bad! Hoorah for the

Duchess of York, and let her detractors be force-fed cream cakes and sweet mulled wine and exiled to Siberia, and if they don't like that then off with their heads!

After the famous 'Pity Poor Me' TV show in November, 1995.

Empress of Hearts

The Princess of Wales unwound herself from her cushions as her TV appearance ended. She had viewed alone. Her therapist had said that was best. She must learn self-sufficiency. She went to the phone. She called her boy William at Eton. But she could only get through to William's housemaster who said the Prince could not be disturbed. He was in bed. No, the boy had not seen the broadcast. William had already used up his TV ration for the week, on the UEFA Cup.

The Princess of Wales put down the phone and vowed to abolish Eton. Come to that she would probably abolish education altogether. Schools interfered so with the proper relationship between mother and child.

Actually, she might abolish football too. The women of the country would back her. It was with the women that her future lay. With every wronged-victim woman in the land, and that was most of them. Every woman who had ever loved and lost, and wept, and survived.

The Princess had banned all incoming calls, but she could sense a kind of astral quiver around the telephone. It would ring if it could; it would ring for ever. The broadcast had been a success. She had won the hearts and minds of the nation. She was uncrowned Queen of the land. Who needed the Palace anyway? The Monarchy wasn't about the past; it was about *now*. And she was the person for *now*. Well, look at her! There was a tap at the door. It was James Hewitt. Somehow, as ever, he had managed to gain an entrance. Moved by her public declaration of love, his arms closed round her once again. She was safe.

'She's such a silly girl,' said the Queen. They'd had the telly brought in so they could all watch over a late dinner. 'But I suppose if everyone in the country caught bulimia the EU wouldn't have to take so much land out of cultivation,' and the assembled company of jowled old men and ladies with noble faces and eager noses laughed heartily. They liked a good joke.

Charles rang from Cornwall.

'Don't you understand,' he said. 'Di's a woman scorned, hell hath no fury et cetera, did you see the look in her eyes? Her body language!'

'If only One understood what she really wanted,' his mother complained. 'One could be more helpful.'

'Mother, she wants your Empire,' said the Prince, and his mother hooted. She'd given birth to an over-reactor, she said to the others. A nuclear reactor. And everyone laughed some more and agreed the British Monarchy could be in no danger from someone so impossibly vulgar. A girl who'd been brought in as a virgin bride to breed the next heir to the throne might thrash about a bit but was inevitably history. Think of Anne Boleyn. But at least this one had had sons.

The Duke said all the same the girl was a loose cannon, but better inside the tent pissing out than outside the tent pissing in: someone had better do something conciliatory, he supposed. Tomorrow.

'Too late!' said the Princess of Wales to her therapist-healer, the next day. She was having acupuncture to improve her self-esteem and enhance her assertiveness. His hand trembled a little as she told him why she'd had to miss aerobics. It seemed a group of Generals had approached her. Fearful of the coming Labour Government, they planned an army coup. They needed the Princess as a figurehead to rally the nation behind them. In return for her cooperation they promised a nation where group therapy was compulsory, education optional, and everywhere the heart would rule the head.

'Ouch!' said the Princess as the acupuncture needle slipped. But the therapist said nothing to anyone. This was the Age of Aquarius, stopped dawning, finally come.

Five years later the Empress Diana, who turned out to be no-one's figurehead (were they *mad*?) stood on the Balcony of Buckingham Palace, with the Prince Regent on one side and her consort James Hewitt on the other. Her adoring people had voted her absolute power in a national referendum, and this was, after all, a democracy: the people's will must stand. She had sole control of the French nuclear weapon, thanks to the love and trust of the French Prime Minister. She announced the secession of Former Great Britain from the Commonwealth, and the annexation of Orlando: it was to be known as the Orlando Purchase. Florida now had the City of London, but we and our Prince had Disneyland. How everyone cheered, and were wholly happy. And why not.

A Christmas letter to Washington, 1995.

Letter from London

The Princess of Wales now roller-blades in Hyde Park, to the alarm of passers-by more accustomed to the tranquil trit-trotting of hooves in Rotten Row. She set the Christmas season off to a fine gossipy start with the BBC broadcast in which she claimed victim status, admitted infidelity, and tearfully offered herself up to the nation's judgement. The nation judged. Women on the whole approved, seeing a feisty young person saying 'up yours' to the pompous old men in suits: if the Prince of Wales is allowed to embrace trees and have a mistress, surely the Princess is allowed a season of bulimia and self-mutilation, and have a lover or so? What else is the girl to do? The men saw a woman scorned and dangerous, an arch manipulator, a vicious ex, and pitied the poor Prince. Many discovered royalist sympathies in erstwhile republican hearts. The media took sides – the Murdoch press acclaimed the Princess as a cross between Mother Teresa and Madonna; the broadsheets huffed and puffed about the threat to the constitution, and, denying the Princess the right to self-volition, detected right-wing (or Australian) conspiracies at work. It was all a great relief from Bosnia and the Budget; and seemed to obscure the humiliating fact that Europe needed the US to make peace in the Balkans, and that promised tax cuts, by a government worried that it might lose power in the next election, did not in fact materialise.

Since news has broken that the Princess creeps out at night, in disguise, to visit the dying in hospital, all have settled down to the view that she's simply loony: convincing extra evidence provided by her sympathy with the homeless, expressed in public this week at a Charity Ball. 'I am appalled,' she said, 'at the sight of young people who resort to begging, or worse, prostitution, to get money in order to eat.' Since she shared a platform with Jack Straw, Shadow Home Secretary, this was construed by the Tories as a political statement and dismissed as irresponsible. It is not easy in this country to speak even self-evident truths – those who do, especially Princesses, are regarded as imprudent at best, insane at worst.

Meanwhile London glitters like the Princess's televised tears. Snow has fallen; skies are bright and clear: the Christmas lights in the West End are, for once, a lavish delight, not a mingy apology for good cheer. For the first time in years you can't get a taxi: smart women run hither and thither burdened with ribboned packages, and no means of getting them home. This year's flu is not severe but strikes suddenly – only one child left to play all three witches in our school Nativity play. You may wonder what three witches are doing in the play in the first place, but Mary, Joseph and Jesus are nowadays avoided so as not to offend ethnic sensibilities, and are replaced by an agreeable postmodern hotchpotch of scenes from Shakespeare, three wise women (rather than men) and general ecological high-mindedness – the children claiming moral authorship; probably rightly, since these days the children lead their teachers in matters of political correctness. The young, trusting, piping voices still have the power to bring tears to the eyes. Parents, if not our Princesses, are allowed a *soupçon* of sentimentality, an armistice being declared for Christmastide.

Finding myself, albeit inadvertently, at the fashionable opening of a new restaurant in St James', 'The Avenue', I was nearly crushed to death by a crowd of the beautiful people, dressed almost entirely in black, with an occasional flicker of red. They arrive like a shoal of fish in a coral reef; one flick of a communal tail and they're off. Setting up a business to pleasure them must be unnerving, so whimsical are their tastes. The men wear lapel-free suits with a glimmer of white shirt here and there: the women have very short skirts, a minimum of glitter but black sheeny pantyhose – opaque are out of fashion – and elegant black suede shoes with chunky high heels. Self-confidence and high spirits make beauties of them all. The space was so echoey, the conversation so loud, the music so beat-ey, it was impossible to hear what anyone was saying. But that's the point: everyone in these places can speak aloud to themselves, as if on a mobile phone, so long as there's enough noise. What happened to dance when the twist came along, and dancing became a partnerless process, has now happened to speech. The young face one another and talk loudly and vigorously into space, requiring no response.

Ted Hughes, the Poet Laureate, hosted a party at No 11 Downing Street, by courtesy of Mrs Clarke, wife of the Chancellor of the Exchequer. This was another kind of party altogether, of the great, good, monied and on the whole elderly, gathered together to raise money for the Arvon Foundation, the creative writing centre founded back in the sixties by the Laureate, then plain Ted. A sprinkling of good-natured writers was allowed to attend this party, to lighten the *gravitas*; I say good-natured because the writers were picked from the lists of those who had in their time taught classes at one of the Arvon Centres out of sheer altruism and the desire to share their art and teach their craft. Thus is goodness in the end rewarded. We stayed too long, as writers will, to finish our conversations, the canapés, and the drink. Arvon was one of the first of the creative writing schools which now proliferate on both sides of the Atlantic, out of which pour delicately expressed novels of exquisite sensibility, proper sentiment and infinite blandness. Perhaps, I sometimes think, putting down some heavy manuscript, beautifully word-processed, dutifully spell-checked, we should have stayed at home. Arvon now looks for funds to diversify, to better attend to the transmission of literary enthusiasm from teacher to student. Admirable! Now we're done with the writers, let us attend to the readers.

The interior of No 11 Downing Street, like No 10 next door, traditional home of the Prime Minister, I would report to be both dowdy and respectable, pleasant but not showy, in a reassuringly English kind of way; one felt Wellington boots and bicycles had only reluctantly been cleared out of the way in order to make room for security, which was tight. The IRA once got a mortar right through to next door's drawing room, launched from a van parked in Whitehall. Enough to make anyone nervous.

But one way or another, and so plentiful and beautiful are the beautiful people, and so long as you can forget the Princess's strictures, London is in pretty good shape. Glittery.

This year's Booker Prize, as ever, disappointed some and gratified others. It has always seemed to me a kind of glorified dog show. A prize is dangled in front of every writer in the land and, like a bone, is snatched away from all but one: the shortlisted are punished by having cameras trained on their faces and the whole nation watch while they lose; they then find themselves apologising to their publishers for having failed. But then I would say that: I was once shortlisted and lost. After that, I was Chairperson of the Judges, in the year Salman Rushdie failed to win it for *Shame*, a glorious novel; and managed to so upset Booker PLC by my 'Chairman's speech' – more of a Writers' Guild rant – that, contrary to custom, I have not received an invitation to the Presentation Dinner since. But there you are. This year's hot favourite was Rushdie's *The Moor's Last Sigh* – as exhilarating and confident a novel as you could hope for, and so good-humoured and generous in spirit, in spite of all, it made you want to weep. A literary establishment, once so grudging about Rushdie's talents, has by and large been won over by their sheer excess. Nevertheless the prize went to Pat Barker's excellent *The Ghost Road* – a more conventional novel, albeit one written out of a male, or at any rate gay, sensibility. Who is to say what goes on in the minds of judges? Even chairing a panel of them it's hard to say: except on the whole the better the book, the more extreme the reaction it produces.

Governments failed to act in the Rushdie fatwa. Five years later they still hesitate. Since then, as Rushdie predicted, it's been open season on writers. In grim Nigeria Ken Saro-Wiwa died, executed by the military regime. The British branch of PEN International, the organisation that works for the release of writers imprisoned for political reasons, had campaigned for months to draw attention to the danger he was in, more or less in vain. PEN report that once the death was announced, they couldn't get the media off the phone. Dead heroes are safe and qualify for column inches and a flurry of indignation. Live ones are just not news. The *Independent*, extraordinarily, having run pages of grief and outrage the week before, and suggesting along with everyone else that Britain cut off trading links with Nigeria, the next week accepted a half-page ad from the Nigerian regime, to the effect that Ken Saro-Wiwa was a terrible fellow who had foully murdered three of his political allies, and deserved execution. It's one of the oldest nasty tricks in the fascist book, of course, to murder a handful of your opponents, put the blame on the rest, and so get rid of the lot of them. But ads bring in the money; and when it comes to it, newspapers understand only too well the importance of trading links. If the space is for sale, the thinking goes, what that space says is not the Editor's business, if that newspaper is to survive. We are all as moral as we can afford to be, it seems, no more.

On the announcement of the Royal Divorce in March, 1996.

A Royal Divorce

Last week, after a half-hour conversation with Prince Charles, Princess Di told the world she had agreed to a divorce. Not her doing or desire, she implied. She had loved Charles and would always love him. He was the father of her children. But it was time for the courts to make legal what had become established fact. The couple had been apart for three years. The marriage had irretrievably 'broken down'. Boringly, the Palace muttered about terms, conditions and money. The Princess, upstaging as ever, went to the heart and talked about feelings.

It seems now only a matter of months before young Prince William, heir to the throne after Prince Charles, and his little brother Harry, share the fate of a third of their contemporaries, and become the children of divorced parents. They are at least not likely to share that of those other two Princes, Edward and Richard, who were imprisoned in the Tower in 1483 and murdered or so some claim, by an uncle in a bitter struggle for the succession. The point being that the crown is no longer the desirable prize it once was. The money is there, but not the power, and a gadfly press drives one to distraction.

Charles married Diana in the best tradition of European royal families over the centuries, the better to avoid such murderous struggles. That is to say he married a certified virgin to beget a legitimate heir to the throne for all the world to see. (Even today, royal births are public affairs, with State officials in attendance.) Fidelity could hardly be expected of him: nor, once she had produced the heir, would it be of her. It was an accepted trade-off. He got an heir, a future Queen and no interruption to his love life: she got a title, wealth, royal children, and a postponement of hers. As a system, it worked well enough. Many of today's English aristocracy are descended from the illegitimate children of kings, by the women they loved and desired, or from their gay favourites. Their wives got by as best they could. Catherine the Great, married off at fifteen, gave birth to the heir, and ended up with a new lover a week and two children out of wedlock.

Either no-one told Diana the rules, or she failed to hear them properly, and had read no history. Or, most likely, her therapists persuaded her that the rules were outrageous. That as a young woman of the nineties, it was her duty to let nothing stand in the way of her own happiness. That for all she had married a Prince, she was entitled to a faithful husband. It was her human right. The Personal is All, she was persuaded, forget any peril to the stability of the State, the tranquillity of nations. For whatever reason, once safely married, the royal heirs born, Diana reneged on the implicit bargain.

More, in the best traditions of the therapeutic age, she felt obliged in so doing to share her quest for emotional maturity with anyone who would listen – millions worldwide, as it happened, with a soft-voiced, gently enquiring BBC acting as therapist. In this painful discipline, the therapee must speak the truth, however painful. Hence Diana's admission of her own infidelity on TV, apparent insanity in a woman already living in the shadow of a divorce. But who, 'in therapy', is altogether sane?

The Princess, we now learn, is a trained marriage guidance counsellor. At her meeting with the Prince, she requested him to appear side by side with her on the nation's TV screens, so they could announce the divorce together. Only then 'could the healing process begin'. But the Prince, who has considerable personal dignity, as well as Royal prudence, would have none of it. God bless the Prince of Wales.

Of course, kings have mistresses and favourites: it goes with the territory. Of course women as fanciable as Diana have lovers. A philandering monarch, a tempestuous Queen, are nothing new to us. Whoever said that Royalty should provide the nation with a moral lead? It's not as if they were elected. 'Divorce' is a pity: it puts the dead hand of respectability and self-righteousness on an institution already burdened with its image of old-fashioned conservatism, in its unlimited embodiment of Church, State and constitution. Let us hope the Monarchy survives the beating of the Princess's pretty hands on the castle doors, and her hapless cry, 'Let me out, let me out, I want to be *loved*. They're all nutters in here.'

A plea to Royalty to rescue the nation, April, 1996.

An Open Letter to the Queen of England

Your Majesty,

Be assured that I address you as a loyal subject. I am no republican. While the anxiety dreams of British housewives focus as they do on the fear that you are coming to tea and will find the house in a mess, we most certainly need you. You are part of the national unconscious. You have a Jungian archetype all to yourself – *The Queen of England* – which combines the infinite grandeur of Elizabeth I with the infinite respectability of Queen Victoria. To do without you, to replace you in Buckingham Palace with an elected President, to start again, as some suggest, to be more in tune with the new Europe, would be disastrous. It would tear our fragile national psyche in two. Are we not panicky enough at the moment, as the actuality of Europe, of a single European currency comes clean, as the prospect of the loss of our national sovereignty becomes acute? What, Britain, joined at the hip with the old enemy, Germany, with only that strip of gastronomic France in between? Ma'am, without Royalty how would we know ourselves in all our irrationality: how would we dare change, what would we dream about?

I do not suppose the women of Germany have nightmares that Chancellor Kohl is coming to tea. They are too sensible and no doubt better housekeepers. But where in the group unconscious, without the unifying mother archetype, can they feel at one? We have the advantage here.

Ma'am, it may even be due to the nonsense of your existence that your subjects manage to continue to be as noisily creative as they are, providing novelists and playwrights, actors, directors and theatre people of all kinds, musicians, film makers and dancers to entertain and even enlighten the rest of the world. The arts do not flourish in sensible, rational societies, or, indeed in societies that overtly honour their artists. Which we most certainly do not. *Sense and Sensibility*, that most exotically English of all films – it won this year's Golden Bear at Berlin, and many Oscars – had to be funded by American money, though energised by British talent. And so on and so on. I have fawned and flattered enough. Ma'am, how your subjects gripe and chatter on! Land at Heathrow from anywhere else in the rest of Europe and be amazed, indeed, gratified, by the sheer volume of chatter. It is your blessing, Ma'am: if only because we chatter so about your children, ignoring all other more serious issues. You keep us gossipy and cheerful.

All that said, Your Majesty, we your subjects are in some difficulty here. This once proud nation bows its head in shame. The International Court of Justice in the Hague declare us to have a bad, bad human rights record. We put the wrong people in prisons and keep the right people out of them: we throw asylum seekers to the wolves, unjustly: we allow dreadful injustices to persist. And the only response of your Ministers is to deny the right of the Hague Court to pass judgement. Please *do* something.

Ma'am, we are in a sorry stage. Our young delinquents languish in adult jails because there is no better place for them, as do the halfwitted. I must rephrase that: we have become too charitable in our speech to refer to the halfwitted, or even to mental incompetents – let me rather say it is the rationally challenged who crowd our prisons, which are sometimes so foul even our official Prison Visitors refuse to enter them. Our prisons float in a sea of excrement, thrown from the windows of people locked up twenty-three hours out of twenty-four, even those who are later found innocent.

We are kind in speech, cruel in behaviour. And we disapprove mightily, by the way, of IQ testing, in case one section of the population is humiliated and the other thinks too highly of itself. And so we find lack of intelligence, for lack of evidence that it exists, no excuse: we throw simple women in prison for not paying their TV licence fee, and keep them shackled with steel chains, to a male officer's wrist, while they give birth. Just in case they take to their heels and escape.

Ma'am, I wonder if such things are even brought to your attention? It is not correct form to bring bad news to the monarch – some race memory of the days of the divine right of kings no doubt, of the absolute power of the sovereign under God, or the cry of off-with-his-head. (We retain the death penalty for treason, but for nothing else.) But Ma'am, these are desperate times: if the truth is not said someone has to do it: or we will lose the respect of the world, forget the minor triumphs of our artists. I know your power is limited by custom and practice, you are not meant to say anything 'political' in public, but perhaps in your weekly chats with the Prime Minister you could say, casually, 'But John, what is this I hear about women giving birth in chains? My civil servants, safe in the remoteness of their office towers, say it is necessary, but can it really be so? I'm sure I wouldn't have liked it to have happened to me.' A small thing, Ma'am, but it would help save us from international disgrace.

Your Majesty, you could give your Ministers the advice which in your human role as older mother of difficult children – forget the archetype of Queen – you must by now be adept at giving. 'When in doubt don't!'

When your Ministers wittingly lie and knowingly prepare to send innocent arms dealers (if this is not a contradiction in terms) to prison for sanction breaking, in the vain hope of saving their faces, all that happens is that they are found out. When they tell the truth, when they say that, yes, there *may* be a link between eating beef products in the years between 1986 and 1990, and ten current cases amongst young people of a dreadful disease – (but no-one can be quite sure), there is the most terrible uproar: a whole industry goes down the drain, thousands lose jobs and everyone feels in general sick at heart and stomach.

Ma'am, people think the green fields of England are grazed by insane cows: they will not import our beef, to the great advantage of their own cattle industries. Ma'am, in this particular case, comfort John Major. He did what he should; he said what he knew, and if the truth was not complete it was not his fault; it was the fault of the experts, the scientists, who turn out not to be infallible, but in their experiments as guided by emotion and wilful thinking as anyone else. 'John,' you must say, 'it turned out badly but you did well.'

Ma'am, take no notice of this sniping about the behaviour of your children: it is a furore whipped up by the republican Murdoch press and TV's desire for ratings. Through history we have all been well accustomed to randy monarchs, from Catherine the Great to Charles II; the more energetic, the more we admire them. It is a conceit of the modern therapeutic age to believe that 'maturity' and sexual monogamy are linked. They are not. And besides, Princess Diana is in deep therapy and shares her emotions with the nation, and wanted to break the news of her divorce hand in hand with the Prince of Wales on TV, so 'the healing process could begin'. No-one can accuse the Royal children of being out of touch or out of date. They are as subject to the flow of social history as anyone else. Don't scold them.

Monarchs are not meant to act as examples of personal good behaviour: *you* have done so, and thank you for your forbearance; but it is not part of the job description, which is Head of the Commonwealth, Defender of the Faith. Now, Ma'am, when the time comes for your son to take over as monarch, the fact that he's divorced might well cause a problem. Though by that time, and may heaven postpone it, your Church – an increasingly gay-led and pragmatic institution – may have given up this particular moral stance as it has so many others. Better still, your Church could be separated out from your State. Dis-established.

Ma'am, please give this matter your earnest attention. The Church is like some old Englishman, devoid of moral stature, swimming in an ancient sea, 'not waving, but drowning', as our excellent poet Stevie Smith describes it. It is the British Crown's close relationship with the Church, some say, which gives it its air of has-been-ness, of profound conservatism. Careful, lest the drowning man does not drag the Monarchy down with it. Re-open the debate on antidisestablishmentarianism. The old arguments still exist, unresolved, from the debates which so invigorated mid-nineteenth century Britain, and also provided the longest word in the English language.

Ma'am, take some heart from the likelihood that the disasters which strike Britain today will strike the rest of Europe tomorrow. We, with our early Thatcherite monetarism; our passion for a fine, sleek economy; our fear of waste, idleness and overstaffing; our panic dread of inflation; our worship of market forces, just got there first. We will have companions in our troubles soon enough.

At first, in the tight, centrally controlled, cost-cutting national enterprise, everything goes well. Then the downside becomes apparent. The division between rich and poor increases: the employed are overworked, tired and anxious in their jobs: the many unemployed exist at great social cost: our young become alienated. The subtle, irrational infrastructures of society crumble. The rat catchers (sorry, rodent operators) are fired because they're a waste of money and where are the rats? Now there's a plague of them and nobody's left who knows how to deal with them. Close the mental hospitals: murderers roam the streets. Little old ladies can't travel by train because there are no porters: the bus takes for ever because drivers and conductors inhabit one body. The train journey sandwich travels by road because it's cheaper: the roads become clogged and impassable. In the world of market forces, the PR which controls the customer is all. The newly privatised immensely rich Yorkshire Water Board, when asked if it had learned anything from last year's inability to keep the supply of water going to its customers, its plans to evacuate a million people rather than cut dividends, replies, 'Yes, we have learned how to deal better with the press.' Britain today, tomorrow Europe.

Ma'am, when at the end of the seventies Europe so ruthlessly broke trading links with the Americas and Australasia, and formed its own internal markets, and there could be no more imports of cheap grain, the farmers of Europe started feeding herbivores a carnivorous, cannibalistic diet. In the interests of efficiency and cost cutting, mid-eighties Britain for a time removed the requirement to heat this revolting diet of dead animals to top temperatures before serving. It tasted okay: so much so it was the habit of farmers to nibble 'cattle cake' when hungry. Now look.

Ma'am, you will have found in your life experience, to use your daughter-in-law Diana's terminology, that when people do morally dubious things, bad practical things result. Please point this out to John Major at your weekly meeting, and to any Heads of State who have the privilege of sitting next to you at dinner. Someone might listen.

Your humble, loyal and devoted servant,

Fay Weldon

On the death of the Princess of Wales, August, 1997.

A City in Tears

All of a sudden you hardly know your own city. The heat wave has broken: rain falls like tears. Young women weep openly on the streets; stricken men stand and stare. This is more than mawkishness, less than hysteria; it is too deeply and sincerely felt to be described as either. It affects the sophisticated and the simple alike. People of all kinds and conditions mill around the green parks and wide malls between Buckingham Palace and Harrods. Traffic is at a standstill: no-one complains. They lay flowers – are there enough grown in the entire world to satisfy this sudden demand? – talk to one another, console one another. Diana is dead. It was our own Princess who died – forget the Palace stripped her of her title. How dare they! We'll have no ill spoken of her – you over there, shut up!

The crowd awards itself a holiday. Everything will stop on Saturday or risk a stone through the window. Liveried Harrods' vans feed the hungry crowds for free. There is a general feeling the Palace should be doing this: isn't it its business to give alms? Who would have thought the stiff upper-lipped British would be reacting like this, feeling all this, working itself up into a frenzy at the hard-heartedness of the Palace, which takes on the same resonance as Kafka's Castle. Though in fact the Palace is achieving a triumph of organisation – an almost State funeral within the week, moving faster than it's moved in its life before, pausing only, stiffly, to thank the country for its support at a time of Royal grief. It is the stiffness the crowd can't stand, and its inability to understand they're not supporting the Palace at all, they're supporting Diana, the wronged Princess. The people have taken it into their heads to elect an alternative Monarchy, and it descends through Diana's line. The final sacrifice has been made, the female God ascends, the gender switch is thrown, and all things and feelings female triumph.

On why the nation grieved.

Loving, Hating and Mourning – Diana, Princess of Wales

Give people permission to hate and they take it. Kill. Kill, kill, they'll cry, on the grounds that their neighbour is the wrong colour, worships the wrong God or is in some other way peculiar. But give people permission to love and they take that too, with all the kindness, softness and ardour of their being, and with as much or as little justification.

With grief comes permission to love. It comes in that order. If we grieve we can only assume, in retrospect, we must have loved. And how we loved Princess Diana. Who was there with a soul so dead who could not grieve when she died? If only for themselves, for noble expectations dashed, for every hope perforce abandoned? The streets and parks of London filled with newly bereft lovers, pale, stunned and red-eyed, clutching flowers. Of course.

But this I think was not a national outpouring: it seemed more like a wandering, drifting crowd of individuals brushing up against one another; the isolated, the orphans, all those in the habit of keeping a brave face on things suddenly unable to do it a moment longer.

Of course. The candle blown out, the vigorous life stemmed, the story stopped mid-sentence. Mother slamming shut the bedside book. No more! That's it! Finished! What did we *do*? We cry into our lonely pillow, for ourselves.

Diana, Queen of Hearts, Patron Saint of Orphans, High Priestess of Therapees, as from 31 August, 1997. The *Hello!* issue of 30 August found Diana (if only by suggestion) to be self-indulgent, an imperfect mother, a self-absorbed divorcee running out of control. The issue, with its cover picture of Diana appearing to look spitefully towards a juxtaposed portrait of a charming, well-muscled, smiling Prince Charles, was withdrawn on the instant. I am glad. Hypocrisy at least acknowledges the existence of virtue. It is always a good sign.

Media celebrities become our friends, our family. Twenty-eight percent of us in this country, live in single-person households, and the proportion of the isolated rises here and throughout Europe. We find it difficult to bear the nearness of others, their emotional working upon ourselves. The doctrine of Therapism, of which Diana is High Priestess, teaches us that we were all born happy and good, and this is the end that nature intends for us. And if we find ourselves not happy and good, why someone else is to blame. Spouse, parent, lover, friend. Prince Charles, the cold Windsor in-laws. Look for the culprit – and never see ourselves. Diana believed that morality lay in authenticity of feeling. In her famous TV broadcast she used the camera as therapist – self-pitying, self-righteous, self-absorbed, supremo of all victims, all tearful eyes and picking fingers – as she related her woes. Of course women everywhere identified. She was all of us. Every woman who ever threw up in the bathroom after dinner, or thought she couldn't face another mouthful, or had visions of knives cutting through skin, who hysterically shrieked, wept, fell about and threatened suicide. That was us. Every woman going through a bad divorce – as if all divorces were not bad – in pursuit of the integrity and dignity of aloneness.

Everyone unable to understand where the dream went, why no-one understood the specialness of the self, the totality of the offer made to the other, only to be rejected. Every woman who married the wrong man. Every women who expected love after the one-night stand, because she felt it and did not get it. Every wife/mother when the husband/father leaves and seems able to forget, and be happy (as Charles was succeeding with Camilla), as if a woman not under the nose was no woman at all, and the gift of her years, of her very life, to no account. As if the very sacrament of the joint bringing of new life into the world was meaningless. After all that, was there to be nothing?

All such women identified, and groping for words, unable to explain, left the home and wandered around in the city parks, brushing up against others, buying second-rate, factory-processed flowers, plastic-wrapped, believing sheer emotion would render the gift valuable, make the petals rich, nature's bounty. But of course it couldn't. The crowd murmured. 'She touched us. She held out her hand to us. She was one of us, the people.' 'The people' is a false grouping. There *is* no such thing. There is only you and me and me and you, in single-person households, making friends with people we see on TV and in the newspapers because there's no-one else.

When Valentino died in the US, Stalin in the USSR, the Ayatollah Khomeini in Iran, there was similar mass hysteria. Nations do this kind of thing. The dynamics of social change get focused on an individual, an icon. See Valentino's death as signalling the end of male eroticism; Stalin's the end of the idea that someone up there, not God, could be trusted to look after you; that of the Ayatollah Khomeini marking the end of the hope of paradise if only you kept to the rules. En masse, we rush to lament what we only vaguely understand. Diana's death signalled a beginning, not an end. I fear its name is loneliness, and it's international.

Shock, disbelief, anger, depression, acceptance. Public grief followed the stages beloved by the counsellor. Disbelief focused at once into conspiracy theory. Many of us went into 'grassy knoll' mode (Who stood on the 'grassy knoll' the day Kennedy died?). *Qui buono?* Everyone! Many of us still haven't moved out of this stage. The death of the Princess will join the other great World Mysteries. Who killed Kennedy? What happened over Lockerbie? Was Gorbachov a CIA sleeper? The kind of thing we need a Day of Judgement for, when all will be made clear; the Great Debriefing. Some of us are tempted to believe the world is in the hands not of God but the great scriptwriter in the sky, who is no great writer, merely a B-picture movie-maker, who perpetually sacrifices believability to drama.

As for the astrologers, they say it was bound to happen; Diana had a Pluto square Mars that evening: sudden, forceful death. If it's written in the stars that's it. We have become a gullible nation: that's what happens, as the psychoanalysts complain, now that the superego is no longer encouraged to exist, in individual or national life, only the id and the ego.

Public emotion, thus uncurtailed or governed by reason, swelled; anger was directed at the House of Windsor for failing to 'show their feelings' properly. (All of a sudden it is emotionally incorrect not to show feelings let alone not have them.) The Palace conceded and flew a flag at half-mast. Anger died. It had to. What were we going to do? Replace the dysfunctional House of Windsor with the dysfunctional House of Spencer? The spirit failed.

Depression ensued. All movement in the property market, lively through the summer, stopped on the first of September: a sure sign of loss of heart.

So she mourned? Everyone you knew. Everyone who had ever lost a loved one – in the sanctimonious phrase of the undertaker – and had not enough time to mourn, or thought the funeral was a farce, or found society wouldn't allow them to shriek, and wail, and tear their hair for ever, or jump on the funeral pyre and burn because really when the other life ends, yours does too. All of us. All of us who've been taught to reconcile ourselves to death; when really death is such an outrage, a wonder of such barbaric proportions it denies the point of our existence on this earth at all. Death is intolerable but we have no choice but to tolerate it.

Since Diana died the country has suffered a few more aftershocks of group emotion – the ripple effect to be expected after any earthquake. There was a surge of xenophobia when the English nanny Louise Woodward went on trial in Massachusetts, accused of causing the death of the baby in her care. It was for a brief time the British equivalent of the OJ trial: partisan as the US black community, all common sense abandoned, we took to the streets and the airwaves to declare the girl's innocence. *Bring Louise Home! She didn't do it! How dare they!* placards and banners everywhere. What she didn't do, or how, or why, was neither here nor there. Louise's meekness, downcast eyes and tentative body language, which to the class-ridden English denoted innocence, registered with the US jury as devious complicity. Guilty! Louise's fate is still undecided: she is already forgotten by the headlines: the trial of a nanny is minor stuff compared to Royal drama. But her troubles served to replace grief with indignation.

And the time for reconciliation was approaching. The property market picked up. More ripples when Prince Charles, with a new PR man, appeared in public with the Spice Girls and Mandela, looking positively groovy. He turned up in Africa – no-one was quite sure where – to apologise for Britain's past behaviour. We were not quite sure why the apology was required but we felt good about it. And Prince Philip himself appeared in public to apologise to the Queen, his wife, for the error of his ways: '*She's had a lot to put up with.*' That was the occasion of their Golden Wedding Anniversary. The Queen glittered terrifically and smiled. These days everyone Royal is saying and feeling the right thing and in clothes acceptable to their subjects. Prince Harry was seen recently at a school outing to a football club match – Arsenal, London's favourite – and held his head high as Princes, if not nannies, are expected to do.

But what has steadied everyone up is the very public divorce of the Earl of Spencer, Princess Diana's brother. It seems he made a declaration of non-love to his wife from his bath, there was talk of twelve mistresses; and he was seen to be mean about money. This within three months of his appearing in the Abbey, at the Princess's funeral, as the archetypal hero: a *deus ex machina*, the handsome young brother came to bear his sister's body away, claim her back for his family, in death as he couldn't in life. And what does he turn out to be? Just another man-behaving-badly. We inspect ourselves for signs of delusion and folly, and find many. We calm down. All in all here in Britain we have had the most remarkable autumn. In the New Year we, the people, will turn our attention to the government, and the various follies being perpetrated there.

This Way Madness Lies

Having made the villains of a novel of mine, *Affliction*, a couple of black-hearted therapists, I found myself in deep trouble with the profession. I had, it seemed, insulted a new priesthood. Never out of sympathy with the struggle of the mad to be sane, or the unhappy to come to terms with their lot, in fighting my corner I came to doubt the validity of the new religion.

The long, echoing corridors of the madhouse, the jangling of keys, the sense of madness as sin . . .

Money, Law and Madness, A Sample of One

In 1965 my older sister Jane wrote a poem. She was a brilliant and beautiful young woman, with three small children; she was married to an artist. There was no money; no way of earning it: no dole for the likes of her: life was a struggle for both of them. She had left school at fourteen, got her exams by correspondence course, taken an English degree at Exeter University, by way of scholarships, and now here she was, trapped in the nursery, trapped by her love for an impossible husband, whose situation she understood very well, as we can see from her poem. It is called 'The Poet to his Wife', and this is what the poet says.

Money and law
Stands at the nursery door
You married me – what for?
My love was not to get you clothes or bread,
But make more poems in my head.

I've fathered children
God!
Am I to die
To turn them out as fits a mother's eye?
I wanted mothering, and they, this brood,
Step in and take my daily food.

Money and law
Stands at the nursery door
Money and law, money and law,
Has the world in its maw.

By the time my sister died of cancer in 1969, still not yet forty, money and law had defeated her husband, my brother-in-law. His works now hang in the Tate, posthumously. He had no recognition during his life. Both Jane and he saw the reality of art: she of poetry, he of graphic design, but not much else. Sometimes I think this couple could, as a double act, justify the myth of the mad artist: they fed into each other's fantasies, they were not as others were. That the not quite sane, as others reckon sanity, have a particular vision that the sane don't, some apprehension of the aesthetic world denied to the rest of us, was a view propounded by R. D. Laing in the sixties, at a time when a great deal of social stigma still attached to any form of mental illness. It is hard for the young to realise that in those days even the word 'cancer' couldn't even be said aloud: it had to be whispered: there seemed to be something so obscene about what was both tragic and incurable: insanity, cancer: an affront to God himself, who was meant to be good. The devil abroad.

It is thanks to R. D. Laing and his view of the mad as saner than the rest of us, merely driven to distraction by the power of their own talent and creativity, that mental illness lost so much of its stigma. Think of Blake, walking in his garden, talking to an imaginary Swedenborg, driving the neighbours mad: think of Strindberg, his hand covered with sores from heavy metal poisoning – Strindberg had a passion for alchemy, believing, even in the late nineteenth century that he could turn base metal into gold – Strindberg, afraid to cross Westminster Bridge because he believed seven hundred angry feminists with axes waited for him on the other side: think of Jonathan Swift, founding the asylum he in the end would inhabit. In the Laingian view the mad are the great amongst us, the poets and painters, the visionaries, at war with their mothers and a respectable and repressive society. And a tempting view it was, to anyone who had taken hallucinogenic drugs

– most of the student population, that is – who realised how shifting and temporary the markers can be between what is sane and insane, what is hallucinatory vision and what is reality. I never held to the Laing view myself – the artist is good in spite of the episode of manic depression, schizophrenia, paranoia, not because of it – but I remain grateful to Laing and his followers for what they did. At least now the sense of shame, and of being somehow polluted, grimed, is no longer added to the burden of those who give birth to, or are children of, or deal with the deranged.

I had a long correspondence, over years, with one Marlena, who typed her letters but signed in green ink. She first sent me a beautifully written story, about a sexual encounter between a girl and a man. There was an agreeable simplicity about it, a clarity of expression, hard to put your finger on: a kind of William Blake-ish-ness; I wrote back to her, in appreciation. She sent me another story, and another; they were getting even better. But now she was writing faster and faster; more words, less meaning: she had peaked, was becoming difficult to understand: the stories were now simply verbose, then studded with capital letters, and underlinings: the simple Saxon words became overlaid with hard, brisk, Roman ones; lots of Cs and Ds and abstract words ending with -iction and -ation all piled up on one another: the sex became seduction, violent, horrific, unkind; its source was evil, corrupt: the Whore of Babylon from the Book of Revelations made her appearance, Mrs Thatcher's Brothel: Dennis Potter and Fay Weldon appeared as divine beings, posted at the gate with swords: and now she was writing not from home but a psychiatric ward. What I was reading was Marlena's descent into madness, into the unhingedness of a mind which attaches itself to language and uses words instead of meaning, not as the expression of it. A desperate act of writing by an overactive, furious, mechanically obsessed mind, wheels whining, writing furiously: trying to relieve itself, getting words out before the head would burst. As if the original beauty of thought could not be contained, but was doomed to be overwhelmed, driven out. Typical schizophrenic writing, people said.

I do wonder about the minds of those we call insane, and who certainly deserve our pity: perhaps in the overlaying of cultures, the splitting and sharing of genes through the centuries, there is just too much to be born. Odd that in Marlena's writing the simple Saxon usage was overwhelmed by Roman, the Roman by the language of the medieval church; then an element of Victorian romanticism enters in; almost in historic sequence, until arriving in the present there is no meaning at all left. Perhaps madness has a kind of vertical layering, back through our family pasts, as well as the horizontal one we somehow conceive of. Here be sanity. There be madness. But who knows what goes on? What is mind, what is brain: what is personality? Or creativity for that matter? The making of something where there was nothing before. The cosmos forms, with in-built imperfections, whether the creator is God, or nature, or the poet.

Opening salvo in a debate at the Central Hall, Westminster, presented to a vast and hostile audience composed mostly of insulted psychotherapists, after the publication of the novel, *Affliction*.

Mind at the End of its Tether

Once there was religion, then there was science, then there was Marxism: now we have therapy, which, in its wider political and social context outside the consulting room, I shall call Therapism. Our belief structures rise and fall with the centuries. We feel safe in servitude, whether it's to God, to knowledge, to patterns of history – overlapping but seldom coinciding – but now turning inwards, serving the inner self. I give Therapism perhaps another fifty years before our brave new caring society collapses under the weight of its own by-product, an excess of empathy – as shatteringly and suddenly, no doubt, as did the Berlin Wall, leaving the human race to find itself some new wheeze in its quest for purpose. What next, once self-understanding fails to bring about heaven on earth? We'll think of something. The human race is ingenious in its search for explanations and solutions.

In the meantime, Therapism offers a new idea of what people are, one which denies God, denies morality and is 'value free'; Therapism replaces the old doctrine of original sin, that notion that we were born flawed but must struggle for improvement with the idea that we were all born perfect, bright, happy and good, and if we are not, why then someone or something – harsh circumstances, faulty parenting or personal trauma – is to blame. Freud's concept of the superego, the controlling conscience which accompanies the id on all its errant voyaging, seems now an unnecessary concession to the old religious ways: even this has drifted from our thinking. Jung wins, okay!

It is a cheerful enough doctrine, this Therapism, but it is also a dangerous one, if in believing that the original bliss of being can be regained by kindness and talk, we also believe that society can be left to get on with itself. It can't.

In the world of extreme Therapism the physiological is denied, and genetic determinism ignored; and the psyche is all. To suggest that the human condition is incurable, that discontent is endemic to the species, that not feeling properly loved is inevitable – inasmuch as it takes two to make a third, and we all know two's company and three's none, so how can any of us be truly satisfied as parent or child – is the equivalent in Therapism to the Pelagian heresy. To suggest that nature did not create us to be happy, but simply to survive long enough to procreate, that discontent is endemic to the species, is pretty much the Manichaen heresy under a new name, and the response the same. Burn the wrong-thinkers alive!

Otherwise Therapism is a kindly and hopeful doctrine, espoused by the nicest and most intelligent of people, and on that very account the harder to refute. See the extremes of Therapism in, say, the happy idea that the fat aren't greedy or genetically doomed; no, eating disorders are caused by abusive fathers. See it in the idea that – as in *Erewhon* – criminals are mentally sick (and conversely, as in AIDS, that the sick are criminals); that depression is a curable disorder, not a natural response to circumstances; that schizophrenia is caused by psychogenic mothers – always the mothers, God bless 'em. That, solipsistically, we do better to fit ourselves to the world, than the world to ourselves. In the refusal to acknowledge that the paedophile and the rapist are merely dwellers at the extreme end of the bell-curve of sexual inclination, and in the insistence that they are 'curable' by talk: let the world be what we'd like it to be, not what it is. Hit on the head? Burgled? That wasn't *real* – that was trauma in the head. The police run a Victims' Support Group – that being a cheaper and simpler solution than employing more policemen, let alone changing the society which produces the crime. The NSPCC now asks for money not to rescue, feed or save children at home or abroad, but to 'counsel' them.

Therapism suits governments, is cheaper than change, and stops people rioting in the streets. The energy of thought is turned inwards, not outwards; too many are too busy coming to terms with their true selves to have time left over for judgemental thoughts about society. In Texas today, those who can convince a counsellor they are in touch with their inner child are allowed to carry concealed weapons. Make of that what you can. The reversal is complete. The inner child, the tumultuous id, becomes the saving grace; it's the controlling superego becomes the murderer.

Therapism demands an emotional correctness from us – we must prefer peace to war, tranquillity to stress, express our anger, share our woes, love our children (though not necessarily our parents) and sacrifice our own contentment to theirs, ban guns, refrain from smoking, give voice to our low opinion of men (if we are women), refrain from giving voice to our low opinion of women (if we are men) and agree with one another that we were all born perfect, bright, happy and free and, what is more, equal. We produce our own inner Prozac: how we smile and drift, while enemies hammer at the gate.

Therapism murmurs in our ear that certain research should not be done in case it reports things we do not want to know: that, say, the reason men get more first-class degrees than women is not that examiners are biased against women, but that when it comes to intelligence the bell-curve of distribution flattens for men, so there are more very bright (*and* concomitantly more very stupid – no, forbidden word: more less mentally-able) men around than there are women, and that these men on the outskirts of normality tend to end up in Oxford taking degrees and getting Firsts. Don't even think about it. Easier just to conclude women are victims and discriminated against. Or if the reason women don't do so well in Finals is these are exams, and men do better at exams than women, then abolish the exams and judge the pupil on course work, until the result is equal attainment for males and females. Who cares about any objective reality. In this morning's paper, there's an account of research coming out of Sweden which suggests that those of us who go to the opera and enjoy cultural pursuits live longer than those who don't. Research acknowledges, but only as an afterthought, that income may have something to do with it. It is not fashionable to say, simply, 'The rich live longer'; though it is observably true. One of the truisms of the New Age, the New Therapism, is that money doesn't make you happy or healthy: 'love' does.

In the Age of Therapism it is assumed that we have reached the pinnacle of wisdom, and that there is nothing more to be learned, just some things to be unlearned, and that if facts are unpalatable it is better to disregard them. In this climate it is difficult for social and educational policies to be effective since they are based on wishful thinking rather than on what actually goes on. The conservative government must test seven year olds and rate schools as if all seven year olds were equal in intelligence: the fall-back position being that, yes, true, some children may be socially disadvantaged and so don't do as well as others – background will be blamed, or uneducated parents, or bad teachers; but the fact that children are born within a wide range of intelligence will be ignored. The word 'intelligence' must be used cautiously: there is something here that smacks of unfairness; of things inherited rather than merited, of a problem that cannot be cured. In the Age of Therapism-out-of-Marxism all of us are equal – in the Age of Therapism-out-of-Science all folk are curable. In the Age of Therapism-out-of-Religion love is all you need.

Psychoanalysts are the new popes: psychotherapists the new priests and counsellors, the lay workers of this dangerous religion of Therapism. I exempt psychiatrists and psychologists since they belong to a different genus: they have come down to us through the medical line, their aim is to heal the body; they see the mind as a physiological entity called 'the brain'. Snip that synapse, change that dose! In the eighteenth century the College of Physicians and the College of Lawyers argued over which of them should claim the mad as their particular areas of concern. In those days insanity presented itself as a legal problem as much as a medical one, to do with an incapacity to make or honour contracts, rather than as a falling-away from a physical, albeit mental, norm. (Some people are just like that.) But the doctors won the argument, and since doctors 'cure', they have been trying to 'cure' the mad ever since. And though with modern medicines symptoms can be subdued, behaviour moderated and distress relieved, 'cure' remains elusive. Some people just go on not knowing how to behave. If they were dangerous we kept them locked away and as happy as we could, according to the standards of the time: now we try to 'cure' them, make them live as we do, and they are wretched and fill the prisons.

A cure by means of talk also remains elusive; unprovable. That is not to say that the conversations are not profoundly interesting: they are, to all concerned. this is not to say that an inspiring body of work has not been built up in relation to the way the human mind works. Of course it has. Our lives are illuminated and enriched by the ideas of Freud, Jung, Kleine, Adler, Eric Berne, among others. Of course. Of course. Some patients report 'cure', though I suspect them of being the ones who end up in love with their therapist. A positive transference, in other words. Some patients report failure, but tend to be the ones who enjoy victim status and have no intention of relinquishing it. Far too many brave and lonely women living desperate lives come up to me and say, 'But it was my therapist gave me the courage to leave my husband.' And others – well, after two hours on a British Airways counselling course to cure fear of flying, most reported greatly increased fear, not less. Make of that what you will.

Anyone can set up in their own front room as a psychotherapist – and the length and structure of their training probably has very little to do with the degree of their insight or their ability to influence others or cheer them up. I am not going to posit here the desirability of registration, let alone declarations of ethics as a solution to the anyone-can-join problem. Anyone can set up a register: anyone can pull down some terminology from the sky and assemble a collection of pious ethical statements. While sanctions remain unenforceable, while the occupation of healing others by talk remains *not* a chartered profession, such as the psychiatrists and psychologists enjoy, letters after the name and noble talk and earnest dedication mean nothing.

Rather see the practising psychotherapist as narrator, and 'good' or 'bad' as writers are seen to be. Many, I suspect, are indeed thwarted novelists. The patient comes into the room and delivers a halting, unprofessional, emotional, inexact narrative of their life to date. Boldly and professionally the psychotherapist rewrites this narrative, giving it a proper beginning and middle, sharpening the plot points, interpreting the tale according to professional training or their own obsessions, whichever is most powerful, and directs the story towards a desired end. Change the therapist and you change the narrative. But perhaps any will do. The therapist validates the client's right to be the central character in the drama; absolves the client from guilt, denying 'ought', gratifying 'want'. (Satisfying, at least temporarily, to the client, though probably not to spouse, family, friends or colleagues, those who constituted the 'family' pre-therapy.) The psychotherapist undertakes to draw the narrative to the right conclusion in due course, at so many pounds the chapter. 'It will take us six months to work through this', or 'This will be two year's hard work on both our parts.' A living novel to be written of so many words, long or short, as dictated by the decision of the publisher! If the psychotherapist is writing in a certain genre, sexual abuse by the father always makes for a dramatic, satisfying and lucrative resolution. But the genre is rather less acceptable than it was.

In the heyday of religion we had a Father God, whose good work was being spoiled by witches: now we have Mother Nature as the benign creator whose work is being spoiled by abusive fathers. Well, men's turn, I suppose. Confession was the mainstay of the Catholic Church; it seems to be in our natures to need to confide in others the sins which bother us; we want to be granted absolution, and pay a price (once Hail Marys said, now money handed over), and forget them. Finite, like a one-off TV drama. Begin again. And why not? Therapy is our contemporary version of confession: the non-stop soap opera of the soul. Except that in the New Confession it's not what you did to others but what they did to you, that must be so mulled over. The therapist offers absolution in the same way as did the medieval pardoner. Mind you, the pardoner was at the sleazy end of the clerical profession. Licensed by a corrupt pope, he was entitled to offer you time off purgatory; your sin could be purged by a money payment. 'What, left your children? Oh dear! Well, cheer up. That's normally five years in purgatory before you can go off to heaven, but give me a couple of guineas now and God will let you off with three years. I have His assurance of that.' The modern equivalent is, 'What, left your children? Oh dear! £1,500 – say fifty sessions at £30 a go – and I'm in a position to relieve you of guilt and sorrow.' If happiness and peace of mind is on offer, we pay up, as then. So little changes. We all need someone to talk to.

Only now (thanks partly, I suspect, to Therapism, and our growing worship of 'aloneness' and 'independence', and our growing disinclination to put up with one another, and our habit of blaming others for our own discontent) twenty-eight percent of us live in single-person households. We are worse off than we were in the old days: there is often no-one to talk to; no friends, no priest to hear confession, and a doctor who can give us only seven grudging minutes of his time. So we take ourselves off to the therapist, the pardoner, and pay, humiliatingly, to be listened to and shrived. No longer a miserable sinner, just someone seeking the validation of his or her own conduct, searching for the authenticity of their emotion, in the name of which all things will be forgiven. Even leaving the children, in the search for the hidden self.

There was a time, of course there was, when I saw psychoanalysis, psychotherapy, as the way forward for humanity. A group therapy on every street corner! That was in the fifties and sixties. Psychotherapy was then indeed a subversive force for change, working away on the edges of a stubborn, reactionary, militaristic, punitive, patriarchal society. It was everything that was progressive, radical; therapy stood for change, understanding, for personal and social advance. But it just isn't like that any more. Psychotherapy, like feminism, has been absorbed into the mainstream, has become a tool of the establishment, part of the establishment. This of course is the fate of all revolutionary movements. Revolution works away hidden for years, then seizes power, becomes that power, is in itself the new reactionary force, and has to be resisted. The wheel turns; the truth, as Ibsen remarks in *An Enemy of the People*, in the end becomes the lie.

By all means let the intelligent help the not-so-bright, let the informed pass on their knowledge to the uninformed, the competent guide the incompetent, the middle class help the underclass out of the black pit of incomprehension. '*If you hit your wife, of course she'll give you a hard time.*' '*What, doesn't she like it? No? Oh, I hadn't thought of that. I'll stop hitting her.*' Of course those who know should help those who don't, and always have, and of course it will 'work'. Call it 'cognitive therapy' if you like, because in the Age of Therapism even the word 'guidance' is suspect, and the idea that someone might know more than anyone else, other than by 'training' which is open to anyone on equal terms, isn't quite on.

Look at it like this. At the turn of the century when Freud and Jung acted as midwives at the birth of psychoanalysis, their baby was born into a room of Stygian black. We knew nothing, nothing, about ourselves. To help us we had the merest glimmer of light, produced over past centuries by poets, playwrights, novelists; just enough to help the baby into being. But the glimmer grew into a brilliance, and thereby changed the world, as much as ever did Jesus, Darwin, Marx. But now it's so bright it could blind you.

I heard a story ten years ago: in 1938 eight psychoanalysts fled Hitler's Germany and set sail for Australia and safety. The ship was diverted to New York, the psychoanalysts were obliged to disembark there, and that's why New York is what it is, and Sydney is what it is. One subtle and alive with self-knowing, the other energetic but blind. That story is outdated now: Sydney catches up with New York. The arcane knowledge which was once the preserve of psychoanalysts is arcane no longer. It is everywhere. Insights and opinions pile on top of one another, battling for space. A *soupçon* of *Women Who Love Too Much*; a dollop of *I'm OK – You're OK*; a shot of *The Cinderella Complex*; of Freud's *Interpretation of Dreams*; of the twenty volumes of the *Collected Works of Carl G. Jung*, and the brew's just fine. (An owl flew in my open window and left its droppings [as it flew] on every single volume – what are we to make of that?) Find the new knowledge in every magazine, on the *Oprah Winfrey* show, in the pop-therapist, on the radio show, the agony aunt; in the rows upon rows of self-help books on the bookshop shelves. But on the whole it is still the bright leading the not so bright, the cheerful cheering up the sad, the ingenious leading the plodders, in the new world order Freud and Jung created (and don't forget Adler): which in time, I fear, will collapse under the weight of its unthought of and unpredicted by-product, that is to say, an excess of empathy combined with a belief that language and reality are the same thing. Talk doesn't pay the rent. Understanding is no substitute for benefits. Fine words, that is to say, butter no parsnips.

From a lecture at The Royal Society of Medicine, in May, 1995, attended mostly by psychoanalysts.

Mice in Mazes – Ourselves Confused

I sat on a platform last week with Stuart Sutherland, Professor of Psychology at the University of Sussex. I heard him say there was still no evidence whatsoever that psychoanalysis worked, or psychotherapy either, though he was prepared to make a grudging exception in the case of behaviour therapy and cognitive therapy. You could, he admitted, with a lot of talk achieve a little desensitisation. But then he is a behaviourist, a Rats-in-Mazes Man. There are his areas of study – he's bound to come to positive conclusions. We all of us tend to believe what we want to believe; that's the point I want to make here. And I certainly don't deny it, that by talking and reasoning, wheedling and pleading, we can cure someone's phobia of spiders. So in the end they can pick up a tarantula. Which could come in useful, I suppose.

Lithium works for Professor Sutherland: self-revelation, talking to superior strangers, never did. We all have our samples of one. I may say we on the platform that day were soundly berated by the audience; fans of psychotherapy, devotees all, samples of ones. '*I know I help my patients.*' '*I love my psychotherapist.*' '*Without my counsellor's help I would never have had the courage to leave my wife.*' The audience out there was oddly angry with us. The writer Jenny Diski, also on the platform, was obliged to say, 'If you're all so therapied-out, wherefore this rage?' And we could not help but believe there was a new religion out there called Therapy; and that we attracted the wrath reserved everywhere for blasphemers.

I know of a psychoanalyst in Israel who for decades has worked with survivors of the Holocaust, mulling over with his patients their horrific traumas and griefs. In the end he concluded that his treatment made them worse, not better. He came to believe that the best thing he could do for his patients was to help them not to remember but to forget. He came to believe that our yearning to uncover the truth, detail the past, lay horrors out on a plate for our inspection, is the real twentieth century insanity, and that it is misguided and misplaced. The mind has its own safety net.

It is called forgetfulness. It is in forgetfulness that health and happiness lie, not in remembrance.

So I would like you to bear these two points in mind. First, how gullible we all are, how difficult it is to escape our own sample-of-one: how we share, even here in this hall, educated and sophisticated though we may be, a universal wish to be unaware of our own unconscious. And that – leading me to the second point – it might not be so bad to gratify that wish, because we may well be running up a peculiar twentieth century dead end, in our hope that, knowing ourselves, understanding the patterns of our mental processes, will somehow make us whole. Enable us to take up our beds and walk, and keep walking. The Temple inscription 'Know Thyself' at Corinth, at the Delphi Oracle where Oedipus went for advice, was never meant to solve all problems. I have no quarrel with Freud, none at all: with what he said or did or wrote. His inconsistencies don't worry me. There is no great virtue in consistency. Psychoanalysis is, was – before the reductionists got hold of it and delivered it up as a series of intellectual constructs and deprived it of any sense of marvel, denied the role of inspiration, decided it could 'cure' – is, was, great fun; intriguing; an examination of and a challenge to, feeling, intellect, compassion. Freud's view of the human psyche still seems apt and poignant enough: so does the language he devised the better to discuss the hitherto undefined and therefore undiscussable. The very notion of the unconscious, which we now all use so freely: fine. The Ego, the Superego, the Id – inefficient translations of the *Ich*, the *Uber Ich*, the *Es* – which in their original forms had a suggestion within them of aspiration – remain workable enough even in their debased English. We all know what we mean by them. But psychoanalysis, in Freud's usage, stood for the excitement, the marvel of the attempt to examine the nature of the soul. Psyche meaning soul. All language is to one degree or another a translation: a vague account of what we think we mean when we talk, loosely but never exactly communicated. Fine. I don't care about Freud's personal habits: the exposés, the scandals, the cocaine habit, the neuroses. I don't care if he was a bad man. But then I never minded David Mellor having a mistress. These things are irrelevant, so long as you're not the wife. Or the mistress. I don't care if Freud was working in old Vienna; people don't change that much; only the framework round them. Freud is not to be taken literally. Not his fault that his successors did, and not his folly either: just unfortunate. Jung observed that literalism was one of the worst enemies of the age; a disease.

I don't mind Jung either. I understand what he means by archetypes; I can claim the novels I write come from the group unconscious. Animus and anima are as useful as the signs of the zodiac when it comes to we laypersons trying to explain ourselves away to others. Though I must say that in the old days when friends went into Jungian psychoanalysis – oddly, Jung seemed to own that word then; the Freudians spoke more of analysis – friends in Jungian psychoanalysis emerged from it just as neurotic or neurasthenic (good Victorian words) as before, but now possessed by a smug if woozy self-esteem and with no conscience at all, just an endless capacity to behave badly. Whereas those of us in Freudian or sub-Freudian psychoanalysis – I was with a Kleinian for eight years: a lot of good-breast, bad-breast stuff – tended to stare into space and do nothing; exhausted by peeling off the onion layers of the self.

I didn't want to be cured, I wanted to understand. And this is at the root of my problem with psychotherapy. Isn't it enough just to use it, enjoy it? Why do you lot have to spoil a perfectly honourable preoccupation, occupation, by alleging talk can cure? Because only thus you can get funding? Because otherwise departments and units of psychoanalysis would disappear? As happened to philosophy? Couldn't you be arguing for it as a pure – not science, I won't have that – discipline? A legitimate field of human concern? Why do you want it to cure? Or have you been forced into this position by dire necessity? In which case fudge the statistics all you like, and we'll shut up. We don't want to lose you. Not altogether.

Back in the eighteenth century, as the hegemony of the Church diminished, lawyers and doctors argued about the category into which mad people should be placed: who was to make money from this obvious deviation from the behavioural norm. The lawyers wanted madness defined as legal incapacity: they could then define degrees of it. The doctors wanted it defined as an illness: they could then describe disorders. The doctors won. We now see madness as mental illness; illness must be cured. There is, we now assume, an ordinary condition known as mental health: anything other than this must be treated; with knock-out drugs which can destroy the physical health, and indeed the mind, and thus tend to throw the baby out with the bath water; or with the talking cure, or the retraining cure, which are at least less dangerous than drugs. And more and more people babble in the streets, and schizophrenics try and make go of it in bedsits, deprived of bedlam, of asylum, of sanctuary, because we can't bear to admit defeat. If it's an illness it can be cured. We see suffering and want to stop it, of course. And where the alternatives are pills or prison, because people must not be allowed to be a danger to themselves or others, and neither pills nor prison cure either anyway – though pills can alleviate distress, and prisons keep offenders out of circulation for a time – then of course try the talking cure. Try protective custody. Try anything. I'm not knocking it.

Sit down with this trusting person by all means and talk, give him the benefit of your wisdom, your sanity, your particular training, your ability to assess the pattern of his words and make sense of them according to your lights. According to your particular discipline. Feed into him and into society your own emotional correctness. Let there be no more obsessions, you cry, no anxieties, no guilt, no excesses, no addictions. Just normality, whatever that is. Because thou art emotionally correct, let no one else be otherwise.

Psychotherapy. I wish I knew what it meant. I wish someone would define it for me. Psycho meaning soul, or have we lost track of that? Psycho meaning mind, these days. Therapy meaning healing. An attempt to cure. What's the illness here? Unhappiness? Obsessive behaviour? Who said people who wash their hands once a day are happier than people who keep anxiety at bay by washing their hands forty times a day? Who's defining it? A deviation from the norm? That norm is healthy? You're joking. What's normal in Rwanda isn't exactly welcome here.

Priests used to heal the soul; priests talked of conscience, guilt, expiation, sacrament. Now we have psychotherapists to heal this guilt slipover from the soul to the self. Conscience becomes unnecessary guilt; guilt becomes free-floating anxiety; forget expiation, forget a hundred Hail Marys, now it's, 'I must be true to myself.' No uncomfortable emotion allowed in the healthy human being. Forget 'original sin'. We were born happy and good, by God we'll stay that way.

How do I, as a customer, define a psychotherapist? Is it someone who the admirable Peter Fonagy, who heads this society, decides is one, someone trained in the methods he declares okay? What are these methods, please? Can we know? Can we have a leaflet? Are you so insecure you cling to the notion that yours is an arcane knowledge? Is a psychotherapist someone 'registered' with some self-elected body with a 'code of ethics' drawn up on a wet Sunday afternoon by someone with a couple of A-levels and a belief in astrology? Most registering bodies seem to take in hypnotists. Jesus! What a field day for charlatans. I know one, a taxi driver who, working from first principles, 'cures' children of stammers by taking them back to traumatic childhood events, telling them this caused the stammer, and altering the plot of the event so it ceases to be traumatic. Bingo! No stammer.

And most codes of ethics I've encountered in the field suggest that the psychotherapist's duty is to the person who comes through the door; that alone: forget their children, spouses, families, friends. Just the one who hands the money over. Yet no one comes through that door alone – they bring a host of unseen, hopeful, living, breathing, albeit invisible, others with them. None of them can sue for what you did, when you came trampling uninvited through their lives. Most therapists I have encountered lately see their function as encouraging their clients to stand alone, independent, proud and free, shaking off the trammels of the past. Jesus, again! People were born to live in families, groups, tribes. Yet now twenty-eight percent of all households in this country are one-person households. Not one-parent households, but one-person households. We begin to find one another intolerable.

Please tell me. What is a psychotherapist? What is your aim? How do I find a good one? Because the field out there is now so littered with baddies, fools and rogues, I have no doubt the good ones do get overlooked. You can't judge a profession by its practitioners, or can you? If you as psychotherapists can stop stutterers stuttering; cure people of disliking tarantulas; raping their own children; cure agoraphobics, claustrophobics, make the lame walk and the blind see, believe me I am entirely glad. If you can do that without exploiting the gullible, making your clients so dependent they grieve when you're off on holiday, loving you so much – positive transference – their lives and families fall to bits, well, good for you. I just get rather a lot of letters from the ones whose psychotherapy didn't go too well – who become suicidal, desperate, lose all self-esteem, who left partners and now regret it – who find the therapist's talk of aloneness has translated terribly into loneliness. The word idiot, by the way, comes from the Greek *idios* – alone. My Kleinian analyst told me we define each other, as the shore defines the sea, the sea the shore: you don't hear this kind of talk much these days.

And those others, who made a mess of things, why weren't they good therapists? You tell me! They seemed good enough to the GPs who recommended them.

Translate this as 'a complaint about low standards in the profession'? Too right.

In Professor Fonagy's letter to me, asking me to deliver this lecture, he says that psychotherapy is turning out to be one of the best evaluated medical treatments currently available. Treatment for what? Tonsillitis? Are we to talk patients out of sore throats? But I don't think that's what he means. Rather: psychotherapy is better than any state-of-the-art medication for mental distress currently available. I don't think that necessarily means psychotherapy is so good, just that medication is so bad. All patients get the same recommended dose, regardless of size, weight, gender. Whether antidepressants or antibiotics. Always struck me as strange, that. But, as I say, if the alternative is pills or prison, talk away. Professor Sutherland puts his faith in Lithium, however, and Professor Sutherland is an honourable man.

Back in the thirties Aleister Crowley, who described himself as the Beast 666, upset everyone by inscribing above his Mediterranean temple the words, not 'Know Thyself' but 'Do What Thou Wilt Shall Be All Of The Law.' Everyone was dreadfully shocked. This was a doctrine which could only emanate from the Devil. We accept it now. It sounds quite ordinary. 'Know Thyself' has somehow drifted into this new doctrine of supreme selfishness and self-approval, without social, sexual or family conscience – 'Do What Thou Wilt Shall Be All Of The Law.' In other words, 'I must think of myself now, not others.' Or the familiar phrase, now normal reaction to another's distress, 'That's their problem, not mine.' When psychotherapists feel brave enough to say the words 'ought' or 'should', as the priests did; or counsel self-denial or self-sacrifice or duty to others, I will begin to take them seriously. Otherwise the psychotherapist is just like one of those debased priests, the pardoners, who went round offering a term off purgatory in return for money. The more you paid them, the shorter your torment would be thereafter. The pardoners promised. People believed. 'Pay me,' says the shoddy psychotherapist, 'and I will give you happiness.'

Now I am in a pretty poor position here. You're obviously all at the top end of the therapy market: responsible people, good analysts and therapists; yes, and even hypnotists; determined to relieve human suffering, and not paid much for your pains: working through State organisations, not charging clients direct. And you've seen psychotherapy work. And I'm glad. I feel rather like someone from the Department of Health explaining to a group of doctors in the mid-nineteen-eighties that they must stop prescribing antibiotics in the public good. Not very popular. And hard to believe, for those doctors, who'd seen penicillin work, just as you've seen psychotherapy work, that what was so good once, such a blithe and obvious solution, in overuse was bad. Save psychotherapy for extreme cases, for God's sake, before it turns us into a nation of solipsists, who believe that self-discovery equals contentment. Save us from a society in which our government won't spend money or risk votes by bringing in legislation enforcing seat belts in school coaches but eagerly puts in grief counsellors after an accident occurs. Save us from schools where there's no money for paper or pencils or inside loos, let alone teachers, but enough for a mighty team of counsellors sent in to adjust children and parents to their lot. Lateral thinking. Don't raise the bridge, lower the river. Don't get rid of horror, persuade us to accept it. Don't address the social problems which lead to divorce – women who work too hard, men who don't work at all because there is no work – give them a counsellor so divorce happens easily, smoothly: society fragments more.

Once upon a time I, too, saw psychoanalysis, psychotherapy, as the way forward. It was a subversive force for change, working away on the edges of stubborn, reactionary and militaristic society. It was something progressive. But now it seems to me no longer subversive: it's mainstream, establishment. This of course happens to many an idealistic revolutionary movement. It works away hidden for years, then seizes power, becomes that power; is in itself the new reactionary force.

I, too, had a moment of insight: a revelation, an anti-conversion experience. You know the archetypal haunted house? The castle of the demon lover? On top of the hill, mean and craggy against a sinister skyline? Every now and then the attic windows open, and flocks of black demons, shrieking, stream out across a stormy sky to do all manner of ill. You see it in *The Wizard of Oz*, you see it in *The Addams Family*: it's in our fairy tales, it's in our psyche.

Well, there I was, a couple of years back, in this perfectly pleasant house upon a hill: headquarters of a very respectable association of psychotherapists, addressing a gathering of their literary society. They wanted to know – or said they did – about the function of the archetype in my novels. And this house was a hive of industry, full of soft-voiced people brimming over with good intent, and every room had some kind of training course or other going on inside it, with an official certificate at the end of it – courses in therapy for probation officers, stress counsellors, policemen, magistrates and the like – and of course it was a hot-house for the creation of yet more therapists. Money was changing hands like no one's business – these courses are not cheap – and every now and then the front door opened and a stream of the certified poured out into the world to spread their talking cure abroad – and where I once would have seen soft-voiced angels of mercy, now I saw demons. And I saw a business, not a healing profession.

And, probably unfairly, as I talked to my group of therapists, most of whom seemed to be would-be writers, about the archetype and so forth, it occurred to me that that was exactly what they were: failed novelists: they had taken to psychotherapy in order to write living novels in the minds of the helpless and unhappy. This was why they did it; why they chose this profession. They would write in the genre in which they had been trained: they would invent and define their client's past accordingly, give a running account of the client's present which suited their view of it, and move the story through to its future, its climax, happy or unhappy, as they projected it ahead. And they got paid week by week as they did it, and didn't have to wait to be accepted and published before being paid. While the client lived the story out, according to the chance which brought them to this particular therapist, this particular form of cure.

After the talk we all went out to a Chinese meal and there, when their guard was down, I listened while clients were freely named, individual cases were discussed – 'So and so must leave her husband; he's a horror.' 'Yes, I know him: he's a frightful bully – after the same job as me, actually.' – and all manner of confidences were revealed: all at the level of simple, smug and cynical gossip. Not even the rules of the confessional applied. And these were the professionals teaching the professionals; and I wondered, what does this training you talk of mean? Exactly? Who's training whom, and for what, and why? Are the intelligent helping the not-so-bright, the informed passing on information to the uninformed, the competent looking after the incompetent, the happy taking the unhappy in hand, or what? What does go on when these two people, one in charge and one not, sit down in a room together and talk?

The Changing Face of Government

Essays out of London, written for Abroad.

Written at the height of the sleaze scandals, which afflicted the Tory Government and were destined to bring it down. Or at any rate marked its fall from grace.

Kissing-and-Telling in Britain Today

Over here in Britain there's a new game called Kiss-Tell-and-Out-You-Go which is all the rage, and has been since our Coolidge-like Prime Minister John Major unveiled his Back-to-Basics campaign at the Conservative Party Conference in 1993. (By Back-to-Basics Mr Major meant a return to Victorian values; a period when, allegedly, family live was stable and people could tell the difference between right and wrong.) In this game a scorned woman runs to the press with her story, the press publish, the public salivates, a wife weeps, a man in a good grey suit resigns or is sacked, his skills and energy are lost to the nation, and the rest of the world think we're insane.

(I have remarked before what's to happen in the wider world happens first in Britain. The Houses of Parliament today, the White House tomorrow.)

Nor any more is the game confined to Westminster: it now preoccupies the City. Not enough that nine members of Mr Major's government have lost their jobs by way of sex scandal; yet more notable scapegoats are required. The nine that went were not lacking in political acumen or significance – they included a Minister of State for National Heritage and a Minister for the Environment and Countryside (new PR-friendly Ministries pop up all over the place, these days) and only this week one Richard Spring, a Parliamentary Private Secretary, resigned within five hours of a three-in-a-bed scandal breaking in one of our more salacious tabloids, the *News of the World*. (Murmur as one might that all three were unmarried and consenting adults, the fact that the one in the middle was a Sunday School teacher was more than flesh or Mr Major could stand. Mr Spring had to go.) But now that the skills of Mr Pennant-Rea, once Editor of *The Economist*, until very lately Deputy Governor of the Bank of England, have been lost to his employers, and to us, it is clearly time to take the matter seriously and wonder why it has come about, this new and unpleasant British penchant for scapegoating powerful men and humiliating their wives?

Do we all feel better because Mr Pennant-Rea was made ridiculous for being a man unusually capable of love – albeit of a too transitory kind for his own good – and displayed the usual folly of the lover in his letters over the years to Mary-Ellen Synon, financial journalist? It seems so. Why are we so mean? Perhaps we dislike men who seem to have everything – good looks, good suits, good money, good homes, good wives – and if they have emotions too, just naturally rejoice in their comeuppance.

Some see the British tabloid press as to blame: the press here is currently beside itself with a kind of hideous excitement, having discovered its power to ruin careers, marriages and governments. To the despair of all serious journalists, at the annual Press Awards ceremony earlier this month, journalistic Oscars went to *The Sun*, for its scoop 'CAMILLA TO DIVORCE!', to the *News of the World* for 'ROYAL SENSATION: DI'S CRANKY PHONE CALLS TO MARRIED OLIVER' and named as Newspaper of the Year the lurid *Daily Mail*. The unfortunate Lord Wakenham, chairman of the Press Complaints Committee, found himself standing on a very public platform and handing out these awards, approving by implication everything his Committee stands against – the notion that it's the business of newspapers to expose the personal lives of others and to arbitrate public morality from the standpoint of the gutter. Reluctance to appear discourteous – the worst crime in the best circles – kept Lord Wakenham standing there, no doubt as the organisers had anticipated.

But newspapers have readers, and up to a point readers are responsible for the contents of newspapers – as the tabloids' editors keep saying.

Perhaps envy is a peculiarly British vice? Other Europeans – the French and the Italians in particular – rejoice when some grey old devil of a politician, financier or newspaper proprietor is shown to have some life left in him. But not us. It's not even as if Mr Pennant-Rea had been telling us what to do or how to behave. The glee was understandable when Tim Yeo, a member of Mr Major's cabinet, who used up much airtime inveighing against the single-parent family, was discovered to have created one of his own outside wedlock. But Mr Pennant-Rea? What did he ever do to us? His hypocrisy was never more than personal. A few might think he was at fault in presiding over an economic system of which the averred aim is to achieve nought percent inflation, when everyone knows that low inflation means high unemployment – but the populace in general is not so sophisticated. No, I think we just like the perpetual rerun of the soap opera: we're used to it; the secret, the revelation, the staged family photograph – with dogs if possible – of reformed husband, deceived wife and startled children. We appreciate opening the newspaper and thinking for at least this one morning, 'My life is better than theirs.' We are at the moment an anxious nation – half of us working twice as hard as we should, the other half lucky to have any work at all; told on all sides that we can none of us have a job for life but must be 'flexible'; and with an increasing sense of powerlessness as the connection between work and reward grows flimsier by the minute. Lucky those who can surf the chaos: redundant those who can't! But still this is no excuse.

Had Mr Pennant-Rea been inefficient, dishonest, drunk or mad, precedent suggests he would have stayed in his job. But not if he rolls round on the floor of the Governor's dressing-room with an Irish redhead, elegant and intelligent though she may be, and an old friend from his days at Trinity College, Dublin. Jilted, Mary-Ellen tells the press; not for money but because she wants justice done. She's Irish, she feels people need to know what goes on behind the marble pillars of the

British establishment: Pennant-Rea needs punishing: he promised her marriage and he didn't follow through. She feels thoroughly Irish, in fact, and persecuted: she says those who have powerful lives should not use their power over those who have weak lives, and she is right. But it is a kind of Irish romanticism, a raising of simple sexual betrayal to a theoretical, even religious, level, that sounds strange to British ears. Easier for us to see a vituperative woman getting her revenge, than see a woman trying to right a natural balance. Mary-Ellen now says of herself that though she has been much criticised in the UK, at home in Ireland she has found sympathy, support and understanding. Of course.

No doubt the fact of Mary-Ellen Synon's Irishness weighted heavily upon the Governors of the Bank of England when they decided Pennant-Rea must go. It was an IRA bomb a couple of years ago which destroyed the NatWest Bank Tower in the City, blowing out every pane of glass in the building, bringing financial centres to a standstill for months, and in effect bringing the British to the Conference Table. One death but all that money! (The story goes that the bomb was meant for the new Lloyds Building, where a janitor told the driver it was more than his job was worth to let them park their van outside; so they drove round the corner to NatWest. Bang! Lloyds were not best pleased. They could have claimed on someone else's insurance.) The idea that Mr Pennant-Rea had rashly exposed the Bank to a security threat was not to the Governors so far fetched: what's more, Ms Synon was a journalist. He should at least, the feeling was, have kept sex off the premises, and not cavorted up and down the solemn corridors and in and out the Governor's chamber. And had he not lost dignity by the press exposure and was that not bad for business? Do not people in charge of money need to be in charge of themselves, even more than do those in charge of running the country?

Any man must lose dignity if a spiteful or angry mistress tells all. David Mellor, an excellent if short-lived Secretary of State for National Heritage, had to go because Antonia de Sancha, kiss-and-tell girl *par excellence*, told the press it was her pleasure to suck his big toe; that made everyone laugh. He has been very popular ever since, on TV and talk radio, but not in Parliament.

Some also say, of course, that Pennant-Rea was happy enough to resign: he could continue with his lucrative lectures on the State of the Economy and not have to pay over the money he received to his employers at the Bank of England, but that's probably just envy talking. The rest of us talk about the state of the economy nonstop, and don't get paid for it, and resent it.

None of this explains to the rest of the world why the British are so nervous about sex, why the play *No Sex Please, We're British* was for decades a smash hit in the West End. We are not in reality prudish or over-respectable. On the contrary. The British are as randy as anyone else, have almost as many babies out of wedlock as within, happily cohabit without marriage, terminate pregnancies almost at will, lose our virginity in our early teens; our pop stars and celebrities change partners as if there were no tomorrow, no children and no social disapproval. Few of us go to Church. Creationists and Salvationists are almost unknown outside the Afro-Caribbean community. We laugh merrily about Back-to-Basics, which might actually have done us some good. The US, I believe, is a far more puritanical and respectable nation than we are, but both nations like to pretend it's the other way round.

The US certainly worries if its President shows signs of sexual restlessness, but the discussion focuses on an apparent anxiety that the rules of gender politics are being abused; that there are undertones here of sexual harassment or a possible offence against doctrines of Equal Opportunity. America used to be less censorious; easily forgiving Jack Kennedy his satyriasis (blame it on the cortisone jabs) and rather admiring him over the Marilyn Monroe business. Until now the US has readily accepted that men in power will attract beautiful women – even that that's why men seek power in the first place. But at least it was always more likely to reject a presidential candidate who was ill or mad, than because he was sexually active outside marriage. Good Lord, it would think but not say, in many another country he'd have had four wives in the first place, and if you were saddled with the good, kind, intelligent but hardly sexy Eleanor, what would you do if you were Franklin?

It is the distinction between how both nations see themselves and how they are that fascinates. I spend some time in Europe, some in the US. It seems to me that the US lives in the present and the future, and this is what gives the nation its peculiar cheerfulness. The weight of group guilt and past failure does not press down upon Americans; they are not weakened by angst. It is as if you have used a computer mouse and picked up an icon labelled 'The Past' and shifted it over to Europe and left it there. It's our agenda alone; and we have no energy left to deal with present and future. If it's revenge for George III's tea taxes, it's a good one. You have reduced us into a kind of Disney Theme Park, and how readily we lap up the role. In the postmodernist sense we dwell in a meta-past. We believe, with a little help from Mr Major, that somehow we still live our public, if not our private lives in Mr Gladstone's era. It is our duty to tut and cluck our disapproval at sexual goings-on. In our group head we still put frills on the piano legs so as not to shock the ladies, still put unmarried mothers in lunatic asylums on the grounds that they are Moral Imbeciles.

Louis Malle picked up on this phenomena in his film of Josephine Hart's novel, *Damage*. Malle dressed his hero, a British politician bent on an incestuous affair, rather as Gladstone or Disraeli would have dressed, and had him stalking the contemporary London streets in what amounted to a frock coat and top hat. Mr Major picks up on it by firing his best and brightest as if the very survival of the nation depended upon rooting our sexual misdemeanour whenever it surfaces. I don't know how we're going to get back into the present, persuade you conscience-free lot to take your icon back.

But I do not suppose Mrs Mellor, posing for the family-together-again press release photograph, or Mrs Ashdown, wife of the leader of our third party, (whose current title I can never remember), posing likewise, or Mrs Pennant-Rea, a stunningly beautiful woman, one of the Jay family of *Heartburn* fame, as they murmur their, 'I stick by my husband' lines, are much comforted by notions of meta-pasts and Sexual Theme Parks. Their misfortunes are real, plain, and unnecessary enough; and compounded by a hysterical and disgraceful press. The phrase 'dwindled into a rejected wife' is much used by the broadsheets in their comments, as if to underline the fact that we're still really in the old days, when a woman was defined by her husband, and the sexually rejected woman is meant to hang her head and stumble out into the desert sands, to be stoned by others. The only women who seem to have shrugged off the epithet are Lady Mary Archer, whose novelist husband Jeffrey sues everyone in sight and wins, and Mrs Norma Major, whose husband John does his best to close whole publications down if scandal so much as teeters at the edge of his life. Mr Spring's real error, I suspect, was to suggest to the Sunday schoolteacher in the middle that John and Norma led a less than rampant sex life and this was repeated in the press. Perhaps Mr Spring should have talked less and concentrated more.

On the publication of the 'Kiss-and-Tell' revelations, concerning Mr John Major's remarkably decent early life.

Goodbye, John Major

One day, I fear, we will look back on John Major's reign (these days we time our centuries by Prime Ministers, not monarchs) with affection. Such a steady, quiet, respectable man, we will say. We should have thanked God for the greyness, not knocked it: and at least the guy was capable of falling in love. Remember even farther back, we'll say – that man who loved opera, what was he called? Edward Heath? Didn't he play the organ, go to the theatre? Just think of it, a cultured Prime Minister! Those were the days . . . Tried to save the nation from, what was it? Unions? Anarchy? Something! Wanted to put the nation on a three-day week – an excellent anti-inflationary device come to think of it – and got driven from office for his pains. All that art stuff had evidently gone to his head. What was Major's error? Why did we get rid of him? Ah yes, didn't he walk the borderline between democracy and populist fascism? Never quite let it topple over? Very boring. He had to go. He wasn't a leader: he didn't have charisma, not like Hitler or Stalin, he wasn't exactly memorable. Mind you, he didn't flail about: he was single-minded, ruthless; when he was still just a bit of a lad – if we're to believe this week's kiss-and-tell revelations in the *Daily Mail* – and political ambition called, he swiftly got rid of his first girlfriend. She was a Seventh-Day Adventist, a divorcée, a mother of two; it simply wouldn't do. That was back in the sixties, in Brixton. He was in his early twenties, she was in her mid-thirties. 'Getting a bit haggy around the eyes, Jean,' he remarked, allegedly, towards the end, preparing her for the blow; next thing: 'We're not going to make love any more.' Then no more kisses, no more sofa-sitting, no more anything. Gone. Goodbye John. Into Norma's arms.

Oh yes, I remember it well. Not John Major, of course, not my scene – I didn't belong to the Young Conservatives, but to the Young Socialists, and it was all love amongst the artists, and we were ahead of our time. But the horrors of the male dumping technique that prevailed in the fifties and sixties permeated all circles. That was before the arrival of the pill put contraceptive responsibility firmly in the woman's court. Before that, for a young man, it was all fathers with shotguns or one-night stands and fake names and addresses. (A wise girl checked the driving licence.) And since sex was on the whole in the missionary position and men were impulsive, and like the girls, never believed that what happened would happen, relationships all too often ended with pregnancy.

While men had the responsibility of *not* getting a nice girl pregnant, or at least trying to, girls had the responsibility of not leading a man on. We thought it was the natural order of things. Just as we thought if we did get pregnant outside marriage, we'd have to have the baby adopted – in the total absence of Social Security Benefits – and the punishment – to keep and feed the baby for six weeks before it was taken away – was natural and inevitable too. In other words, we didn't think.

And the young man's dilemma was, as John Major found, now I want to break off this relationship, how do I do it without breaking the girl's heart? And, what is more, particularly once she's dumped, how do I make sure she doesn't turn up in three months' time saying 'I'm pregnant, it's yours, now you have to marry me.' Girls would – even nice girls – and on purpose too, if they saw your interest flagging. So first, male theory went, the decent guy would warn them they no longer attracted you ('a bit haggy around the eyes, Jean') – then you'd confirm it by stopping sleeping with them, then you'd ease off altogether, over three or four celibate months, thus saving her pain, and yourself possible future embarrassment. The delayed exit hurt more than anything; but it was considered kinder, and more gentlemanly than the sudden break, which could drive a girl mad. (Male conceit had, mid-sixties, risen to a peak, a crescendo!) Jean suffered. John went, piously correct in his behaviour, and into Norma's arms.

It seems to us now a strange and passionless world, in which the young man always goes home before dawn, in case the children find out, in which the girlfriend's mother comes on the Spanish holiday too, and takes the bed in the middle. But Jean's mother, like her daughter, did seem to be a pleasant woman, and she and John got on well, and after all a chaperon was required. Not so strange in context! Unmarried sex, mid-sixties, could still raise eyebrows, especially in places like Spain. Had mother stayed home, the young couple might not have found a room.

And what in the world changes, other than detail? For many of us, no matter how liberated we feel, sex stays in the head: wherever we go, mother goes too. We put on the Wonderbra but sue for attempted rape, if the man we get into bed with naked makes so much as a pass. The girls on *Blind Date* offer all kinds of lurid and sexy goings-on to the invisible man Cilla Black provides – but the minute the screen's away, the minute he's real, natural selectivity is the only thing that rears its head. *Blind Date* outings end up respectability itself. Friendship, yes – but if the certain necessary *frisson* doesn't happen, forget the sex.

The world of Young Conservatives remains pretty much as it ever was – the lads are loutish, when together, timorous when apart: the girls well groomed, hoping for engagement rings and longing to be wooed. We get our view of how others live from the media, and the media are not interested in the world of mixed choirs, sports club, prayer meetings, kisses on doorsteps, the tender and cautious exchange of feelings, the nervous buying of Valentine cards, of secret hopes and undisclosed longings: where's the drama here? Where's the story?

The placing of a Georgette Heyer novel (don't mock it!) on a pillow as a gift, as John Major did for Jean, is touching, not absurd – something she remembers to this day. Ordinary people do not need the censure of society to keep them tentative in love and steady in habit – it's the starchiest couples now live 'in sin' – with a wary eye on the divorce statistics, what a costly and troublesome business! – it's the wild ones who take the plunge and get married. Total madness, marriage, these days, with an almost one in two chance of ending in tears.

Mind you, mind you, the young John Major knew how to control a girl. 'I'll only say I love you if I'm going to marry you,' he'd say. And she waited and waited and he never said it. Does he control his Cabinet in the same way? If Jean ever had an idea, it was another of 'Jeannie's homespun theories'. Does anything change? 'Ah, Mr Portillo, another of your homespun theories!' John would be irritated if Jean's teenage son didn't clean his shoes. 'What, Mr Clark, not balanced your budget yet?' Young John Major didn't like Sundays because according to Jean they didn't have enough structure in them. Try searching for Sunday now, in these days of seven-day anxiety, seven-day work, seven-day search for profit. Oh yes, the lad grew up to win a victory or two; I hope not wholly at our expense. Young John Major became perforce wary of scandal: all that youthful slipping home in the early hours, trying not to be seen! Decades later the *New Statesman*'s sued and *Scallywag*'s stopped.

Jean looks a nice steady brave responsible girl. If she uses her youth to fund her old age who can blame her? And the young John Major did dump her, albeit in as kind a manner as he could; she in return speaks about him as kindly as she can, and I reckon they are quits. And if the *Daily Mail* articles are part of a putsch, to mock John Major out of court, it doesn't work. He comes out of it too well.

Leading up to Labour Victory – Innocent Days of 1996.

White Hope or Sell Out?

Does the hour find the man, or the man find the hour? Is Tony Blair the committed leader from the left our society requires if it is to survive, the healer of all political and social woes, or is he a politician of astonishing and ruthless ambition? Here in Britain, where this innocent-looking, bright-eyed, lean young man now leads that weary, stuffy old man the Labour Party by the nose, the jury is still out. My mother, aged eighty-nine, and from the old intellectual left, watches Blair shake hands with the enemy, the bankers and industrialists, and trusts Blair to behave like a socialist once he is elected. Just promise everything, please everyone, and get the Conservatives out. Perhaps Oskar Lafontaine in Germany should do the same? Depoliticise, and win.

Or perhaps not: others are not so sanguine. My husband, in his mid-forties, sees Blair as a dangerous populist, a Ross Perot with a party behind him. When Blair was first elected as leader of the Parliamentary Labour Party, two years back, the first thing he did, or didn't do, was *not* support the railwaymen's union in a strike which, for once, enjoyed massive popular support. To woo the employers and marginalise the unions seemed more important at the time than justice for the working man, or even temporary popularity. What new kind of devious socialism was this? Why use the word in the first place? My grown children are grateful for 'a leader' but wonder about the integrity of a man who defies the principles of his own party and sends his child to a school for the privileged; and my best friend says darkly, 'Have you noticed that the two sides of his face are entirely different?' There is worry about the national dumbing-down over which Blair presides, the marginalisation of the intellectual wing of the Labour Party, the notion that plain everyday response takes precedence over informed opinion, the mockery of the aspirations of the educated.

But all agree that a change of government is necessary, and Blair is the one to bring about the change. The Conservative Party have been in power since 1979, first under Thatcher, then under Major. They are seen as a mendacious, bungling lot, who have to go, before the nation loses all credibility in the eyes of the world, and 'mad cow' and 'Britain' become synonymous. The sight of the Conservative government trying to bully the rest of Europe into eating beef it doesn't want to eat has distressed and humiliated sensible people on all sides of the political spectrum. The reliance of government on the sound bites of expediency has lost it all dignity. But the party of the right still has enough energy left to create a little turmoil. Our losing to Germany in Euro '96 was greeted with relief by those on the left who feared that a football victory would leave the British so bullish they'd have a referendum – the blind leading the ignorant – and vote against staying in Europe. Then what? It doesn't bear thinking of.

Tony Blair and his advisors spent their summer holidays in Tuscany, the traditional haven of the chattering, garlic-eating, wine-drinking middle classes – the decision so to do seen by some as just another nail in the coffin of the pint-of-beer-down-the-pub straightforwardness of 'Old Labour'. Just before they packed their shorts and left, New Labour published a document, 'New Labour, New Life for Britain', in which it became apparent that what many had suspected was true; New Labour is really Old Tory Mark II. Difficult enough as it had been for the left to distinguish itself from the right and vice versa – just as First Class on an airline has difficulty these days differentiating itself from Business Class (you can stretch your legs only so far, consume only so much champagne) – now it became all but impossible. Here are the old sticks of the right re-presented; the hard, tough, no-nonsense hand; swift punishment for young offenders, tight control of government spending, a curfew for children, a return to family values, better training for the young and so forth, and as carrots nothing more exciting was offered than a shorter wait for hospital treatment and smaller school classes. Such complaints as were heard from within the party were about lack of consultation, not the abandonment of socialism.

A word analysis of the 'New Labour, New Life for Britain' document proved that 'new' was the adjective used more frequently, then 'positive', then 'constructive'. 'Stakeholder' appeared frequently, as in 'stakeholder society', as did the word 'challenge'. The sound bites of expediency, rather than a policy, perhaps; but it seems to have worked. Traditional Conservative voters, osmosing the great Blair PR putsch on radio and TV, breathed a sigh of relief and decided there could be no harm in voting New Labour, while lifelong Old Labour voters breathed a sigh of sorrow for lost illusions and decided to go on voting labour, to keep the Conservative Party out.

We can have it all ways, Blair suggests, in a flurry of platitudes, if only we think positively, and meet the challenge of the new. We can keep our lean, keen enterprise culture, but without the underclass this culture has created, and without extra taxes either. Of course everyone wants to believe him. Utopia!

Blair, with his talk of morality, his genuine Christian beliefs, his halo of righteousness, waits in the wings of government like a *deus ex machina*, to lead us to a new society. A leader, a recognisable leader! A firm one too, who will allow no dissent amongst his traditionally quarrelsome and outspoken MPs. All now speak with one voice. Clare Short, the one vigorous freethinking member of the Shadow Cabinet, already in disgrace for suggesting that marijuana could possibly be legalised, found herself demoted to Shadow Secretary for Overseas Aid, for suggesting in public that the master's style of leadership was 'macho'. The hope is that, under Blair, the left won't for once destroy itself through ideological argument, factionalising and splintering, won't waste its anger on its allies, not its enemy, and thus allow that enemy to seize victory. It will take a leaf out of the book of the right, which, dedicated to the principle of self-interest rather than communality, has traditionally had an easier time than the left in agreeing where it's going, and thus in getting itself elected. To gain power by telling lies, by telling an electorate only what it wants to hear, is tempting, and easy, but very, very dangerous. What happens before the election, continues to happen afterwards.

The background fear of all our Western democracies is this – that the voter can so easily be conned. We look at the posters and TV slots which feature our hero and notice how the shoulders have been subtly broadened, the jaw strengthened. We worry. We suspect politicians with too idealistic a turn of mind; we like them going to Church but not to have too much faith, and is not Blair going for instruction to a Catholic priest? The man actually *believes* (which makes the paranoic fringe suspect an elaborate Opus Dei plot to finally destroy the left). Since the Third Reich we have preferred pragmatists to Utopians: we have played safe and confined our notions of 'progress' to technological matters. Perhaps we have been over-cautious in refusing to envisage any kind of glorious future for humankind; lest in our attempts to achieve it, we sacrifice our political and personal freedoms. Perhaps we've been wrong: perhaps it is possible.

Be that as it may, here in Britain we look at Blair's bright eyes and wonder what it is we're seeing – a good family man who goes to Church but who believes, like all dictators, that the end justifies the means; or a man ambitious for himself who will say whatever it is his audience wants to hear; or a genuine socialist playing a game he'd rather not play for the sake of the future.

One of the old guard Labour Party, a former Shadow Home Secretary, said to me the other day that there was a hair's breadth between the policies of the Conservatives and that of Labour, but in that hair's breadth he was content to live. Space for manoeuvre between left and right, even inasmuch as these old definitions apply, seem to be so small once a party comes to power, we may just have to put up with that ungenerous hair's breadth, hope Blair gets elected, and be prepared to throw him out if he *doesn't* renege on his pre-election promises. And there's a fine irony!

Written for *The Guardian* on the euphoric occasion of New Labour's victory, May, 1997.

Over to You, Tony

This is an exhilarating day for the nation, by a large majority. The electorate has flexed its muscles and found its power. It put up with the Tories for eighteen years, took a collective breath, and decided to get rid of them.

People under thirty-five feel all their problems are about to be solved. Their children will be educated and their illnesses cured; to them the change of government feels like a magic bullet. Those of us rather older take a slightly more cautious view. We welcome change – everyone does; and the feeling of togetherness is something that hasn't been felt in the land for a long time. All of a sudden in throwing out the government that tried to make us one nation, this is what we became.

Once the euphoria has died down, more realism will creep in. Will Tony Blair make out in Vienna next week? Perhaps he should take with him Mr Major, who knows the workings of that particular and terrifying committee. New brooms have the same old rubbish to sweep up.

The areas of manoeuvre that any government has are small in the modern world once power becomes a reality. But at least those familiar terrible faces are gone. There is a satisfactory sense that some individuals found their comeuppance: though as we watch them on the television facing defeat and humiliation, we could even feel generous towards a handful. The few whose private habits we knew and despised them for at least have gone.

The Thatcher-Major term ran concurrently with great technological changes. It is easy to blame them for everything that has gone wrong in our attitudes to one another, in the triumph of self-interest, the growing up of the 'me' generation, the general lack of social cohesion, and a strange sense that a kind of anarchy has prevailed alongside a loss of our civil liberties. Thatcher was all-round bad, but the electorate didn't throw her out. Major was an improvement, kept a handful of right-wing extremists under some kind of control, and will probably be seen by the future as a shrewd and able man. That's being generous. Look around the south-east and see prosperity. Go North and see poverty, disillusion and brave people making the best of a government frightened to spend except on the wrong things. Look forward to what Labour will do? Of course. But such a large majority! They could do all kinds of things which in theory the populace has wanted. Cancel the Criminal Justice Act; legalise drugs; spend the Lottery money on education, not the arts. Why not? But when it comes to it, it was easy to have the Major government to blame for what in fact for most citizens conveniently reflected their worst will, not their best. I'm glad the Liberal Democrats did so well – they will exercise a restraining element. They're really nice people – perhaps, as the electorate sensibly enough understands, too nice to trust with total control. Government is the art of the practical, and we are unaccustomed to having ideologues in power. We will have to see what happens next. We may well find politics here following Clinton's pattern, in which the enormous enthusiasm is moderated, but the relief after the Reagan years remains.

It is an exciting moment. The sun is shining. People walk around in shirtsleeves, smiling; even the tourists in central London seem aware of the change. Think of it: you could go to the polls and alter the course of your nation's history. It's like writing your own episode of *EastEnders.*

For such a long time, we have felt that things have moved outside our control, and not with the will of the people, and not in the best interests of the people. They have talked to us as if we were children.

They have told us what is good for us. They have interfered with our freedoms. They have logged us and examined us and told us where we were wanting. They have classified and categorised us. They have assumed we all lived in the same way and wanted the same thing. They have dared to castigate single mothers. They have encouraged us to abort our children in the short term to save the NHS money in the long term, and didn't tell us. They made us eat infected beef to save a scandal, and to save money. They have cut where they shouldn't have, and spent where they shouldn't have. They burned lots of money up in fireworks. They planned impossible and grandiose millennium projects. It's easy to hate them.

If New Labour can undo some of what was done to us, restore our freedoms, see themselves as administrators rather than as a government – what are we, children? – we will love them. Over to you, Tony.

When the banning began, July, 1997.

Protector Blair's Britain

To ban or not to ban? Hardly a question at all in today's new Cromwellian Britain, not when it comes to fox-hunting. Or smoking. Or 'selection' in schools. Or single stay-at-home mothers. Banned they will be. The people want it so; it shall be so.

No-one likes posh upper-class men on horses chasing a wretched fox and encouraging dogs to tear it to bits. Nor, for the record, do I. But it's not the fright and distress of the fox that gets New Britain sufficiently riled to do away with this centuries-old custom. No-one's (yet) suggesting that the terror of the pig standing in line for the abattoir is a reason to ban meat-eating. Rather, it's the pleasure the fox-hunters take in the chase which is their undoing. They have too good a time, and it shows, which is deeply suspicious to Britain's new puritan heart. Time for it to go.

Three-and-a-half centuries ago Cromwell banned maypoles, theatres and bright clothes as overheating the public imagination; the times go full circle and now the puritans are back. The lean wholesomeness of Tony Blair is welcome to the people, after the complacent stuffiness of the Conservative government, after years of sexual and financial scandal – culminating in money in brown envelopes being exchanged in Harrods in return for convenient questions asked in Parliament, and such like. As welcome as the Lord Protector Cromwell was after Charles I, who got his head chopped off, not just for being 'tyrant, traitor, murderer', but for running a lavish and idolatrous court.

Let Prince Charles marry Camilla fast, or the people will want to know why. They want him married, settled and respectable. In the meantime they clamour for the fox-hunters' blood and have their own way.

Protector Cromwell had a victorious army to back him. Protector Blair has his overwhelming victory at the polls. Blair occupies not just the parliamentary but the moral high ground. He announces his government's plans to the media first, before legislation is even proposed to Parliament. Since the House of Commons votes exactly as it is told to, and has done for years, what's the point of going through the motions? Let's just get on with it: save time and argument, announce intent. And already the saddlers, the clothiers, the barriers, the blacksmiths are shutting up shop, while frothing at the mouth. And civil libertarian issues are hardly mentioned.

The right of a government to interfere with the personal habits of its people, to take the place of individual conscience, seems now fully established. No-one must go to hell in their own way: they must go to heaven under government protection.

The civil libertarians can argue 'til they're blue in the face that to hunt or not to hunt is a personal issue, that paradox and dilemma are best solved on a personal not a mandatory level. That to say, if I weigh my pleasure in the balance against the pain of the fox, and it seems to me to be okay, that's my business. Do we not drive cars in the same way – my convenience pitted against another's lungs, and does not my convenience win? So what's with the fox?

Here in Britain, back in the sixties, we abandoned the pursuit of excellence in our educational system, said down with the convenience of the few, the high flyers, and abandoned the eleven-plus; the dreaded exam that sent a few to grammar schools, the majority not. Now we find ourselves horribly low on the international ranking league tables when it comes to adding up and spelling. Most destructive over-political-correctness derives from a noble aspiration to spare the disadvantaged humiliation: to save Monsieur Renard from being torn to bits. The road to social hell is paved with an excess of empathy.

One hundred thousand of the most unpopular people in Protector Blair's New Britain gathered last week in Hyde Park to protest at the proposed ban on fox-hunting. They mightn't have bothered. Too rural, too rich, too intellectual, too 'luvvie' – the word now popularly used to describe anyone in the arts – too civil libertarian or too dependent on fox-hunting for a living to be liked or listened to. Fifty thousand hounds, they say, will die because without the hunt no-one will be able to afford to feed them, and goodbye to John Peel and tally-ho, and Olde England will be no more, except in theme parks. No fox was harmed in the writing of this piece.

Brushing Up Against the Famous

Far more terrifying to be the interviewer than the interviewee, to initiate rather than respond, to form a view rather than provide one. Especially with the voice of the mother echoing in one's ears: 'If you can't say anything nice don't say anything at all.'

Written before viewing the film of the novel, She-Devil, *in 1990.*

Roseanne Dances

If, in Hollywood, in the golden dusk of a Californian evening, you look Westward towards the Pacific, you will sometimes see a great shining disc rising in the sky. 'Look, look, a flying saucer! A UFO!' cries the exulting visitor. But no, it's merely the planet Venus rising, seen through the polluted atmosphere of this exhausted and exhausting city, the world centre of fantasy. The evil motes in the sky magnify the star, so that it appears swollen and a little sinister, gone wrong somehow but still magical, still promising love.

The pole of the film industry moves little by little Eastward to New York, leaving the West Coast to get on with the dispiriting grind of the fearfully written, low-budget, highly profitable, and occasionally brilliantly acted, TV shows. But Hollywood is still the birthplace of stars, and Roseanne Barr, Mormon trailer-dweller made good, rose lately there like a new Venus, a distorted, swollen star in the galaxy of perceived female perfection which customarily twinkles from TV sets and makes the real women of the world, from Helsinki to Cape Town, by way of Manhattan, feel wholly inadequate. We are scarcely even aware, I sometimes think, of the impossible standards we set ourselves. Lately I went to a rehearsal of a radio play. 'Who are all these freaks?' I found myself thinking, before recollecting these were just ordinary actors of normal human physical diversity. I was ashamed of myself. I had caught the bug. Go too frequently to TV rehearsals, and you become infected with the notion that good looks, straight noses, even teeth, regular features, are the norm and not the exception: you come to believe that the human race is beautiful; possessed of a miraculous symmetry. Some usually quite sensible people, I am sorry to report, announced themselves quite outraged that the tall Julie T. Wallace, who in fact looks a great deal more symmetrical of body than most of the women queuing up in my local rural supermarket and built on no larger a scale, should show her not quite conventionally pretty face on TV and demonstrate that a person outside the accepted TV norm of size and shape can have feelings. As if some artist had painted the crucifixion and made Jesus overweight. Bad taste! Invoke the blasphemy laws! Fat is the worst of all sins. Yet the majority of women in this country are size sixteen and over. What is going on here?

But perhaps something begins to give. In the TV series of that name, Roseanne more or less plays herself. The current series she is unemployed, looking for work, reluctant wife of an amiable slob as overweight as herself, reluctant mother of three underweight, horrendous kids. Roseanne is unashamedly fat, unrepentantly mean, loud-mouthed, cynical and has (perhaps this is the secret) no intention whatsoever of making herself over, in a society which makes self-improvement a religion. She is wildly sexy and wonderfully popular, and no one can quite understand it, not even the audience. She is a star. That means she can do as she likes. She does. She is (they say) divorcing her stage and real life husband: it is (they say) costing her $16 million so to do. That means (I presume) there's double that at least in the kitty, though I daresay I presume too much and it's no business of mine – except women who earn a lot remain a puzzle to the outside world, which has a kind of instinctive feeling they can only have come by it by being up to no good.

Roseanne's wisecracks are repeated up and down the land, wherever in the world she appears. On the whole it is women who do the repeating. The wisecracks are anti-man, anti-matrimony, anti-child. Research on her stage show reveals that all-women audiences laugh most, all-male audiences next, mixed-audiences least. Naturally.

'Are you sorry you married me?' asks the nice-guy TV husband, rashly. Roseanne thinks. Beat, beat, beat – 'Every second of my life,' she responds, just when we think she's forgotten her lines. Shrieks from the crowd. See! The true answer at last! All is not for the best in the best of all possible worlds, as the other family TV shows would have us believe . . . The kids misbehave. Roseanne observes them. Roseanne is silent. Roseanne thinks. Finally Roseanne speaks. 'This is why some animals eat their young.' Everyone roars. Oh, the relief of it! The unsayable said. Wives and mothers can be people too, if only for a moment, and husbands and children won't fall down dead.

It's as if TV itself has played too pappy a maternal role in all our lives for far too long. We're tired of it. TV tut-tuts at atrocity, famine and war (well, other nations' wars), encourages good behaviour, applauds achievement, presents happy endings as the stuff of life: saying that's what audiences say they want so let them have it: but audiences can only know what they already have. Theirs is not the power of invention. Perhaps we all, programme makers and audiences, begin to think it's time we grew up and left home. Let's not have the Cosbys, let's have Roseanne.

Roseanne Barr, her TV star in the ascendant, has done just that, grown up and left home, gone to New York and into films. Currently she's in Orion's production of *She-Devil*, a loose version of my own novel *The Life and Loves of a She-Devil*, as the wronged wife. Not the monster as she appears in the book, but as an angel who both avenges and eventually blesses, whose husband (Ed Begley Jr of *St Elsewhere* fame) is rash enough to run off with his romantic-novelist mistress (Meryl Streep). Susan Seidelman directs. The Seidelman-Streep-Barr combination had created what is known as 'great interest' – the expectation, the hope, was that the Titans and Gods would surely clash, shoreline and sea, as the old aristocratic film world met the new raunchy nouveau-riche tide out of TV. The script, as it happens, keeps the two women very much apart. But Barr's bright eyes soften when she speaks of Streep: 'She's just wonderful!' And Streep likewise of Barr. Reports to the contrary flowed from the studio – of rows, storms, slamming off sets – and certainly Barr is easy to misrepresent. Her language is not ladylike. I was on set for a day: just a day: I met her briefly. She arrived like some dancing whirlwind beating up a placid cornfield. She was hungry – 'Isn't there any fucking food?', she demanded. It was all around. But New York film caterers, sweet lads, are into cuisine *minceur*, decaff, melon cubes, chicken bites, grapes and wholemeal cookies: none of your bacon butty stuff this side of the Atlantic. But Roseanne is mocking herself as much as them; the sweet lads merely moaned and laughed. And the rest of us felt not outraged, but hopelessly genteel, mingy-mouthed, unconnected with the real world, or only via the bits of paper, the script, we happened to hold in our hands. Our failing, not hers. Roseanne had an air of desperate kindness, the easy irritation and impatience of someone who has come to understand the world too well: she doesn't care what people think: too late for that: her function now just to speak the truth and earn millions.

She is a gaudier star than Streep. She looks at her functionaries askance (Roseanne, please, your hair. Roseanne, please, your limo. Roseanne, please, the photo call) and tells them foul jokes to cheer them up even while she insults them. For a decade or so films tried to do without stars – became writer-based, director-based, and one can understand why. The whims of the star are as terrifying as the whims of the absolute monarch. Upset the latter and you lose your head; the former, only your job it's true, but with the job goes your income and status. The stars are back, and with a vengeance, and of a different kind, and with them, I imagine, film audiences. Without them, life just got boring. Safe, but boring.

As for the film, well *She-Devil* opens here in May. It received mixed reviews in the States. The Mediterranean countries love it: audiences stand and shout and applaud their approval. Meryl Streep is indeed wonderful. Roseanne Barr has been whipped into shape as an angel of light and decency; though heaven, one feels, is probably not her natural habitat. It includes some quite brilliant set pieces – Meryl Streep hearing bad news from her agent in a smart restaurant: Roseanne burning down the matrimonial home. The ending of the film is as ideologically sound – good woman (now economically and emotionally free, to suit the feminist lobby) waits for reformed husband (now understanding what's valuable in the world, to suit the traditional lobby) – as the novel was ideologically unsound – (woman achieves feminist goals but then turns herself by means of cosmetic surgery into husband's mistress). And if you're Susan Seidelman, and you have to raise Hollywood money to make the film, and your task is to make something which will sell in Gaza as well as Sydney, not to mention these days Tashkent, you had better be as ideologically sound as you can manage. Films change people's lives, as once novels used to. Oddly enough in these bright new days of 'corporate responsibility', when the multinationals vie to plant the most trees and take the fat out of the fried potatoes, to want to be ideologically sound is not an automatic shooting in the foot when it comes to the raising of money for the making of feature films. Those who control large funds and major studios are not automatically either stupid, greedy, irresponsible or insensitive.

Of the film, when asked, and I am often asked, and bearing all this in mind, and mindful of the fact that I signed a contract – raising my hand in front of the US flag and declaring that I was in my right mind, and selling the idea of the novel, its characters and events, throughout the universe and for all eternity – and then took the money and spent it, I say, 'Thank you, Miss Seidelman. You did a good job there. How did I like the film? Why, I am reminded of something Oscar Wilde said, when asked how he liked a new production of *The Importance of Being Earnest* – "Just wonderful! In fact it rather reminds me of something I once wrote."'

In August, 1995, when we lived in a big house.

Guess Who's Coming to Lunch

Jamie Lee Curtis came to lunch.

She came at short notice. Her people and my people had been trying to set up an interview for weeks and failing. (That, reader, is the essential nature of 'people': this is what they *do.*) Jamie Lee Curtis has been working with Kevin Kline, John Cleese and Michael Palin at Pinewood Studios, on the sequel to *A Fish Called Wanda.* This new film is known by everyone but John Cleese, whose film it is, as *Death Fish II.* John Cleese wants it to be called *Fierce Creatures*, and though these days well-therapied-out, kind, gentle, furry and infinitely charming, they reckon Mr Cleese retains enough fierceness to have his way. The film is about a private zoo on the eve of a take over: all the gentle furry creatures must be got rid of, because only fierce creatures pull crowds. (Make of this what you will.)

Jamie Lee Curtis phoned on the Sunday, a known voice yet still unknown, as is the fate of Hollywood stars. She said she was Jamie Lee Curtis and my husband said, 'Oh yes, tell me another.' Since she was going home to Santa Monica, Los Angeles, mid-week and was busy, I said why not come to lunch tomorrow and she said yes. I know enough to know that the famous cannot eat in peace in restaurants. Staff are obsequious and people stare. Homes are best. I explained I knew nothing about her other than that she was Schwarzenegger's wife, Helen, in *True Lies*, in which film she had done a striptease so erotic I had to parentally-guide the children by standing in front of the TV set and blocking their vision: and the criminal American girl in *A Fish called Wanda*, who so stunningly and ruthlessly seduces an oh-so-English barrister, and the little all-but-androgynous female cop in *Blue Steel* who single-handedly takes on a vicious if sexy serial killer and succeeds. A routine film, made startling by her presence, and with a few very good lines which Jamie Lee Curtis delivers so beautifully and precisely you remember them. I apologised on the phone for my ignorance. She said that was okay; all she knew about me, come to that, was the books I'd written. She'd once read eight in as many days when stranded in London and tried to buy the rights to one of them and failed. I never got to know that, at the time.

Jamie Lee Curtis, said my husband, impressed, is coming to *lunch*? What shall we eat? Bread and cheese, I said, as usual. Jamie Lee Curtis seems to impress everyone, especially men of a certain age and sensibility. My grizzled accountant, hearing on the Monday morning that she was on her way, reeled around the kitchen gasping and biffed my husband on the shoulder, in a mannish sort of way. (Most meetings at my place happen in the kitchen.) I felt a little piqued, reader.

But I knew so little about her, other than what I'd seen on the screen, that when she came to the door at one o'clock, perfectly on time, I called her Jamie Lee. I had at least cottoned on to the fact that she was Tony Curtis's daughter. She referred to herself as Jamie. It transpired that her mother is Janet Leigh. You will have seen Janet Leigh in *Psycho*. Of course Jamie Lee Curtis would be just 'Jamie', otherwise she would feel more her mother's than her father's child. Her father came from the Bronx: he started life as Tony Schwartz; her mother came from Idaho; if it hadn't been for films, she would have been called Helen Schwartz and been brought up in Idaho. She said this rather wistfully. She really liked acting women called Helen. That was why she'd agreed to play Schwarzenegger's wife in *True Lies*, now she came to think of it.

Jamie Lee Curtis dominated the screen in that film too, and made the unbelievable believable and the absurd moving.

But I gallop ahead, reader. She's happy for me, and thereby you, to know these things. This is no insightful, scandalous, or revelatory piece: just an account of lunch with the star. She inspires fierce loyalty. She is stunning, skinny and well-bosomed. She is sinuous as Jim Carrey, but without the grotesquerie. Amazing. Monday was very hot – we've been having a heatwave here in London. She wore a navy, scoop-necked, very short-sleeved linen top and navy slacks, and a plain high straw hat with a broad brown band around it, invincibly plain and enormously stylish. She'd passed the hat in a shop window every morning for months and finally that week had gone in and bought it. It was its first day on. She had a neat backpack (Prada, I daresay) from which she took a gift: a children's book she'd written, inscribed from her to me. It is charming, and called *When I was Young*, in which a very young child looks back on herself yet younger. Now many a star writes a book, and many a publisher sighs and publishes out of a sense of deference and self-interest both, but this work's not like that. It was a proper idea, the real writerly thing. Just as father Tony Curtis is a good painter as well as a true actor, she's a good writer as well as a true actress. Or 'actor, female', to be correct. (Actors, female, reject 'actress' as a description of their profession, finding it diminishing and pejorative. 'As the actress said to the bishop.' 'Actor' will do well enough, they say. It's just hard, sometimes, to get sentences to balance, and of course 'As the actor said to the bishop' gets you in worse trouble. But correct is correct and must be observed!)

We sat in the kitchen. Lunch was late. My husband was delayed up in leafy literary Hampstead. He'd said, rashly, up at the deli, Jamie Lee Curtis is coming to lunch, I want the best bread, salad, cheese, cold meats, fruit. There was such a flurry of response, all efficiency was lost. I had no idea, neither had he, or he might have set out earlier. Sharon Stone could have come to lunch and no-one turned a hair.

She said could she snoop: she liked snooping? She examined the bookshelves, the mulberry tree in the garden with its crimson dropping fruit: she introduced herself to my stepchildren: she ran her hands over the littlest, and his eight-year-old face lit up from inside and became translucent and stayed like that for days. Truly. She gave the thirteen-year-old a guitar plectrum used in *This is Spinal Tap* by Nigel Tufnel, actually her actor-musician-writer-producer husband Christopher Guest, and the boy beamed all over his face, abandoning all accustomed cool.

Now it is a strange thing to say but the only other person I have encountered who has this effect on people was Jerry Garcia of the Grateful Dead. Strange because he shuffled round in old canvas shoes and stared, albeit wisely and benignly, out at the world with prematurely-aged and rheumy eyes, and Jamie Lee Curtis bounces round in a well-exercised fashion and with very clear eyes. Nevertheless, both have the same peculiar quality of being a focus for and transmitter of the light. Don't ask me what I *mean*, reader, I scarcely know myself. Except that one of the Grateful Dead songs, written after the traumatic rock festival in 1970 at Altamont when a Hell's Angel knifed a fan just in front of the stage, has a chorus which suggests that one way or another, in the end the darkness gives. It's repeated as a kind of chant against evil. There are just a few people around who seem to keep darkness at bay, and Jamie Lee Curtis is one of them. Jean Paul Gaultier has something of the same quality, but not in such intensity.

She said she ate anything. She did. She put butter on her bread, ate the meat and liked the cheese. No wine, though. She is disciplined. She is not conventionally pretty: her face is all planes and angles, her forehead is high and domed. The children of Hollywood stars are usually extremely well organised in their looks and are born with or end up with regular and boring features. Physical symmetry – coming down to them from both parents – has a lot to do with good looks but also seems to create, on the mental plane, a conventional frame of mind which drugs, alcohol and excess do little to disturb. If she missed the symmetry she also missed the urge to do the expected thing and self-destruct. The best scene in *Blue Steel* is towards the end where Jamie Lee – sorry, Jamie – trapped in a car by the mad psychopath, bullets flying, lifts her head in its cop cap to stare out of the window at the world with unforgettable, unforgiving, accusatory eyes. That's her, we feel; that's what Jamie Lee Curtis really thinks of us. She wears a hat well. She kept hers on during lunch.

She called the boys in and put food on their plates, feeling, rightly, I was neglecting them. She has an eight-year-old daughter, Annie, with her in London, but for the day with friends. Annie spent some months at the Mount School behind Harrods where they wear a uniform which dates back from the eighteenth century and causes tourists to stop and stare: knickerbockers and floppy velvet Rembrandt hats. Annie, after some initial confusion, coped well enough with the insaneness: of course: she has a good mother. Jamie Lee Curtis is taking next year off from Hollywood, to stay home, write books and have a good time with Annie.

She talked about her father, whom she clearly loves. He's 'landed' now, she says. Has a house and a home and a girlfriend, and a 'proper' life. But in her mind he's still the original, exotic, talented, unlanded man she remembers; living in hotel rooms out of a suitcase. No fuss. Ten white pairs of shorts, ten white shirts, twenty white socks. Off to the laundry when required. He'd get the hotel staff to bring up flowers: from the lobby, anywhere. He'd take out his paints, his brushes, a canvas, and he'd paint. His proper occupation, he believed, was painting, and you can do that anywhere, when it comes to it. They can stop you acting by not giving you a part, but they can't stop you painting. Like writing, it is a primary creative act: you don't have to be part of a team, you don't have to hang about to be asked. If he hadn't been Tony Curtis the actor he'd have been Tony Schwartz the artist, and happy with it.

Tony Curtis has a gift for arranging things, says his daughter. He can place things just so. He'd put a scrap of paper with a telephone number, a postcard, an invitation, any old thing, between the leaf and the stalk of a flower and it would look important, special, considered, given grace and *gravitas.* Jamie said she always used to try and do this too. As she spoke, she placed a postcard between leaf and stem of a single sunflower in a long thin dark olive oil bottle I use as a vase and which stands on the table. It looked pretty good. There was, of course, a card to hand. I have a long kitchen table – to eat we push the papers, the contracts, the bills down to the far end and put on a white cloth this end and use a lot of glass and it looks okay, I think. I said my former husband had the same gift for placing things just so: at least one of my sons inherits it. I could try and try myself and never get it right. It was to do with defying symmetry; you were born to the art, or not. We agreed. She looked at my eighteenth century Welsh dresser, with its original square not rounded hooks, where my failure to avoid symmetry with the old blue-and-white china was evident, but masked by so many dentist's appointment cards, invitations, vouchers from the Indian take-out, postcards, bits of paper with telephone numbers, who would notice? (Ours is a very English house: we – or at least I – live with clutter, and in the constant apprehension that if we put anything away we will lose it, and in the un-American fantasy that the past is important, and what is cracked and chipped has added value, not less.)

Jamie Lee Curtis, she of the grace and *gravitas*, said she had spent years trying to arrange things on shelves as magically as did her father, and finally she thought she'd got it right. But when the LA earthquake hit – as it hit hard in Santa Monica – everything had fallen off the shelves and broken anyway so she swept the lot away into black plastic sacks, and threw them out and the past with them, and had begun again, finally understanding she did not have to try to be like her father and could be herself.

She said can I snoop some more? I said yes, and she did. She went upstairs into the bedroom – we have been living here for two years, and we took down the curtains a year ago because we didn't like them, and the decision of what to choose which we *would* like has been too much for us. We put Japanese screens up instead, through which the moon shines, making pearly latticed squares of light throughout the room and which are okay in winter but hopeless in spring, before the leaves have come out on the copper beech outside the window, or in late summer, when the sun shines directly in; then light wakes us up too early. But you get used to these things, until you see them through a stranger's eyes. The floor was littered, as ever, with clothing. And she went into the bathroom where the shelves are crowded with cosmetics of every possible make, without apparent consistency, and as many without lids as with, mixed up with toothbrushes out of their mugs, earrings and plaque-disclosing tablets. You know the kind of thing, I daresay, reader: the universal look of the bathroom that tries but fails. But if she wanted to look she had to put up with what she found. She seemed satisfied, having prowled the edges of the territory.

Half-past-three and time to go. There was no limousine circling the block. She took her backpack, some signed books from me, and loped out to find herself a taxi. She kind of moves on the soles of her feet, like a wild animal, swiftly and with precision.

Over here in England people have an archetypal dream: that the Queen is coming to tea. It is an anxiety dream, a pleasing-mother dream: knowing you have to get it right you try and try and clean up your house – how guilty you must be – and fail. All kinds of people have this particular dream: anti-royalists as well as royalists. Everything goes wrong – you move in slow motion, your hands are on your arms the wrong way round, giant wasps devour the food, some of your teeth just fell out, filling up your mouth – that kind of thing – but when finally the Queen arrives, she doesn't notice. She is charm itself. Well, there you are. Jamie Lee Curtis came to lunch.

A meteor, anyway, surging over the horizon, glittering brilliantly for a while, fading away until next time. That's show-biz.

A Star is Reborn in 1997

'Time to move out,' says Patti Lupone. 'The performances are outgrowing the space.' Patti Lupone, Broadway star, is in London rehearsing at the Maria Assumpta Convent in Kensington Square. Terence McNally's Tony Award-winning play *Masterclass* moves here from New York to open at the Queens Theatre on 8 May – the event of the West End season. Patti Lupone plays the great diva Callas, as back in the fifties, at the famous Juillard School in New York, she puts young opera hopefuls through their paces. Takes a star to play a star. It's not surprising the convent space begins to seem small, as day by day Lupone takes on the divine mantle. Lupone herself is no mean personality to start with – emotional, intelligent, passionate, effervescent.

'I understand Callas,' Lupone says. 'I know what it's like to be her. I share the temperament. I have the same lung configuration – perhaps they go together?' (Lupone has wit and humour – being funny is not a quality one associates with Callas.) 'I even have "the voice",' she says. 'It was just never trained for opera.' Those who have heard the Lupone voice (I haven't) say it's stunning, flawless, to die for. In her career – she started in musicals, and only then went on to straight plays; Chekhov, Arthur Miller, Mamet: serious stuff – she's starred in everything from *The Beggar's Opera* to *Oliver* to *Les Miserables* to *Evita* – mostly to cheers, occasionally to boos. But then someone once threw spring onions at Callas, instead of flowers. That voice could be really chancy. Audiences are notoriously picky when it comes to singers. 'They never forgive you the high notes,' says Lupone, 'the low notes they don't notice so much.'

Seven elderly nuns still live at the Maria Assumpta. The place smells as convents do, of dignity, old age, goodness and cabbage. Rehearsals are just finishing; this room at least still vibrates with energy.

'In fact I sing only one line as Callas,' Lupone explains. 'The singing in *Masterclass* – and there's lots – is left to the young hopefuls' – Sophia Wylie who plays Sophia de Palme, Susan Roper as Sharon Graham – 'and as it happens they're brilliant, astonishing. Singers who're suddenly called upon to act – and find they can. I love them!'

We go off to the Kensington Palace Hotel for a drink and a rest before she has to go off to a photographic session, in the company of her assistant and her PR man.

Now there are stars, and there are celebrities who pretend to be stars, and it's important to distinguish them. Stars serve their own genius; celebrities serve themselves. Stars do their own thing – act, sing, dance, make you laugh or cry, whatever – with an intensity which lifts them into outer space: to be in their company, in person or in an audience, is to be raised likewise. Celebrities just have the skill of getting noticed. Stars can be beautiful or plain, it doesn't seem to matter: they light the universe, the nearer you get, the more they dazzle. To be in the company of celebrities is to feel twitchy and doubtful. Stars suffer. Celebrities pretend to. Stars are ruthless; so are celebrities. Stars behave badly: so do celebrities. But you forgive the star; you don't the celebrity.

I ask Patti Lupone if she ever behaves badly. 'Of course not,' she says. But I think I saw her young assistant blanche, and her PR man moisten his lips. Patti Lupone noticed too. She re-phrases that. 'Whatever it takes to get me on stage in good order,' she said, 'to give the audience what it is owed, then, perhaps yes.'

Patti Lupone is a star, not a celebrity. Everyone relaxes. She is not just forgiven, she is loved, she is worshipped. She has beer: I ask for tea.

The PR man blanches again. 'What can I do?' I ask. 'I'm English. The English drink tea.'

She understands that. She comes to London lots. She likes playing to audiences over here. 'They make up their own minds,' she says. 'They don't wait to be told what to think. They haven't yet been dumbed-down.' Which is what she fears is happening to New York audiences. Feed them pap, they grow to like it. Nothing by Terence (*Kiss of the Spider Woman*) McNally is pap. She describes him as an Irish cherub.

What can it be like, I ask her, thus to share her own head with that star of all opera stars, Callas of the glorious but chancy voice: Callas of *Tosca*, Callas the passionate, the bringer of beauty and joy; Callas the tragic, the lover of Onassis, who dumped her for all the world to see for Jackie Kennedy (who complained of the size of the diamonds while Callas just *loved* – oh bitter, bitter!). How do you take all that on board? Aren't you somehow swamped?

'Look,' she says, 'this play is about dedication to a profession, the sacrifice any true artist has to make. What's so special? In *Masterclass* you get not just the tragedy of the woman and the terror of failure, not just the pressure of other's expectations, but the glory too, and the sheer joy of having found out so much and doing it so well and being able to teach it to others.'

Swamped? On the contrary.

In New York recently a man came up to her after a show and said, 'You've made me want to do a better job at work.' He understood what had been going on on stage. She'd felt she'd really accomplished something. She doesn't like applause to be too easy: she wants to deserve it.

She tells the story of how at a tense moment in *Masterclass* in New York a mobile phone rang. She waited: then mid-curtain call she addressed the culprit from the stage. 'What a bore you are! You spoiled this play for everyone else. Go home at once.' He rose. He left. Was this behaving badly, I ask? She doesn't think so. Nor did the audience. They cheered and cheered. I'm glad I wasn't that man.

Patti Lupone lives in a Connecticut farmhouse two hours out of New York. She and her husband keep hens. Her husband used to be a cameraman, now he looks after her. She has a son aged six, Joshua, who 'comes with', but soon the need for education will keep him at home. Then what will happen? Lupone worries. She frets. Will she choose art, or the child? Which will win? It will be art; I tell her so. 'But you're the one who will suffer, the boy will be just fine.' I know all this; I once put art before the needs of little children, who in the end scarcely noticed. I too kept hens; I too had a farmhouse in the country. Patti Lupone and her husband keep Rhode Island Reds, Andalusians, Blue Anconas; Marilyn the feathery blonde Blue Rock is her favourite. I had a little red Bantam called Rita who lived in the house and sat on laps. I had foxes as enemy; she has racoons. The Lupones don't believe in guns: they had to get a murderous racoon, a serial killer, with a pitchfork. At least foxes run off when they see you coming. Enough of all this; we are talking about Callas, not poultry; theatre not farmhouse.

McNally the writer knows all about opera: no simple playwright he, she says. He's an opera buff. He even represents the New York Met in their annual Opera Quiz. But frankly, opera as such bores Lupone. She prefers musicals. More goes on on-stage. Yes, yes, she has the diva's temperament, the lung configuration, the 'voice' inherited from her great grand-aunt the coloratura Adelina Patti, but so what? When she was four she took tap-dancing classes with Miss Marguerite and thereafter that was the way she went: theatre not opera houses. At seventeen she got into the Juillard School – in the company of a lot of six-year-old cello players – prodigies. 'I felt so *inferior*,' she says. Even there she did drama, considered a lowly discipline, not music. She never *developed the voice*, in the opera sense. Her father never approved: her mother, who was a frustrated basketball player, an athlete, always did. The family lived in Long Island. Grandparents on both sides emigrated from Italy at the turn of the century. Her parents divorced when she was twelve. She took not much notice, she was too busy, she says, following her destiny.

Which brings us on to the sensitive subject of Andrew Lloyd Webber and *Sunset Boulevard*.

'How do you get on with Glenn Close?' I ask, cautiously.
'She can't sing,' Lupone responds, which is just about the worst thing she can say of anybody. She amends this, hastily. 'Well, I suppose she can sing, but not in the Callas sense, not in my sense, that is to say, not just the singing of notes, but feelings.'

Lupone, like Callas, has had her public humiliations. At the mention of *Sunset Boulevard* her expression does what Callas's did when Onassis married Jackie Kennedy. The eyes widen, the mobile, powerful face is suddenly still, and vulnerable: the horror of betrayal speaks for itself.

The show opened in London, and the critics here loved it but those in New York didn't and when the time came for it to open on Broadway Lupone was, brutally and without warning, fired. She found herself replaced by Glenn Close. Glenn Close who can't even *sing*. These things happen in the world of theatre, true, but Glenn Close didn't warn Lupone, speak to her, consult or commiserate. She could have, should have.

'Not a single word,' Lupone says.

The humiliation was extreme, the press had a field day. Lupone is known not to forgive, let alone forget. Does she still have fantasies of revenge? I ask.

'Fantasies?' she cries, scornfully. 'I am *Sicilian*!'

The vehemence is frightening.

'Oh well,' I say, 'all the better to play Callas in *Masterclass.*'
She brightens at once.
'Of course,' she says, 'I know that. If I hadn't lost that part how could I be in playing this one?'

She's off to have her picture taken by Terry O'Neill, once Faye Dunaway's husband, and good on cheekbones. If she's exhausted she doesn't show it. She's ordered sandwiches for seventeen at his studio. *Seventeen* of her people will be with her. the *Mail on Sunday* marvel. Isn't this an excessive sense of stardom? No, I say. Lupone has to be photographed as Callas in full regalia. It will be the portrait of a decade, the spirit of one of today's great theatrical stars, informed by that amazing one of a generation ago, with a wealth of human aspiration and theatrical achievement in between. Seventeen people, if you ask me, is peanuts.

Leading up to Independence Day, 1997.

Mindy in the Nashville Night with Fireflies

One o'clock in the morning in Nashville, Tennessee. Mindy McCready, aged twenty-one, is laying down vocals for a new album. Outside the studio this small, graceful city sleeps. People go to bed early here: the summer days are hot and humid. But Mindy McCready likes singing while others sleep, so this little patch of town is awake, wide awake, waiting on the whim of a shrewd, slender girl with an intellectual's face and a habit of popping gum.

Mindy McCready, they reckon, is the one who'll bring grace, myth and magic to a country music business bored by its own competence, its own sheer commercialism, its capacity to make money by getting the market right.

McCready herself is well aware of it. When someone remarks that Garth Brooks, Nashville's biggest star, who sells scores of millions worldwide has a degree from Oklahoma State in advertising, she laughs, and says with a flash of vehemence, 'Maybe that's all you need to know.'

Mindy, they say, doesn't have to calculate, she works by instinct. She's the real glittery Monroe-ish stuff, the once-in-a-lifetime star who isn't just more conveyor-belt talent, but who'll end up spawning a thousand imitators.

Nashville these days produces young men with rosebud lips a-plenty. And tough guys under black hats with soft hearts. Clint Black: Tim McGraw: killer eyes melting as they sing about the work they have to do on their relationships, and somehow, mysteriously, getting a real erotic intensity going. (The power of love to soothe and control the phallic beast, perhaps: another female victory.) There's a host of successful girls with therapised hearts and great voices, who sing their own material. Not to mention the Judy Collins-ish phenomenon of Matraca Berg, songwriter turned singer, who not only had five No 1 hits last year, but also won 'Song-of-the-Year' award at the annual Country Music Awards ceremony this September, for a definitive losing-your-virginity song called 'Strawberry Wine'. Matraca is a local Nashville girl made spectacularly good – her mother a hillbilly and her father a nuclear physicist. He came to the city to work for the Oakridge Nuclear Facility – set up as part of the Manhattan Project – and stayed for the music. Nashville is a complex town.

But like Steve Earle, the Johnny Cash of the nineties, who busted through raw from the heart, McCready didn't have to be constructed: a girl who came ready-made, as befits her name, complete with a Cherokee grandfather, from the depths of the Florida Everglades. By some cosmic mixture of chance and intent, she knocked on the right Nashville door her first day in town, the Gods who control these things being awake for once.

Mindy McCready, they say, hasn't ever had to learn how to behave in an interview; she simply speaks a short-term truth as it occurs to her.

'Do you have any ambitions, Mindy?' *the usual interviewer's question.*

'Get married and have a couple of kids.' *Not the usual answer.* 'Oh, and I'd like to do a Spielberg movie.' *Hang on a minute, Mindy. Isn't country music meant to be tops, as far as you can go?*

'I guess I just want to be Lois Lane,' she adds, wistfully.

So long as she can bewitch an audience and control the airwaves as if she were Dolly Parton, Callas and Marconi mixed, that's okay by her management. What does it matter what she says? Here's power indeed.

But at one in the morning, at the studio, she's in her element and her small production team is in a state of elation. 'Singing like a bird,' says Doug Casmus, her manager. He's come to fetch us to sit in on the session, en route to finding his singer the strawberry milkshake she's asked for, and with the whole town closed down. Casmus can't wait to get back. What mightn't he be missing? 'How's she doing?' he asks Jimmy Nichols, McCready's band leader, musical director, and at the moment soundmixer, when we finally get back. 'Awesome,' says Nichols, throwing hands in the air. 'She's awesome.'

Here in the studio are tough, accomplished music men: strange to see them practically with tears in their eyes at the sound of yet another female voice, another pretty girl. But from the moment the heavy soundproof door swings open into the damp, black fireflied night, and a snatch of the McCready voice drifts out, on playback, cut short, repeated, over and over, with the kind of lyrical, angelic merriment you'd think to hear on Mount Olympus on the Gods' night out, you understand why. The McCready capacity for mirth, irony, cleverness, not qualities usually associated with singers out of Nashville is what gives the girl her singularity. She will have to fight to retain them, as the business tries to iron them out.

McCready's first single, 'Ten Thousand Angels', out a year ago, rose up the Billboard charts to No 6; hers was the fastest selling debut album – (such is the language of Nashville) – by a female country artist in five years. The video – McCready at a point somewhere between Dietrich and Drew Barrymore, suffering lust in a dance bar – was, as they say, a sensation. 'Guys Do It All the Time' (when she had a few beers with the girls last night) got to be known as the US Women's National Anthem. The ghost of Brenda Lee had revisited the nineties.

As it happened, McCready stood in for Brenda Lee at this year's CM Awards, singing 'Sweet Nothing' in her own young voice when the older singer stepped forward to be inducted into the Country Music Hall of Fame. Albums and videos are one thing: even if you don't sing in tune, technology can make you: even if you're cross-eyed the camera can sort it out – but live performance is the test. McCready, having cheekily by-passed the usual training route of singing in bars and clubs, on the road in minor venues, gradually working up from audiences of tens, twenties, to hundreds – went straight from the Karaoke bars of Florida to an audience of sixteen thousand at a Fan Fair show in Nashville.

Not all in the audience will wish such a newcomer well, either. 'How did she get so far so fast?' they mutter. But the magic works on the stage as well as on disc: the opposition faltered and gave up, as the McCready charisma showed itself for what it was. Now they'll stand her on stage in a glittery purplish-blue gown, for a worldwide audience, and even standard Nashville make-up – orange foundation, shaded cheekbones and big, heavy lips – can't take the individuality away, though doing its damnedest.

Tonight she's laying down tracks for the new album, 'If I Don't Stay the Night', out over here this November. 'Kids don't want to offend their parents,' says Mindy. 'I don't mind being a role model for a whole lot of young girls. Suits us all.'

It's taken the McCready team six weeks to get her to this point. She's been ill, upset, family-ridden, whatever. Too busy popping gum, breaking out of a major long-term relationship, and related contracts, keeping a new love affair secret, having a good time, all *Why-shouldn't-I?*, and *Don't-hassle-me*, to turn up anywhere on time. But now at last she's in the studio she can't, won't, stop working.

This is star behaviour; it isn't learned, or affected: it comes as naturally as day follows night, and is hard on all around, and will be until they learn to trust the McCready instinct, understand the pacing. Realise she has it all under control, allow the artist to call the shots. The tracks will be down at the last moment, but down they will be, and perfect.

The strawberry milkshake, it turns out, is a bribe to distract her, make her stop working, leave the mike, and the studio floor and at least come into the soundroom, so they can carefully say, 'Hey, Mindy, there's a big TV spectacular tomorrow night, remember? It's important, make or break time, Mindy. How about saving the voice?' They're wasting their time. 'Forget the shake,' says Mindy from the studio floor, after all that. 'We have to do another take.' She sings the line again: why won't he say he loves her. Repeats it; still isn't satisfied. 'Once again, please. I'm sounding whiny.'

'Try it incredulous,' says Jimmy from the box. 'So this guy's doesn't love you, he's out of his mind.' She tried it. Again the question. Why won't he speak his feelings, same notes, different intonation, and yes, the *he* of the song isn't a hard-hearted no-good bastard, he's just all men everywhere turning down an offer which if there was any justice in the world, any respect for women, he couldn't refuse. Getting it wrong. The art of the country singer is to turn the bathetic into the cosmic.

Country music is no longer sad songs crying into a dark night, relying on the wistfulness of its roots in English folk: it's mood of the moment time. Nashville moves with the decades, it's the music version of Hollywood. Not exactly strong women, not exactly wanting to do without men, just a new breed of girls impatient with men who fail to live up to new female expectations. And young men trying to come to terms with this strange new world, where courage is to do with experiencing your feelings and facing yourself, not toting a gun and riding a horse.

Country music gets a bad press in sophisticated circles on both sides of the Atlantic. Rather like reading *Hello!* – you do it in private but don't admit to it in public. Common practice, when guests turn up, as a US publisher told me, is to push to the bottom of the stack the country songs that really get listened to – with their wistful overtones of nostalgia, longing, elation, the announcement of a common, simple humanity – and put jazz on top. Jazz, which everyone owns and no-one listens to except in smart company. Half the country struggles to remember its roots, this publisher said, the other half to forget them. McCready is the one to somehow bridge the gap.

McCready herself comes out of trailer-park, milkshake, gum-popping land. A stormy background: naturally. A mother, a performer herself, who ran a private ambulance service. (Mindy drove the ambulance from the age of twelve, no doubt with the same wilful, dedicated efficiency as she does everything else: bump, bump, you'd go, but you'd get there.) A charming, handsome, before-long absent father; two young brothers to keep on the tracks, because there was no-one else to do it, minimum education, a troubled adolescence; now Mom's given her a new little brother, a one-year-old, named Sky. She beams when she talks of him. Her face lights up.

But now see her on stage rehearsing, hair tied back from earnest brow, and she looks like Maggie Smith, the fierce dedication, the acknowledgement of craft, the application of intellect, the intuition of greatness; she wouldn't look out of place if this were Racine.

These are rehearsals for an Elvis Presley memorial concert: she, the newcomer, gets to sing 'The Battle Hymn of the Republic' with the established stars to back her, ending the show. Another breakthrough for McCready. Rivals writhe, but acknowledge her right to it. Oh, they're business-like, these people.

Tonight there's a trailer-park live audience in the hall, and it's ninety degrees and there's no air-conditioning. This show is being recorded for network TV; the local crowd's just there to provide the applause but refuse to be relegated. They cheer and clap who they want, not to order. This is their power: they'll make their mark, carry millions worldwide with them. No-one takes it lightly. This is Nashville.

Through the rehearsals McCready was clearly saving her voice. The team grow anxious; so does she. Perhaps she should have stopped for the strawberry milkshake, after all? But time for the show itself and she shimmies out on stage another person – Marilyn Monroe but slimmer, taller, at ease and full-throated. She plays to the camera, not the live audience; insists on a retake for the sake of the film, which annoys them – *they* liked it – but she's forgiven (people who look this good do get forgiven) and leaves the stage to rapturous applause. Other pretty girls have gone on and off the platform on this hot, sticky night, sandwiches between the rosebud men, and have sung okay, with carefully considered emotion and crafted passion. McCready, like Steve Earle, simply delivers the real stuff.

There's some kind of trouble backstage – there always is, it's part of the territory: broken hearts and broken contracts – she's just twenty-one and in love, and there's a drama going on which no doubt will end up in some biopic in the future, but for the moment merely serves to enrich the voice, and heighten the energy. She's hurried out into the night.

The next day we're in a hotel suite in Nashville. This child fits in the interview between the doctor for her throat, another rehearsal, and a secret outing no-one knows where, not even her manager, especially not her manager. She sits on the settee all loose limbs and hilarity, popping gum from time to time, to demonstrate lack of seriousness. It doesn't work. She is profoundly serious. We discuss the possibility of suicide from high hotel windows. Why only throw out the TV, why not oneself? She brings her father and her stepmother to the interview. This part of the family have just moved out to Nashville to be near her.

I ask if she can talk freely in front of her father, since the latest 'Country Babylon' book, out that week, Laurence Leamer's, *Three Chords and the Truth – Behind the Scenes With Those Who Make and Shape Country Music*, presented Mindy as most critical of her Daddy's domestic behaviour.

'Him?' she demands incredulously. 'Him? I don't take any notice of *him*.'

'I wouldn't forgive her if I were you,' I say to the father, aside. 'Ungrateful brats the lot of them.'

He shrugs and smiles peacefully. He's a charming, good-looking guy.

She obviously adores her father, and he obviously adores both her and the stepmother who says not a word but who I suspect of being the real power around here.

Shortly after this interview McCready was snapped by a *Hello!* photographer, out shopping for beds in a Hollywood mall, with TV Superman Dean Cain, hunk of all time and ages. So that's why the longing to be Lois Lane. Makes sense. And it looks as if she's neatly slipped out from under family once again. They'll just have to follow her out to Hollywood, and then there's not much further you can go.

Now wonderful to have a child like that, who pops some gum, tra-la-las a bit, hitches you to her coat-tails and takes you along for the ride to the stars, making it seem so easy.

Mindy pursues her career in the chancy summer of 1998.

Mindy Over Tea with Minders

'How's the voice?' I ask.

The voice is one of the most spectacular I have ever heard. It's alive with an eerie, spine-tingling quality. Buffy St Marie, melodic folk singer, meets seamless, sophisticated Madonna. Perhaps if Madonna had Cherokee blood, as Mindy McCready does, she too would sound like this. In McCready's songs to date we've had only about thirty percent of the voice, and that's enough for this slip of a twenty-two-year-old, this Mindy, to have burst into the Nashville scene, untrained and under-rehearsed in its professional ways, and taken the place by storm.

Now she's in London promoting her single 'Oh Romeo', just released.

'The voice is great,' she replies, suddenly beaming. It's like the sun coming out. No modesty required. Those few who by the grace of God possess this vocal instrument, do tend to talk as if it belonged to somebody else. They cherish it, refuse to overwork it, get neurotic about it. Nobody else ever seems to quite understand. The voice owns them, they don't own it. It doesn't care all that much about promotion. If the voice needs to take the next flight home it will.

And promotion is what she's doing now, here in London's grey summer, so far from home. Her team, the other side of the restaurant in the Kensington Palace Hotel where she and I are talking, are looking distinctly nervous. Not just the single 'Oh Romeo' but Channel 4's

Naked Nashville, in which she's featuring, is currently screening on Saturday nights. The smart bet is to watch *Top of the Pops* next week. She's making it big in this town. Of course she loves it, looking out over Kensington Gardens, but she'd rather be back in LA with her boyfriend. Of course she would.

'What, in California?' I ask. 'All those storms, houses falling into the sea, earthquakes, fires?'

'Look,' she says, 'I come from Florida. It's Florida that's scary. California's nothing. In Florida we have hurricanes, and infernos. California has storms in teacups, bushfires. Forget it. Nashville's the real problem. Soggy and damp, though I love it in the spring, and bad for the sinuses.'

'How are the tonsils?' I ask.

'Fantastic,' she says, 'Gone!'

Last time I talked to her was a year ago, in Nashville in July, sultry and swampy as it was. As well as sinus trouble, she had a strep throat, one of a series: she was on antibiotics, she was white and translucent; she had an album to record. How was she going to find time to get these tonsils removed? Let alone the courage? Knives snipping so near the vocal chords? Yikes!

Mindy McCready disappeared for a time. Studios, managers and PR folk pursued her, tight lipped. She surfaced in Hollywood, hand in hand with TV Superman Dean Cain. Her tonsils were gone. The voice was stable. She runs her own life and she does it well. The team ought to relax.

A year later she looks more substantial, much happier, twenty-two and palely, stunningly beautiful. Now she's with Dean Cain. They live together in love and tranquillity, in a house on the beach in Los Angeles, leading she promises me 'a quiet domestic life'. She flies in and out of Nashville, where the country music business is centred: where her beloved father now lives and the two younger brothers she brought up, are all 'doing well,' thanks to Mindy's new position in the world. Her mother still lives in Florida, where Mindy was bought up in a trailer park, now, at forty-two, with a new baby and in a good new relationship. This whole family has staying power.

I have a feeling she probably would give up her life for Dean, forget what the lyrics say. And he for her. There's the truth of the song and the truth of real life, and girls in real life, in these days of girl power, are often soppier than their lyrics allow them to be. Do you reckon any one of those Spice Girls would give up true love for the sake of their friends? If you want to be my lover, you'd better get on with my friends. Don't you believe it.

Dean would be with her on this tour but the start date of a new film he's starring in came up. They were both meant to be 'doing the lottery' this Saturday, up in Glasgow. He was picking the numbers, she was singing live, and just off the flight from LA. Nervy stuff. A footballer was brought in to do the numbers. She sang 'Oh Romeo'. 'How did it go?' I ask. She smiles. She has a singularly pretty smile. 'It seemed to go down okay,' she says. 'They clapped and clapped. It's the first time I've sung live in front of an English audience' – she corrects herself. She learns fast. '– a European audience.' (Scotland ain't England.) I bet they clapped. It's a terrific song, and a new English mix for the single (from her album 'If I Don't Stay the Night'. Will she, won't she, sleep with her boyfriend? Is it how to lose him or how to keep him? – a little too near the knuckle, it transpired, for US 'country' radio stations) which now has an almost Brit-poppy sound, and the voice: well, we're getting about forty percent of it, I reckon, now the tonsils are gone. One hundred percent and you'd be quivering at the back of the Opera House.

'Did it hurt?' I ask, 'having them out?' She looks about twelve, suddenly. Last time I saw her she was popping gum like some careless teenager. None of that defiance now, just perfect polite poise, but the mention of the tonsils reduces her to positive childhood.

'Hurt? It was terrible!' says Mindy McCready, 'I've never known anything like it. If I knew then what I know now I'd never have had it done.' But I bet she would have. The singer serves the voice, not the other way round. That's how you tell the star, and why the world sits up and takes notice when a slip of a girl turns up one day in Nashville, and gets a record contract just like that. Because even the hard-nosed businessmen of New Nashville, making their millions these days out of soft men in black hats and nice girls into twangy therapy, have a race memory of the old days when stars were stars and took the world by storm, and would like it to happen again. And with Mindy they think it just might.

Channel 4's current Saturday night series *Naked Nashville* tells you all you need to know, if you don't already, about the life and times, and the state of singer and song, in today's Nashville. The romance may be drifting out of Hollywood, but it's still going strong in this small swampy Southern town, out of which for some unknown reason, all the emotions of America, set to song, have been pouring for decades.

After interviewing Dolly, the first of the truly cloned, a sheep, a sweet creature, in the summer of 1997.

But Has Dolly Got a Soul?

Dolly the famous sheep has two dads. One is Dr Ian Wilmut of the Roslin Institute, the other is his fellow scientist and colleague Dr Keith Campbell.

Dolly has two mums: an anonymous egg cell from one sheep and a mammary cell from another, already deceased when Dolly was conceived. (I am sorry to tell you that the name Dolly derives from Dolly Parton, for obvious if lamentable reasons.)

Dolly, in other words, is a brainchild – in all her woolly, sweet, affectionate, soulful, bleating being.

She is the product of an advance in genetic technology so staggering that even Dr Wilmut and Dr Campbell themselves scarcely seem to have taken it in. They have freely detailed their work in the international science magazine *Nature*, as good scientists will, and now the whole world is free to develop their ideas, and will. Dolly doesn't care. She munches on. The cloning of human beings looms.

Dr Ian Wilmut is as far from a mad scientist as you could imagine. Steady, responsible, gentle, married, grown-up children, marvelling at the diversity of nature, prepared to see God's hand in the origin of species, worrying about the moral validity of the scientists' current cry, 'We find out, society decides.'

Dr Keith Campbell is wild-haired as a genius should be. Charismatic, inspiring, an ideas man come to this kind of genetic technology recently, a schoolboy so interested in tadpoles that his mother used to have to sweep baby frogs from the kitchen, once Dutch Elm disease control officer of Sussex, now Dolly's dad, along with Dr Wilmut. A realist, a rationalist, who refuses to speak of miracles, only of what is so far unknown.

The Roslin Institute is a highly respectable agricultural institution, registered as a Scottish charity, farm plus laboratories in the flat, windy lands just outside Edinburgh, dedicated to improving the nation's livestock – and doing it to great effect. There is a famous fourteenth century chapel at Roslin, a tourists' favourite, where they say the Holy Grail is hidden. Nothing much else happens here. It's enough.

On the face of it, the fact that a sheep has been grown not from the mating of a gentle ewe and some feisty ram as nature designed, not even from a ewe's egg and a microscopic embryo cell in the very first stage of development – easy-peasy these days – but from a ewe's egg emptied of DNA and an adult donor cell, might not in itself seem so remarkable.

The big breakthrough, however, was the realisation that a fully differentiated donor cell, under the tutelage of an egg cell, however emptied and helpless, would, if encouraged, return to its undifferentiated state, and start over when required. Newton watched his apple fall, Watt observed his kettle boil. Campbell describes his moment of genius as a brick dropping on his head. What you had to do was get the two cells, ovum and egg marching in step as they divided. Then you could fuse them and the process of new life could begin. Out of step, nothing. In step, everything.

And the way to make the donor cell dumb down to the ovum's simplicity was to make life hard for it: starve it a little, freeze it a little, fool it into quiescence, and – bingo – it falls in alongside the egg, keeping pace.

The brick fell. Work began. Dolly was born after two-hundred-and-eighty tries. The world's press turns up at the door. China on the telephone, France, Australia. Film offers. Book deals. Sheep are mammals: humans are mammals. You could make people in laboratories. Fortunes could be made. Hysteria mounts. Visions of genetic monstrosities; soulless hordes; a thousand Mozarts, a million Hitlers.

The reality is different: expensive, difficult, still in the future. Wilmut and Campbell fear a backlash, in which public alarm, whipped up by the press, provokes governments into embargoing legitimate and important biological research. They are right to worry. Back in 1989, foreseeing much of all this, I published a novel called *The Cloning of Joanna May*. Joanna May, aged sixty discovers her scientist husband, Carl May, had her cloned thirty years back.

This is his rationale:

I see a world of accident and not design, never perfectible left to itself. So I intervene. I can make a thousand thousand of you if I choose, fragment all living things and recreate them.

I can splice a gene or two, can make you walk with a monkey's head or run on a bitch's legs or see through the eyes of a newt: or smell like a rose. I can entertain myself by making you whatever I feel like, and as I feel like so shall I do. Whatever I choose from now on forever.

That's Carl May in mad scientist mode. He blames Joanna, naturally, for his behaviour. In actual fact the clones, being reared in different wombs, having different life experiences, turn out as markedly distinctive individuals. Nature counts as much as nature.

And Joanna answers (she always has an answer):

Do what you like but you can't catch me, you'll never catch me, I am myself. Nail me and alter me, fix me and distort me, I'll still have windows on the world to make of it what I decide. I'll still be myself.

I will watch the world go by in all its multifarious forms, and there will be no end to my seeing. I will lift up my heart to the hills, that's all, to glorify a maker who is not you. I should carry on if I were you, cloning and meddling, you might end up doing more good than harm, in spite of yourself, if only by mistake.

For all Dolly is a clone, she's a most agreeable sheep: one might almost think she had a soul.

My dear, the style, the terror, the knowingness – this totally unknown world of fashion, suddenly revealed.

Gaultier's Halo

Jean Paul Gaultier has a halo. I saw it. You know? The kind the saints wear in Renaissance paintings? A circle of light around the head? This one was at an angle like a well-placed hat, encompassing the big ears, the cropped blond hair, the cartoonist's dream of a face.

The only other person I ever saw with a halo was Mick Jagger, so we're not necessarily talking goodness here. That was years back. I saw this guy walking down a London street towards me, and I thought what's that kind of bright light circling the head? I didn't realise who it was until he was almost past me: the light was so bright it got in the way of recognition. Mick Jagger.

I told someone about the experience: she was into all kinds of mystic comprehensions at the time. 'That was no halo,' she said. 'That was an aura. You get them in all colours. If the aura's brilliant and without colour, what you're seeing is the sum of other people's attention. Whoever has it is famous and everyone's thinking about them. Not many people see auras. Perhaps you're one of the talented? Would you like to join my aura classes? Yours is a lovely bluey-greeny shade, with a lot of quiver. Only $100 a session?'

I said, 'No; if mine is bluey-green and quivering, forget it.'

And then when Jean Paul skirts-for-men Gaultier comes walking towards me down the stairs of his workshop in Paris, just after the autumn's fashion collections, when the magazines, the newspapers and the TV screens are full of him, and he's clearly the hit of the season, there he is, shimmering and glittering round the head with this stylish colourless light. But I find myself thinking, forget public attention, that's no aura, that's a halo. This guy is an angel, a saint. And so by the end of the interview I am convinced he is and if anyone says to me, Jean Paul Gaultier I go 'a-a-ah', goofy and soppy.

I was nervous. It had taken months to set up this interview. 'His people' and 'my people' had trouble matching schedules. We were given half an hour. 1.30–2.00, Paris, on a Friday before a Bank Holiday. We flew over in the morning. The new Gaultier studios in the Bastille area are barely finished. The district is fast coming-up in the world, having been in a state of depression sing 1789, when the revolutionary citizens tore down the famous Bastille prison, symbol of despotism, brick by brick – just as they did exactly two-hundred years later with the Berlin Wall – and carted off poor fashionable Marie let-them-eat-cake Antoinette in a tumbril to the guillotine. 'Fed up with your fancy clothes, your fashion-plates and powdered wigs,' the people cried, 'let's have jobs and food instead!' The district's been a long time recovering. But now Gaultier and Galliano have moved in, and fabric stores, milliners and boutiques follow. And the intertwined metal initials JPG stand on this tall narrow building like a symbol of the right of frivolity to exist and prosper.

The JPG building has at first sight a twenties look, all steel and rounded edges – then you double take and realise it's actually a mid-1990s view of how the 1920s thought the 2020s would be. But that's Gaultier's style – old-fashioned futuristic adding up to state-of-the-art plus. If you've seen one of the Gaultier spectacle cases – my husband has such a thing – you will know what I mean. I use the word 'spectacle' advisedly. 'Glasses' is too casual. You have to open such a case carefully, ceremoniously; you don't just snap them open and shut. Take me seriously, Gaultier's designs demand, even though the designer doesn't quite. It's the Zen approach to high fashion. You do what you do with focused concentration, total dedication and high professionalism, and you laugh merrily and forget it, tossing the moment aside. As no doubt Madonna unhooked her famous conical bra, the first of the wear-outside, not inside, garments, and tossed it aside, laughing, while the world gaped and blinked, as the moment came and went.

Go through the front doors of the JPG building and you are faced by an old-fashioned elevator, crimson double-gated barred doors of the kind you have to clang-to in order to make electrical contact. You get in, opening and closing the gates with raised eyebrows. More old Paris than state-of-the-art, you think. You press the button. Nothing happens. Press again. Whereupon an electronic voice tells you in French – so you might be imagining it – to quit the elevator at once. It is a design statement, not a mode of transport. So you leave the elevator at once, foolish, and climb the stairs, and through the Gaultier doors, and is this the actual workroom or is it a set up?

Infinitely courteous and personable young men man telephones and computers, but there are velvet sofas too, and an odd mannequin, velvet-clad. Is that the latest look? It all looks 1890s to me. We will have to wait a little. Filter coffee? Espresso? No thanks. Water. The heart's racing enough: is this what celebrity does to others? Apparently. An entire wall turns out to be a flat TV screen. Someone puts on a film of Gaultier's latest fashion show, just a week back. Yes, there's the circus theme the papers were full of: horses rise and fall, carousel blares, the models parade in clothes that look quite ordinarily wearable to me, but the heightened nature of our actual surroundings, the sense of expectation, keep filmed reality firmly in its place: second best. Though one ummed and ah-ed in polite admiration.

I was once with a rather famous screenwriter once at a TV party: the Head of the Network was present, not to mention a royal or so. I found the screenwriter standing in a corner slapping her own wrist. 'Are you okay?' I asked. 'I just hate myself,' she said. 'Why do I find myself sucking up to these people?' Slap, slap! I knew what she meant. We crawl to others as others crawl to us. Hateful.

So there we were, nervously sitting on designer steel chairs – the sofas turn out to be design statements too – doing our ah-ing and umming. Lionel, Gaultier's assistant, beautiful, deadly serious in defence of his employer, has given us a quick once-over to assure himself we are not serial killers, scum journalists, spies from other fashion houses, lawyers delivering writs or other malcontents.

And then this guy comes down the stairs. Jean Paul Gaultier.

He was wearing cuffed black boots, any old jeans, a T-shirt and a combat jacket with ink-stains on the sleeve. He's strong-featured, good-looking, cropped blond hair, an earring in one ear and has a look of simple kindness about him. He made me laugh. And he had a halo. Well, he's an angel, I thought. That's no aura, that's not the effect of celebrity, that's a halo, that's goodness.

I tried this notion out, tentatively, on a transsexual friend. Was it possible that Jean Paul Gaultier had a halo? 'Oh yes,' she/he said, 'of course. He is a Saint of the Third Sex.' I was into deep waters here. What do I know? Does giving men permission to wear skirts necessitate, or qualify for, canonisation? Then I remember the shock-horror when women first began wearing trousers. People thought the sun would go out.

'Well, anyway,' I said vaguely. 'I thought Gaultier was an angel!'

'Everyone I know does,' she/he said. 'Don't tell too many people about the halo, though. Might not be wise.'

As for the laugh which spring unbidden, that might be less to do with Gaultier's saintliness than the fact that he comperes one of the funniest late-night TV shows over here – *Eurotrash* – along with Antoine de Caunes, another bad lad from a good family. (Jean Paul's father was an accountant, his mother a good wife, his grandmother a wild, fortune-telling beautician.) De Caunes appears on screen beautifully suited, Gaultier anticly attired. The very first time I focused on JPG he was wearing a kilt, yellow socks and a striped red and white shirt. His bare knees were strong, male and knobbly. He was making so bad and belaboured a joke, in so strong a French-English accent, so wilfully making a fool of himself, so exactly right was the gap between hem of skirt and top of sock, and so trashy was the programme – as I remember, a guide to the strange toilets of Sweden – it was impossible not to be riveted. Gaultier was both performance and presentation incarnate: a send-up of himself: bashfully ridiculous. What was this popstar/fashion guru, this young king of couturiers, *doing* on this programme exactly? A saint on his day off. I ask him. He just *likes* doing it, he says, and as we're in the age of a purpose to everything and no point without profit, this too makes me believe Gaultier's ripe for canonisation.

Gaultier is the Guide of Grunge, the young person's designer: in his Carousel show he borrowed ruthlessly from the past – Victorian walking suits in denim, a black monkey fur coat, *fin de siècle* in punk lettering across the back, worn with a twenties turban – and moves the moment on into the future. You wouldn't catch JPG casting straws into the fashion wind to see what he could profitably do next; no, he does what feels right and, in doing it, finds himself ahead of the times, which plod laboriously after him.

Ask him how he sees himself and he replies, simply, 'Someone who sews.' He was born to sew: it is a vocation. In this simplicity lies his sainthood: around this simple desire to sew a good seam an industry grew up, a web of PR and business enterprise in which he sits cross-legged like a smiling haloed spider, if you will forgive a mixed metaphor or so.

What Gaultier likes is a good seam on a cheerful garment. He may have to invent a garment or a style, simply for the sake of the seam. I suspect that if it's now de rigueur for the young to wear their shirts hanging out below the edge of sweater or jacket, it's because Gaultier likes as many seams showing as possible. That's what you get with the layered look. Lots of seams.

Who does he admire? Vivienne Westwood, John Galliano, Jean Muir. (Thank God, threadbare, worn fragile from overuse though it may be, I'm wearing Jean Muir. Perhaps he's being courteous? He would always rather please than make insecure.) He admires anyone who thinks a good seam is important.

How does he make enough money to keep the whole thing going? I ask the difficult question head on. Not from selling couturier clothes, presumably. A few thousand dollars from a few rich stars isn't going to keep the carousels whirling. Gaultier's up front about it. You franchise designs, sell the logo, name the perfume, take commission on everything; you keep going. One show's just over – that's six months minus one week till the next one: he's already had to order the fabrics, select the yarn. The ready-to-wear collection must be revealed six months in advance. He was late to see us because he was on the phone to Japan: problems with the production of JPG shoes. And so on. He's serene, infinitely patient with us. But you understand, if he's so busy, why he has ink stains on his sleeve as well as a halo round his head. Though the halo is no longer visible. You have to see halos and auras kind of sideways; or they disappear, not open to rational scrutiny.

'So what's new, Jean Paul?'

'Nothing new left,' he says, 'just new ways of looking at things.'

'Skirts up, down, full, narrow?'

'Forget it, he says: there is no such thing as fashion any more.' Except we tend to all move together, some a little further ahead than others, and Jean Paul's plotting the route. 'Have some fun,' he says.

Growing Up and Moving On

Snippets of autobiography.

Written in the autumn of 1997, when the trees in the parks were golden.

The London I Love

This is my city. Our fortunes are intertwined. Soon London is to have a Mayor: its split personality will no longer be tolerated. It is to exist as one coherent body: one concept: one self. No longer divided into separate identities – Westminster, Camden, Wandsworth, and so on: the languid Thames carving irrationally through its middle – the city will lift its head as London, simple and indivisible, with even its parking regulations consistent. I try to be happy about it. For London to have found itself, in the best psychotherapeutic sense, discovered its true nature, no longer in need of treatment for a fragmented identity, to be declared whole – wonderful! But what about me? Will the same thing happen to me? If I come to my senses, what sort of writer will I be? Writers are in essence neurotic beings, multifaceted. The unification of the self is not their aim.

I first set eyes on London fifty-one years ago. It was love at first sight. It was on my fourteenth birthday; on 22 September 1946, to be precise. I stood on the deck of a liner out of New Zealand as Tilbury, on the Thames estuary, hove into view. Whoever'd heard of Heathrow then? Tilbury Port was London's gateway. Grey hillsides loomed through fog, covered with even greyer, sootier, overlapping shapes which turned out to be dwellings. An all-female family, my mother, my grandmother, my sister and I, we stood at the rail of the *Rangitana*, and marvelled. Such an intensity of grimy living! Unbelievable. The *Rangitana* was the first passenger ship to leave New Zealand after the war ended; built to carry one hundred and fifty passengers, on this voyage she carried two thousand. A nightmare! We'd crossed the

Pacific in almighty storms, with one engine failed. We were penniless and homeless, all our worldly possessions in two trunks in the hold – 'not wanted on voyage' – but my mother's one ambition was to escape the Antipodes, so here we were. I loved it. My city, I thought. Home at last! Sirens hooted, ropes were thrown, the massive, exhausted vessel safely docked.

That was the London of the late forties. A hungry, dirty city, pock-marked by bomb craters, families broken, traditions disrupted, feeling the pangs of a bitter victory. The first night in London my sister Jane and I slept on the floor of the one house still standing in a bombed-out square. There was a full moon. I couldn't sleep – I sat in the window and looked out over rubble and ruins which pierced the air like church spires, and saw the wild cats play, and thought again I love this city. I will always love it.

There was no food; or what seemed to me, fresh from New Zealand, as no food. Bright yellow egg powder from the US, a strange powdery pudding called Cremola, also yellow. I was given a ration book and an identity number. I belonged. I was thrilled and proud. A Londoner! Two ounces of butter a week. You could hardly see it. (These days how I still pile butter on my plate.) I ate my first herring. Bones! I choked. In the dreadful winter of forty-seven we lived in a single bedsitting room in Belsize Park, on the way up to Hampstead. The tube station roared hot air out onto the street, melting icicles. We'd stand at the entrance for hours. There was no electricity and just a flicker of gas: we stayed in bed a lot of the time, for warmth, and read the socialist *New Statesman and Nation*. Labour was voted in, with a tremendous majority. I went for an interview to the vast, rambling County Hall, opposite the Palace of Westminster, and there from a dark little cubbyhole was awarded a scholarship. I was a bright child. 'I will get the better of this city. I will show it who's who,' I remember thinking. London and I were more or less married by then.

Our family fortunes improved. My mother got a job as a housekeeper in a pretty house in St John's Wood. We had three whole rooms in the basement, dank and dark as they were. There was a rat. I stopped screaming, feet up on the iron bed and attacked it with a broom. The rat fled. I won. I went to a posh school and passed exams. My big sister, at seventeen went on a 'country holiday' (all available young that year were sequestered to get the harvest in) and came back with straw on her back and a thirty-four-year-old Communist teacher whom she insisted on marrying. Oh, the danger of out-of-London! It dawned on me then. The marriage lasted six weeks. She didn't like sex after all, it seemed.

The fifties. The city, recovering, lifted its head and looked around and saw a future. The 1951 Exhibition on the South Bank pointed the way ahead. We built ourselves concert halls, theatres, pleasure palaces, fun-parks. Rationing ended, but smog descended, to remind us citizens that nothing's easy. I choked and wept in the thick yellow air of Regent Street, oppressed by memories of the past. Thousands died. I rather liked the drama. That was the decade of bedsitting rooms, of housing shortages, of communal bathrooms, of barely hot water trickling miserably into chipped basins, of tiny wages, but cheap living. I lived with my mother and my baby and no husband in Notting Hill in a room where the furniture was nailed to the floor in case the tenants sold it or burned it. The landlord was notorious: a man famous in the annals of oppression everywhere. His rent-collector had a German shepherd dog, one eye and a wooden leg. Truly. Stomp, stomp, stomp up the ill-lit stairs. We fled to Saffron Walden, a pretty market town in Essex, all Elizabethan timbered beams, from where I commuted to London – two-and-a-half hours there, two-and-a-half hours back – to a menial job in the Propaganda Department of the Foreign Office. How slow, how slow the trains: how early the departure, how late the arrival. Out-of-London was always disaster – the house we lived in was haunted. Poltergeists threw, unseen women wept all night. We fled back to London, where the ghosts are more manageable. This time Strand on the Green, out by Richmond, on an elegant curve on the River Thames. Moving house was easy. We never accumulated more than a trunk or so of possessions. 'Not wanted on voyage.' Sometimes

I thought that was me. I never owned more than two pairs of shoes. Who did? That was the fifties, that was.

Decade of drear, of building political paranoia. I married a man twenty-five years older than me to give myself and my baby a home. We lived in Acton, a grisly suburb, as far from London's centre as I was ever to live. I was fat and miserable. There was no sex. He was a headmaster of a technical school and reported any suspicious activity in the Teacher's Union to MI5. He wouldn't let me work – 'No wife of mine works' – or join the Labour Party. Too political. He made me go to classes funded by the CIA on the Rule of Law. We sat under trees on the pleasant green swards of Holland Park and fuelled our national and individual paranoia. Reds under the bed! They gave us wonderful sandwiches. They bought us. At the end of the decade I ran away from the schoolteacher with the child tucked under my arm and four stolen pounds in my pocket. His next wife, like the one before me, I realised, also came with a son. It rendered consistent the forms he had to fill in over the years, when he applied for jobs. Married, one son. Any of us unmarried mothers would do. There are always so many about, grateful for a roof over our heads.

I shouldn't complain. I was hopelessly in love with another, married with three children. I stood in a pub, wearing the black V-neck sweater so popular in those days. You could pull it down over the shoulder to expose as much bare white skin as you felt inclined. It was love at first sight for both of us. He got me a job in advertising. I paid for his holidays so he could affect a reconciliation with his wife. How I wept! Tired of masochism I fell in love with someone marginally more suitable, an artist, currently between marriages. This one lasted thirty years. Oh my city, London, what romances and excitements we have known; what infidelities, yet what consuming loyalty.

The sixties! London's glorious decade, and mine. Darling city of one-night stands, of Carnaby Street, of incipient revolution: how the music flowed out of it, to enchant and seduce the rest of the world. The Beatles couldn't understand why we didn't do it in the road. Look down at your feet and you wore green shoes with satin bows, not straight-up-and-down brown-laced; more still in the cupboard, yellow and pink, psychedelic. We lived in Primrose Hill, by the zoo. We could hear the lions roaring at night. I earned money in advertising selling eggs to the nation: my husband earned money stripping pine and selling antiques, rescuing the artefacts of yesteryear from the depredations of developers. London grew rich and trendy, in step with us, or we with it. Our city! We had children, gave parties, lived to excess. Both of us deep into psychoanalysis: the rich depressives' friend. It had not occurred to either of us that it was the world needed changing, not ourselves.

The seventies. Back to nature. Oil prices rise. Which way to go? London seemed to have lost its zing. Live next to the soil, perhaps, live natural, be part of the breathing, heaving Gaian universe? Turn your back on city life. We made our own wine, baked our own bread. Or he did. That was the new male way forward. But what about mine? Why was everything in the house his way, not my way?

In the fifties, my Professor of Moral Philosophy had told the class that women had no capacity for moral judgement, let alone rational thought. I'd accepted that without question. Women didn't argue, in those days. I'd rolled about in beds as if that only was my fate; my children were my destiny. No more! We women raised our consciousness: we learned to argue. The city stayed oddly oblivious.

It occurred to me one day that in all the 'great' novels I had ever read women were misrepresented. Their story had never been, wasn't being, told. I began to write. Television plays. Novels. About the lives of women as they were, in all their complex glory and absurdity. Men walked out of rooms as I walked in. I was astonished. They weren't intentionally even 'feminist' novels, or only incidentally. It just so happened that the same social pressures which produced the feminist movement had also produced me, a writer. A Marxist concept, fitting the times, the London I lived in. This was the decade of boiler-suits and no make-up for women, or deconstructionalism, anti-deconstructionalism. London grew boring and worthy. So no doubt did I. The seventies, the worthy decade, of full employment, high inflation, industrial unrest and flares. Have another baby, have two, to cement the marriage! I did. Then London, I have to admit it, I betrayed you. I forsook your pavements and went to live in Somerset, in the country, where it seemed for a time the moral high ground was.

But I always kept a London foothold, this time in Kentish Town. I'd travel by train into Paddington, and breathe in the rank sulphurous fumes of my city and rejoice. The polluted air seemed stringent and exhilarating, after the soft depressing laxness, the emptiness, of wind over green fields and farmhouses. A virtuous, dull decade.

The eighties, not so dull. The decade of self-interest triumphant. London under Thatcher, unemployment, soaring house prices, city hype, designer clothes. New developments and demolition. Canary Wharf: the Thames Flood Barrier. Flashy living for London, and me as well.

I have a book here before me, contender for this year's Whitbread Novel Award. Its title is *Bleeding London*; it's a kind of fictionalised street map, written by an excellent young author, Geoff Nicholson, who is clearly as enamoured of the city as am I. His characters define their social status by marking with a cross on the map of London the locations of their sexual encounters. By how they cluster, you will know the kind of person you really are, understand where you belong. (A vulgar pastime, but fun.) His heroine, if such she can be described, travels all the way across London in order to gain a Hampstead cross, and thus improve her profile. Hampstead, where I now live, being the haunt of writers and psychoanalysts.

During the eighties, I admit, subject as I am to the feeling tone of the city, helpless in the grip of its moods, but sanctified, I hope, by the passage of time, the dwindling of all things into the past, I marked up crosses all over London's West End, in its finest, snappiest, trendiest, more designer-conscious, most flourishing hotels. I can tell you about the soft beds of Claridge's, and its lonely marble bathrooms: about awful food at the elegant Savoy: the perpetual lavish refurbishment of the Ritz: the excellent steak tartare (who'd ever eat raw steak in the nineties?) at the Dorchester: of the pinky-beigy boring comfort that is accorded everywhere to the rich and careless, as my lover and I sought illicit literary conversation after work. And I wrote and I wrote and I wrote, escaping into a fictional world.

And as the London of the eighties turned into the caring, sharing, touchy-feely nineties, the decade of self-knowledge, and the Age of Therapism got into its stride, so that now the disabled get free parking spaces and the elderly a free swim down the old Municipal Baths: and there's a giant new Aquarium to encourage the tourists (who now over a year out-number Londoners themselves) in what used to be County Hall, where once I got my scholarship from an ill-lit cubby-hole, I turned with the decade. I too am now a caring, sharing, responsible, remarried, taxpaying person, weeping for Princess Diana.

On a hot London day at the brink of the millennium, you can feel as short of oxygen as you ever did in a nineteen-fifties smog. You still can't get about the place; once it was because you hadn't got the fare, now it's because the city's in gridlock, from too many cars, an overdose of prosperity. But the taxis zoom about the parks, beneath the cherry trees, in what still seems to me to be the most beautiful city in the world, London, my home. And in Regent's Park you can still hear the lions roar, though I daresay only until they're moved to more congenial, suitable spaces, or retrained for return to the wild, and I am excited, exhilarated, fourteen again. My city, my life, intertwined, and I knew it the moment I first laid eyes upon the grey, huddled Tilbury hills.

Frivolity rules!

My Thirty Years in Advertising

Once you've got into it, of course, you don't get out of it. Never. I'm still looking for a the solution to the Aero problem – how to do better than *bubbles with full-cream milk*, and I haven't even set foot inside an advertising agency for a good twenty-five years. Ever since I was fired from Ogilvie and Benson for regularly marking up thirty-seven hours a day on the new-fangled time-sheets we copywriter consultants (ho-ho) were issued with when the American bosses took over. It had to be thirty-seven hours in every twenty-four to bring me in the money I thought I deserved. It was three months before they noticed. (Oh, how frivolous we all were in those days of full employment.)

They didn't say in so many words that was why they fired me, but I think it was. Their story was that they'd lost the egg account – *Go To Work on An Egg* – and there was no work for me to do. But personally I think it was the time-sheets plus the *sin of being right* too often. I'd told them they'd lose the egg account if they lost the moral high ground which kept the little lion on their stale, stale eggs, and wholesome mothers and babies on the posters, and insisted on spending the budget on Egg Chicks. Leggy girls dressed as chickens – well, barely dressed – calling at your door before eight in the morning? If you've egg shells in the bin you get a free half-dozen? I ask you! The whole Egg Marketing Board collapsed, but I did go round with the Egg Chicks and was horrified to discover how thrilled the housewives were to see them coming up the path. Moral: never worry about selling, only about the client. Oh, the things I learned!

They can fire you but you're still there, you just don't get paid. How to improve on *Aero – bubbles with full-cream milk*. Of course cream equals death these days, so how about *bubbles with fat-free milk*? Or could one go for the compromise and have *semi-skimmed*? Try *Bubbles with organic semi-skimmed milk*? No, I think not. So the brain burbles on through the years, brooding over past failures.

Trying to write a Black and Decker TV commercial for Pearl and Dean's new TV department in 1956 (yes, folks, 1956) when ITV was just beginning, and none of us had ever seen a TV commercial, only cinema, and had to work it out from first principles, or hearsay, from New York. I wrote a ninety-second tragi-comedy, I remember, with one product mention. The department closed on Christmas Eve. Out on the streets in the snow with a day's notice. That was *before* full-employment. I had a two-year-old child. If I see a Black and Decker ad today I still cringe and feel fearful.

During my life in advertising I used to try to get into J. Walter Thompson, that mecca of the poetic copywriter, every year or so, but you had to pass an intelligence test which included mirror images. I could not for the life of me work out what a way a curvy line would look upside down and reversed. They never let me in. I hold it against them to this day.

After Pearl and Dean a boyfriend got me a job at Crawfords: that was how it worked in those days. Does it still? Bet it does. The Director who interviewed me said, 'It is a woman's duty to dress attractively, to please men.' I remember asking 'Why?' but copywriters were known to be eccentric so I still got the job. I worked on *Drinka Pinta Milka Day* and moved around for a bit having a high old time, and fell in love with the man who wrote *Have A Break Have a Kit Kat* – and then went to Benson and Mather in the days before Ogilvie came along, where we were far more serious about everything. I learned from the typographers that space on a page is important and I learned from reading-and-noting tests what people absorb from the page (far less than you think); and I learned from having to make TV commercials single-handed (in the days when if you wrote 'a cold arctic night' the whole crew would ship out to the Arctic, and then dump the reels on your desk) how a screenplay related to a film, and how to edit and dub on the Moviola, and then I started writing TV plays – long stories selling ideas rather than short stories selling product – and soon there was no need to go to work every day and anyway they fired me. And that was that – except it isn't. *Aero – still bubbling away in the head.*

The state of writerly play in June, 1998.

Joining the Writers

It was always such a romantic title: *Writers' & Artists' Yearbook*. When I was a child it sat so importantly on the parental bookshelf. This I assumed to be the book of arcane knowledge, the book which magically contained all other books, ticket of entrance to the world you longed for. Just look inside and you were as good as published! And what's more if you were a Writer you came first, before the Artists. Children notice these things.

My mother, now ninety-one, would point out to me that she was born the same year as the *Yearbook*: 1907. The very notion, she claimed, had made a writer of her. She published good novels (*Via Panama* – there's a copy in the London Library) and short stories, and romances in instalments the world queued up outside the news-stands to buy and which thrilled me to the core. (*Velvet and Steel*; *The Cups of Alexander*. Such wonderful titles!)

As of right, a copy of the *Writers' & Artists' Yearbook 1930*, travelled with her from England to New Zealand, where we lived through my childhood. My mother's father, Edgar Jepson, whose novels best-sold in the twenties and thirties (*Lady Noggs Assists*; *An Accidental Don Juan*) always had a *Yearbook* on his London shelves, she told me, 'Well, of course,' though he was always faithful to his publisher Herbert Jenkins. Herbert Jenkins' books, if you disobediently read them in the bath, would leach red dye down your childish hand and all the way down your arm, so adults shrieked if they came into the bathroom, thinking you were wounded. Served them right. Consulting this year's edition I find, alas, that Herbert Jenkins are no more. But yes, there's Curtis Brown, under Literary Agencies, the same firm who handled my Uncle Selwyn Jepson's thrillers (*Stagefright* – which was turned into a Hitchcock film; *A Noise in the Night*): I'm a Curtis Brown client now as well: I still feel the romance of it. This grown-up world of artists and writers, as exciting and mysterious as I had always believed.

Uncle Selwyn always had the latest edition of the *Yearbook* on his shelves, but then he could well afford it, as my mother pointed out. Literature is its own reward: it's detective books and thrillers make the real money. And she was in New Zealand during the war, and she would send her manuscripts off by boat – a six-week journey: well, how else? Those were the days before faxes, let alone e-mail; words travelled on paper, in envelopes, not magically through the ether – and the ships would be sunk, down to the bottom of the sea along with fame and fortune, and only a carbon left a couple of thousand miles behind in the Antipodes – and that was the end of that. And we think we have troubles!

And every decade the *Yearbook* gets better, more informative, more helpful. Flick through it. Specimen scripts; how to run your own Picture Library, Good Lord! How to control yourself on the Word Processor, how not to let it run away with you. All the contacts and addresses you could possibly need the better to get what's in your head out of it and into the outside world.

The problem for new writers becomes not how you say it, but what it is you have to say, and why it should be said, and exactly what it is you have to offer others. What do you know that they don't? – these days people know so much! This alone the *Yearbook* can't tell you. So far and no further. I know that now.

I get asked from time to time if I have any advice to offer new writers and all I can say is well, first of all I admire you very much: you have such fortitude, such resolution, such faith. And secondly, if you get to three chapters and are then stuck, you're not stuck, you're finished:

you haven't bitten off enough to chew, that's all: and thirdly, all rules are made to be broken. What others say are your weak points may, if you drive into the skid, be your strongest. I used to frown on the over-generous use of adjectives until one day a student showed me an Iris Murdoch sentence which contained eighteen adjectives in a row for one single noun, and a brilliant sentence it was. That's when I gave up offering advice.

Written on a bad hair day, in damp English weather, autumn, 1995.

Snip-snip

Hairdressers of the world forgive me. I have hated and feared you too long. But now I understand what makes you snip on and on so ruthlessly, deaf to all protests – 'But I said the merest trim, no more, that's enough, stop, please, please!' – I can feel more kindly towards you: yes, even though in the past I've had to go whole weeks before showing my face in public again, so shorn and bereft of hair you've left me. But understanding you as I do now, I can forgive you. You're just obsessives, the lot of you; I recognise myself in you. Enthusiasts. You need to put your mark on me, that's all it is, and you *love cutting hair*.

I might even have been born to trim hair, myself, never realised it, and ended up a writer by mistake. I realised this when I was out in the garden the other day, totally happy, cutting the grass with the scissors, blunting off the frail, tapering, acid-green shoots which, newly sown, now thrust out of the black earth. It is essential to cut if the new shards are to thicken; if the seed is to send up not a single slim vulnerable blade but a whole defiant clump. Or so my gardening book tells me. Only I know the mower's too heavy and could drag the too-young, too-tentative grass right out of the soil. (I dream these days – nightmare – that I get up in the morning to patches of black mud in the lawn; because I used the mower. Mind you when I kept tropical fish I'd dream I got up to find them floating belly-up in the tank – because I'd raised the temperature of the water: it was no longer tepid, it was *hot*. Thus, it seems, our daily occupation can swiftly become our unconscious preoccupation.) The mower's out; I have no shears so what can I do but use the scissors?

And once you're in the garden with the scissors, you choose the lushest and most verdant patch – lift a section with the hand just as the hairdresser lifts a clump of hair before snipping, snipping, more, more – and then, so naturally, before you know it, you the grass-cutter find yourself having to *even-up*. There's no helping it. You can't have anything lopsided: you have to be fair. And then that side's a little bit too short. So then the other side has to match. And then, look, look, see, there's an individual strand to pursue – how did that escape – and before you know it you're practically down to scalp level, or earth level, whichever, deaf to everything –

'*Come in from the garden at once! It's the White House on the phone.*'

'*Tell them I'm busy. I'm in a meeting.*' *Snip-snip! Evening-up.*

I was driven, driven. Compulsive, like cramming M&M's into the mouth with both hands. I understand both myself and you better, now, hairdressers of the world. The sheer pleasure of getting it right.

At Frèdèric Fekkai on the seventh floor of Bergdorf Goodman in New York – where the scent of artificial roses delights the air, ('Through the home-making department, Ma'am, past the special offer gilt chairs and the framed old masters and to the right.'), stylists gracefully twist the hair dryer to flick away any stray snippings of hair which might pollute the glassy clarity of their work stations. A Kate Moss lookalike in a short white coat travels the salon on her hands and knees, with dustpan and brush, in a cloud of snippings.

At Frèdèric Fekkai they will sulk if they can't cut; so you say yes and sit amongst the most confident, the most at ease, the most sleek and stunning women in the world, with the glossiest, healthiest hair imaginable, internetted the lot of them, running the world from manicure stations and the back-wash. (Yes, you tip the girls who wash. There's a little pocket on the shoulder of the pink gown where you can keep ready folded bills so as not to embarrass yourself or them.)

While the Kate Moss lookalike sweeps up beneath their tiny, well-shod feet. It would defeat your self-confidence for days just to sit there, but never mind. You think if Frèdèric Fekkai cuts your hair you will look like one of them. You don't.

At the salon round the corner from l'Hôtel Maison de la Reine, in Paris, near the Picasso Museum, they vacuum up cut hair as it falls, with little custom-made bright pink plastic Hairvacs. They treat you like a collaborator, as if you'd been sleeping with the enemy: they'd shave your head completely if they could. '*Oh chic, Madame, très chic!*' Sez you. They hate me. I hate them.

'*Just a little spray? No? But it's a very good brand. And so damp out, madame. Your hair will fall.*'

Yes, and there's another Fr.30 on the bill.

'What, madame, c'est vrai? *Hair spray gets in your ears and gives you eczema?* Incroyable! . . . *Madame, what is wrong? You have such good ears, it is madness not to show them! But* Madame, soyez tranquille – *hair grows.*'

That's Paris. In Helsinki, in Reykjavik and Bergen they haven't yet got round to back-washers. Inelegantly, you sit with your legs apart, your head forward, while they dunk your head in the basin, and scrub with icy fingers, so vigorously that your chin keeps hitting the porcelain of the basin, and you feel your teeth will go through your chin. In such small Northern seaboard cities, the girls – who always try to make you look like their worst enemy or more lamentably still, their mothers – send you out looking like a fisherman's wife. It's amazing what look you can achieve with rollers: what they've left of your hair tightly bound and baked hard beneath a dryer hood unchanged since 1930. Erratum: a fisherman's widow. Add grief to plainness. In these places your fallen hair stays fallen, multi-coloured snippings to tread into shabby rugs, the sum of all departed clients.

I use my fingers as a broom to dispose of the scissored grass cuttings, flicking the fallen shreds out of the way of what, in my enthusiasm, I've left of the by now severely truncated growing shoots. They must get air and light! I feel tender towards them, though I did the harm in the first place. '*Très chic, mes herbes, très chic!*', I console them, when the first thin wail of protest arises. (Scientists tell us that the grass cries out when cut, in shock and pain: that vegetable life hurts just as does animal life. But then, they'll tell us anything, to get funding and prove a point. I take no more notice of this kind of assertion than does the hairdresser of mine, when I arrive bleating I want only a fraction off, please. A smidgen! And then – What are you doing to me?)

In Sarajevo, back in 1990, my mind simply blanked out from future shock: in Melbourne, accustomed as they are to the harsh dry desert winds, Aussie stylos use the hair-dryer so hot and near the scalp you cry out. Then they despise you. They scorn you for your whingey limey ways. 'Why don't you do it yourself?' the stylos cry. 'Just dunk your head under the tap and stick it out the window to dry. Stick in a few rollers if you must. Self-reliance, that's our motto!'

'I can't, I can't,' I moan. I have never mastered the art of blow-drying, let alone putting in rollers. I have this disability; I can't mirror-image: I can't steer a boat (pull the tiller to the left and the boat goes to the right – extraordinary proposition!). I can't umpire at tennis (if that side makes a mistake, the other side gets a point? *Incroyable!*) If I twist a roller forward in the mirror, it ends up twisted backward? Impossible! It's hopeless. By the time I've said all that the stylos are down on the beach for the arvo with the sharks and the UV rays. I'm an indoor person myself.

In Los Angeles, in a Shopping Mall down the Boulevard from the Château Marmont (a very, very long Boulevard; Hollywood, that's to say) they add spare body parts and automatically give you Big Hair and Long Talons, so you can hardly remember who you are; which can, in the circumstances, be a relief. No questions asked and no comments invited. 'Sit down Ma'am! Thank you, that's you done! Have a good day!' Your hair backcombed into a dry fizz.

At the Beverley Wilshire they give you for breakfast the biggest half pawpaw you ever saw, with a half strawberry in its heart. Very big, very tasteless, too upfront to be erotic. All LA is like that, very big and tasteless, from the films to the hairstyling to the fingernails. I love it.

Though specially for LA, of course, they're genetically engineered a kind of thick, coarse non-grow grass which doesn't need mowing: it quite spoils the look of the gardens of Beverly Hills. (In Bel Air you can't see a thing anyway, let alone the state of the grass, for the high-tech security walls: very disappointing.) I prefer our English lawns: soft, green, smoothly vulnerable, impractical; always ready for a cut. Just beware nightmare patches of black mud.

You may wonder why I get to so many hairdressers, so many cities, so many hotels. It's because I write novels. I get sent by publishers to book-reading centres all over the world. I get to have my photograph taken. I have baby-fine hair. I can't do a thing with it. I gave up trying a long time ago. I go to Reception: check-in; ask the concierge – 'what salon do you recommend?' At the Drake in Chicago they recommend the old-fashioned barber on the lower floor: it's a front-wash joint: staffed by head-dunking, chin-jabbing, strong-fingered Russian beauties whose evident ambition it is to erase you from the competition. Some women are very good at that.

When I was a child my mother would cut my hair. '*I'll just feather-cut,*' she'd say. Snip-snip, she'd go, and then snip-snip again. '*I'll just even up, shall I? Be quiet, you foolish child! There! It suits you really well so short. Now I'll just rub it dry with the towel. I expect it will come up fluffy.*' But of course short and fluffy never did a thing for me, except keep the boys away, with its no-nonsense sensibility; and the rubbing hurt my head. Snip-snip, nearer and nearer the scalp, nearer and nearer to the epitome of loathsomeness, bald-patchedness. Mother couldn't help it, I see it now. She just liked cutting. I've inherited the tendency from her. Well, what the hell, grass grows. Forgiveness all round, grass, and keep your wailing to yourself.

Lamenting a misspent youth in the spring of 1998, clearing out closets; dust motes shining in the sunlight.

Yikes! The Frock in the Photograph

I came across a box of photographs the other day. I wish I hadn't. What a misspent past, couture-wise. Dowdy and distrait, appalling! How had I dared leave the house looking like that, uncombed and crooked-hemmed, let alone stand in front of a camera? Had I never, ever, looked at myself in a mirror and *done* something about myself?

This was not a box of family snapshots – the kind that makes the heart glow or else breaks it – this holiday, that birthday, those clouds from that aircraft, the children when they were babies, the husband when he was still just that. At least family snaps have the great merit of mostly not having the self in them, since the self was the one who took them. No, this was a box of the kind of photographs that *follow after*. The past that others won't let you forget. The pictures people send you. '*Came across this the other day: thought you might like to have it for your archives.*'

The self on platforms, handing out awards: the self as wedding guest, high heels on grass; the self trying to look serious, opening a fete. (Yes, truly it seems I have opened fetes in my time, *and* worn a hat – here's pictorial evidence!) The self being gracious receiving a prize, whatever, but always in the wrong dress. At least with doctorates they cover you up in a gown. Occasionally pretty, often plain, face screwed up into the light, seldom stylish, always younger. Who would want to look at such remembrances of the self?

Did everyone else wear *frocks*, or was it just me? And come to think of it, what became of those garments, those strings of chunky Moroccan beads, the impossible shoes? What happened to all those clothes one once wore, and hated or loved for all the wrong reasons? Black-bagged and binned, or simply left behind when one slammed out? Were they put in the wash when the dry-cleaner should have had them so that was the end of them? Did I ever take them, like a proper person, down to the charity shop? I doubt it. Whatever happened to the silk brocade kaftan which turned from an expensive personal statement to such a fashion joke overnight that even this non-stylish person noticed? Perhaps I gave it to a friend to cut up for cushion covers? That would have been a noble fate – only did I ever have friends who *sewed*? The fate of garments goes unrecorded and forgotten.

When I say 'came across a box of photographs', I misrepresent the situation. What happened was that I took a box-file from the shelf and all the pursuing photographs inside fell out and I sat amongst them and tried to come to terms with them, and even put them in some kind of order. It is current wisdom that the traumas of the past need to be remembered and relived, and in this way spiritual and emotional healing will occur. I have never subscribed to the idea: to my mind the passage of time and forgetfulness are the great natural healers. Better to avert the face from the past than stare it in the eye. Avoid hurt, don't seek it out. Scabs should not be picked. Scars need a dab of concealer not frequent inspection. But here I was, the pictorial past lying all around me, what could I do?

Here's me at six, wearing a multi-coloured Fair Isle sweater, knitted by my father's mistress. I know I'm six, because of the gap in the front teeth. I'm smiling happily, but there is vengeance in my heart. The sweater is hot, tight and scratchy, a perfectly horrid garment. I know now what I didn't know when the picture was taken. (Bet the mistress took it, too, showing off her miserable handiwork.) That I was going to carefully select one of the knitted rows – the most vulnerable because it was a single length of wool – and snip with the scissors and pull.

The garment was then to fall into two halves. She was to knit it together again, and I was to snip and pull once more, and she was to give up altogether and move to another city. My father, who was a doctor, put bitter aloes on my fingers to stop me biting my nails – yes, I can just about make those out too, poor nibbled things – but I told him I liked the taste. He laughed and gave up. We were in New Zealand when I was six. My mother came back from England to rescue me: here she is wearing a little pill-box hat with a veil. How beautiful she was! Much better looking than the mistress. The photograph is shiny black and white, and cracked at the edges, but I remember the scarlet of the hat to this day, colour coming back into the world. Fair Isle sweaters – for those of you who don't know – are knitted to a traditional Scottish pattern – different colours but all of them subfusc. First sartorial mistake – ethnic idolatry seldom works – but I was only six. What could I do? In those days little girls wore what was given to them to put on – they didn't kick and scream if they weren't allowed to dress up like the Spice Girls. If your father's mistress knitted you a sweater you wore it.

Perhaps this is the problem? Why I end up wearing the wrong clothes at the wrong occasion? Perhaps kicking and screaming and choosing the wrong clothes at six is essential to proper sartorial development and eventual fashion maturity?

Here's a packet of postcards, taken from an oil painting by Rita Angus now hanging in New Zealand's National Gallery. My sister and I stare wide-eyed at the world from the canvas. My sister's nine, I'm seven. Our dolls, our love objects, are ranged behind us. There, dear lord, are our *dresses.* Red check, big white floppy collars. Dark green cardigans. We're dressed alike. I hated that. It was always happening. After my father left there wasn't any money; we were always packing up and moving on: impossible to accumulate a thing, not even clothes. We had two outfits each, my sister and I, at any one time. For school – one white shirt, one navy gymslip, one navy jumper. For best – one dress, one cardigan. One raincoat to wear over both outfits, two pairs of shoes so there was always one pair not wet. And occasionally, in times of exceptional hardship, the two outfits would diminish to one. School uniforms only. (Oh yes, and *combinations* – strange itchy wool garments, vest and panties in one, with soft-buttoned flaps in personal places.) If my sister and I wore matching dresses, my mother, now ninety, explained recently, it was because in wartime New Zealand clothes were in short supply and there'd be only one line of little girls' dresses in the shops when buying-time came round, once a year. And anyway art required it. Rita Angus liked it. And that was that. No-one would have asked our opinion anyway.

When I was sixteen I was asked to a party *with boys.* Let me explain that for most of my youth I lived in an all-female household and went to all-female schools. (This was in the school-uniform-only days.) I had obviously 'nothing to wear'. My mother said she would make me a dress. She scraped and saved and sent me out to buy material. I came back with a kind of diaphanous yellow and blue gauze. I was, at any rate in her eyes, a great big galumphing girl. Hopeless. We both agreed. It ended up with me not going at all, pretending to be ill, and because I had such an aversion to lies (as one does at sixteen) actually taking to my bed, and staring out of the barred window which stood between me and the London street, and seeing the brisk legs of passers-by and marvelling at the way everyone else seemed to know how to conduct their lives. I suspected this was to be the pattern of my life to come. And I was right. Mistake after mistake. There is no photograph of me at this party. I wasn't there, and just as well. Diaphanous yellow and blue.

Here's a picture of me in the mid-seventies, at a Writers' Award Ceremony. I am wearing a terrible, expensive, expansive dress with pleats in a kind of grey silky material which makes me look like a house. Prince Philip is handing out the awards. I remember sitting quietly at my table, waiting my turn when a dainty woman from New York, dressed in a gold skull-cap, a slinky gold-encrusted slip, little strappy sandals and with perfectly tanned arms, paused on her way back from the platform and said to me, 'God, you're so wonderful. You don't even *care.*'

'But I *do* care,' I wanted to cry after her. 'I *do*, I *do*! I was four hours in the hairdresser's this afternoon. Doesn't it *show*?' Of course, it didn't show. This was me, all attempts at style forever subsumed into the general *me-ness.* I hate her, that woman in the skull cap. I shall never forget her, I shall never forgive her. I got three awards that night. I got Best TV Drama, Best Radio Drama, and I can't remember the other one. Three Rosetta Stones, in heavy bronze. I expect skullcap got a consolation prize for Best Cracker Motto. The third time I went up on the platform Prince Philip said, 'This doesn't often happen. We've run out of conversation. You say rhubarb, rhubarb, rhubarb and I'll say rhubarb, rhubarb, rhubarb.' So we did, and the flash bulbs popped and the photographers did their stuff. Philip wasn't much on the sartorial front, either. Like me he tried, but like me it never worked. In his head, tux or not, he was a wearer of tweeds and plus fours. That was a comfort.

Here's me at a residential course for creative writers. I remember the faces, the people, even what they wrote. I can't remember their names. I'm wearing a deep-blue, sheeny, silk dress: a shirtwaister. I liked that dress. It had a row of tiny little mauve leather buttons down the front. It probably sounds like hell to you, but honestly it was okay, one of the few successful dresses I ever bought. It even had romantic associations. What became of it? Did I try ironing it and burned a hole in it? Did I forget to pick it up from the cleaners?

Or perhaps because I loved it I saved it, and it was one of the garments which ended bundled up and mouldy in a black plastic sack, along with a Bonnie Cashin pink mohair cape and a Bill Gibbs green wool gold embroidered jacket, and sundry other love objects, thrown out of the house when the marital storm broke? *Out with the trash! That's all you're worth! Goodbye!* I have the bleakest, darkest wardrobe now. Who wears anything but black, especially to parties. Brown sometimes gets a look in, or grey, or navy, then it's back to sinuous black for everyone, and translucent flesh, and long legs and glossy hair. But it's still black. We are all in mourning for former clothes, and past lives, best forgotten.

Of course I'd rather not remember. Every garment, a different resonance. So many other times it was me walking out of the house, taking nothing but a suitcase, leaving the old clothes behind along with the old life. *I want nothing of you, nothing, nothing, nothing!* Then another suitcase in another hall. Except of course it never works. Leave naked if you must, but you take yourself with you. The past catches up. Your medical and insurance records follow after you, pitter-pat, pitter-pat. Photographs find you. Family need you. Friends locate you. Throwing away the old doesn't mean ringing in the new. Since you can't rewrite the past you had better learn to live with it. The photographs go back in the box, neatly collated.

The run-up to Christmas, 1996; the power of prophecy.

The Journey to Mr Fox

Reader, I married him. The ring slips upon the finger. What is *Jane Eyre*, what is many a well-known novel which penetrates the archetype, which tells of transformation and destiny, but a fairy tale bereft of the trappings of enchantment? What we long to know, what we yearn to hear, happy endings for the well-intended, (so long as you keep to the rules, but first decipher the letters of fire) misfortune for the bad, true enough in a Jungian sense, just not in the real world. Swinegirl (little Jane Eyre) catches Prince (Mr Rochester). Froggish Mr Knightley, in Jane Austen's *Emma*, turns marriageable when kissed. Madame Bovary takes arsenic and meets her destiny. A likely and rewarding tale, this happy ever after in the head, and justice done: the unquiet fairy tale settled into novel form. You never know: perhaps the tellers of the tale, bards and novelists alike, in their obsessions, in their imaginings, in their picking up of trifles of misremembered sayings, the collective unconscious forging ahead, dream adding to dream, hark forward into a future, not backwards into a misty past. How would we ever know?

Reader, I married him. In 1992 I fell in love with and married a Mr Fox, in spite of the warnings in a fairy tale I knew well, having written an admonitory novel around the tale back in 1976: calling it, quite directly, *Words of Advice*. In the UK the title, as it happens, was changed to *Little Sisters – Words of Advice* sounding too like a book of moral strictures, which it was, for the comfort of British publishers. The tale was that of Lady Mary and Mr Fox: its instruction and warning – be bold, be bold, but not *too* bold. Evil presents itself as good:

penetrate that evil to discover it: keep your wits about you, and righteous rage will save you.

Let me tell you the story of Mr Fox and Lady Mary, as told by Gemma, rich and beautiful, to Elsa, poor and pretty, in this novel of mine *Words of Advice.*

Lady Mary the High Lord's daughter was betrothed by her father to the noble Mr Fox. The day before her wedding, too inquisitive for her own good, she'd stolen into Mr Fox's house to see what she could see. *Be bold* was written in letters of fire above the first door, and all within was grand and quiet: *Be bold* was written above the second door; and there too all was orderly and peaceful. But above the third door flamed the words *But not too bold.* Just a door, thought Lady Mary, like any other door, and in she went on tippy-toe. The other side of the third door she found a charnel house and her beloved Mr Fox feasting with his friends. A robber baron, that he was, her Mr Fox; the meal he ate was human flesh. As Lady Mary crouched hidden in her dark corner, watching, a severed finger flew across the room, and fell into her lap and on that finger she saw a ring. So she slipped the ring from her finger, and crept away with it and that night showed it to her brothers; and when the next morning came and with it her marriage day, and handsome Mr Fox came up the aisle to marry her, her brothers fell upon him and killed him; and so justice was done.

In the end it is the evil Mr Fox who is too bold, allowing himself to be discovered, and so destroying himself: not Lady Mary, whose boldness saves her: and the ring, of course, symbol of safety, though it clearly failed to help its original owner.

In the novel Gemma is married to a millionaire and is confined by a hysterical paralysis to a wheelchair. She has taken her nineteen-year-old house-guest, Elsa, under her wing, and persists in giving her unwanted advice by means of fairy tale. The author herself does much the same for the reader, using the novel as vehicle.

In familiar tell-tale sing-song rhythms, if not content, the novel begins thus:

> We all have friends who are richer than ourselves and they, you may be sure, have richer friends of their own. We are most of us within spitting distance of millionaires.
>
> Spit away – if that's what you feel like.
>
> But, after the manner of these things, Elsa, who has not a penny to her name (except the remnants of last week's pay packet) knows Victor, who is an antique dealer, who knows Hamish and Gemma, who are millionaires.
>
> And Victor and Elsa, one Friday evening, cursed or lucky things, sit in Victor's big new light-blue Volvo at the gates of Ditton House, where Hamish and Gemma live, and wait for the great teak veneered doors to open and let them through.
>
> Victor is forty-four. Elsa is nineteen, and his mistress. A year ago, when Victor was still a tax accountant, he fished Elsa out of his typist's pool. She flapped and wriggled a little, and then lay still, legs gently parted.

(Elsa – as I describe her, and I come to this novel almost as a stranger, since I haven't referred to it, let alone read it, for twenty years, and I daresay I barely read it then – writing a novel is so entirely a different matter from reading it – is 'abundantly lovely', she is the robust woodcutter's daughter, rather than the princess, who can feel the pea under the pile of mattresses. That's Gemma's style: in *Words of Advice* the two archetypes meet and battle it out.)

> She (Elsa) weighs twelve stone four pounds and is five feet eight inches tall. Her swelling bosom and rounded hips give ample promise of pneumatic bliss. Her skin is white; her cheeks red; her hair browny-gold, and thick, and long. Her face is perhaps rather heavy and her expression sleepy; but whether

that is good or bad depends on what you want her for. Her blue eyes, when she can be induced to raise them, are innocent enough. This evening Elsa is wearing her best: old jeans whose every tattered seam she knows and loves and a faded mauve shirt with a button missing.

Ah, she's beautiful; lush and not louche.

Another button pops now, as she bends.

(Victor is six-foot-two, weighs fourteen stone and is an established antique dealer. He is not a Prince; rather he is Emperor. And swinegirls and kitchenmaids are meant to consort with potential Princes, not established men of middle years. Trouble of some kind is bound to ensue.)

And behold, gliding down the long panelled hall to meet them, her powered wheelchair moving with the silence of the most expensive machinery, comes Gemma.

Seen from a distance she is a child: her smile radiant and full of expectation. As her chair approaches, years pass. She is twenty, twenty-five, thirty, thirty-five – older, older still. Or is that just a trick of the light? Because she lives in pain, or longs for death? And that is all her expectation.

Gemma stretches out her pretty hand to greet first Victor, then Elsa. She is young, after all. Barely thirty.

(After their initial meeting, in which Gemma insists on mistaking Elsa for Wendy, Victor's daughter, Elsa is sent without ceremony to her room.)

Elsa, embarrassed to the point of tears – (how she overflows, always; bubbling and erupting into the outside world: she blushes, she cries, she stumbles, she is sick; she gets diarrhoea or cystitis at the drop of a hat; she coughs up phlegm; her nose runs; as if there was far more of her than could ever easily be contained) – Elsa, snivelling, is obliged to follow the servants along ever narrowing corridors to a small room overlooking the central nexus of the house – the work area where the kitchens are, and the dustbins, and the compost heap, and the coal cellars. This room is as chaste and ordinary as the other was luxurious. It has cream walls, green painted woodwork, a narrow bed with white sheets and grey blankets, a locker, a basin, a plain white towel on a peg and a small yellowy piece of soap in the washbasin. There is no mirror, but under the window stands an old brown office desk. And on the desk is a new typewriter; manual, not electric. On the desk are stacked reams of typing paper: top, carbons, and flimsy in assorted colours. There is a tin filing cabinet – full of empty folders; waiting, but for what? – and a small wastepaper basket.

Elsa throws open the window, and leans out. She is four stories up. Her long hair falls over the sill and down over empty space.

She is frightened.

Elsa lies upon the bed and shivers. She does not like being alone. She is one of seven children. She is not a good typist. She tries, but even if she gets the words correct, sheets emerge from the machine crumpled, untidy and smudged. The typewriter sits on the desk like some unfair challenge; the filing cabinet like some test she knows she will fail: the drop from the window an unspoken threat.

Defenestrated!

A fairy story comes to Elsa's mind: that of the incompetent peasant girl who boasted of her prowess at weaving, and was shut up in the castle by the king and set to work weaving hanks of straw into gold. Has Elsa likewise claimed to be what she is not – a secretary, when in fact she can barely type a line without smudges and mistakes? Is her presumption now to be punished? And who is her Rumpelstiltskin to be; the dwarf who visits by night and performs the impossible task, claiming her first-born child unless she can guess his name?

(Is she to bear a child to Hamish? Surely this too is not required of Elsa?)

Oh, grief so harshly punished! And poor Rumpelstiltskin, fit only to be used and abused! This and many other bitter tales Elsa would later tell her brothers and sisters at bedtime.

But perhaps she is being too gloomy: perhaps the typewriter is coincidental: perhaps her nightly visitor will be the prince whose face must never be looked at, in case he's seen to be a toad after all. Well, easy enough not to look. Just to lie back and accept.

Or perhaps, since she is so clearly now imprisoned in a tower, snatched out of Victor's double bed by the witch Gemma, her prince will come to rescue her, climbing the tower, using her yellow hair as a rope? But how did that story end? Alas, he was toppled from the tower by the witch, and blinded by the brambles below, never to look on beauty again.

(Go too far and fate will get you! If the Prince had been content with serenading Rapunzel, had only looked but never touched, he might have survived with his sight intact: had the peasant girl at least learned how to weave flax into gold – at night class – she might have defied the witch – her mother, the sexual rival – and come down of her own account.)

Elsa shivers. Although there seems little forbidden to her about her own beauty, perhaps God has other ideas?

The door is pushed open. The Prince? The dwarf? The toad? But no, it is only Victor. He has to bend to enter the room. His high-domed, much-scarred head catches, nevertheless, on the lintel: he cries out in pain. Blood flows. Elsa laughs. He carries folders in his hands. Recomposed, he is brisk and businesslike.

'Gemma wants these in triplicate, Elsa,' he says. 'It's an inventory of all the things she wants sold.'

(More flax into gold, if you please!)

'You mean it's a working weekend?' Elsa is plaintive, dabbing his bald landing strip with tissue. 'I thought I was a proper guest.'

'Well –'

'They wouldn't ask Janice to type –'

(Janice is Victor's wife. Of course Victor has a wife.)

'Janice can't type. Women should be useful. You are. It's a compliment.'

(Elsa is mollified, but still complains and protests.)

'I'll make a dreadful mess of it now. I'm much too tired. I'll do it tomorrow.'

'But Gemma wants it by morning.'

'I'll do it after dinner.'

Even as she speaks, Elsa has the sensation that some fixed pattern of events has moved into place, and is now firmly locked, and that whatever she says or does now in this household will be according to destiny, and not in the least according to her own desire.

Or is it just that, throughout her childhood, whenever Elsa said 'I'll do it later' her mother slapped her? But no – our feelings of doom, our intimation of immutable fate, must surely be deeper than this.

(Elsa's suspicions are correct. She is locked into Rumplestiltskin mode. She must turn chaff into gold, or be lost.)

(The next day, the typing delivered on time – Hamish crept into the tower room and did it for her, to the highest standards – Gemma gives Elsa more unwanted advice.)

'You aren't going to stay a typist forever, I daresay,' murmurs Gemma.

'No,' says Elsa. 'Of course not.'

'Be careful,' says Gemma, suddenly and sharply. 'I know what you are thinking and I know where it can end. To be wanton, and yes, you are wanton – with your life, your sexuality, your future – is a dangerous matter. You are greedy and careless at the same time, and have made yourself a hundred times more stupid than you need be. Women do; they have to, if they are determined men shall be their masters; if they refuse to look both into the faces of men and into their own hearts.'

Elsa opens her mouth to speak.

'Be quiet,' says Gemma. 'Say nothing. I know it isn't comfortable. I know that self-knowledge is painful. I know that to think you are a princess and find you are a beggar-girl is very disagreeable. I know that to look at a Prince and find he is a toad is quite shocking. I also know, and you will probably never have the opportunity to find out, that to think you are a beggar-girl and end up a Princess is perfectly dreadful.'

Elsa blinks, startled.

'If I can read your heart, Elsa, it's because I can read my own. I have a story to tell. It's a fairy tale. I love fairy tales, don't you?'

'A bit.'

'I thought you would. Princes, toads, Princesses, beggar-girls – we all have to place ourselves as best we can.'

Elsa has the scent of triumph in her nostrils, the taste of sexual power between her soft red lips. Something instinctive and nasty surfaces, hardens, takes possession. Other women are her enemy, she perceives. Men are there to be made her allies, her stepping-stones to fulfilment and worldly success. Elsa looks sideways at Gemma and thinks 'Why, if I wanted I could have your husband too.' (Thin, dry, husk-like Hamish.) 'Then where would you be, Gemma,' thinks Elsa, 'with your unworkable legs and your crippled hand.'

(Gemma, like Lady Mary, has lost a finger, her ring finger. How she comes to lose it is the tale within the tale, and it is at this point that Gemma tells Elsa the story of Mr Fox.)

'What's so interesting about the story?' asks Elsa.

'What is so interesting about it,' says Gemma firmly, 'is that I heard it one night on someone else's transistor radio, read by Dame Edith Evans. I was on a train: I had a sleepless night in front of me. And the very next morning I met a Mr Fox and fell in love with him; and rings and fingers, or the lack of them, featured prominently in my life thereafter. Had you never noticed the way the secret world sends out signs and symbols into the ordinary world? It delivers our messages in the form of coincidences: Letters crossing in the post, unfamiliar tunes heard three times in one day, the way that blows of fate descend upon the same bowed shoulders, and beams of good fortune glow perpetually upon the blessed.

Fairy tales, as I said, are lived out daily. There is far more going on in the world than we ever imagine.'

'Just a coincidence,' muttered Elsa, disbelieving.

'*Just* a coincidence! I love Mr Fox and you say *just*?' Gemma is outraged. 'It was many years ago, as they used to say at the beginning of fairy tales, when the world was fresh and young – and so was I – but it was not imagination. It was in 1966.'

The tale outside the tale outside the tale, of course, validating Gemma's claim that fairy tales are lived out daily, is the author's falling in love ten years later with a perfectly decent Mr Fox and not a single brother stepping out of line to finish him off. Coincidence, as Elsa would maintain. The world is full of Foxes, and very few are robber barons.

With the relating of the tale Gemma is freed from the bonds of trauma and rises from her wheelchair to walk again: Elsa runs home to her mother and sisters and drinks cocoa before bed. The men drift off into other women's fantasies, circling within their own, as Princes will.

I was brought up on fairy tales – the traditional kind which never made much sense, found in my youth in Andrew Lang's many-coloured fairy-tale books – eleven in all, the Blue, Green, Red collections, and so on – before the days of their literary-academic deconstruction, before Bettleheim, before M. L. Von Franz. Lang was Professor of Philosophy at Oxford at the turn of the century: his view, later demoded, was that fairy tales were mere relics of savage customs and thoughts common to early man – such as the belief that animals can understand and speak with a human tongue.

The effect of these tales, so far as I could see, was to fill the heads of little girls with mystery, and provide them with those archetypes which make for unease – Why am I not slim as the Fairy Princess? Why are the Fairy Godmotherly gifts I proffer not magic? Why do I stay the beggar girl and the Prince just looks the other way? Why if I'm

Cinderella is there no ball to go to? Why are my good deeds not rewarded by fate? Why does my goose not lay golden eggs? and so forth. But these magically-written yet awkward tales at least acquainted me and many others with a turn of phrase which seemed part and parcel of the language of King James' bible. And of course provided us all with the resonances of a common folk history and culture, without which the contemporary young – whose fairy tales have to come in Disney form – are so much the poorer.

There were as well, for childhood reading, those other fairy tales which posed as traditional, but weren't – coming as they did from the clearly tormented minds of the brothers Grimm or the enchanted mind of Hans Christian Anderson, and were, to my mind, the better for their single, or dual, authorship, as a Beethoven variation improves on a folk-song theme. To my mind stories which have been handed down, verbally, over centuries, are on the Chinese whispery side of validity. You can waste a whole lot of life trying to analyse them, force them into genres, picking them over for non-existent wisdom. You need the genius of Jung to do it. For myself, as a child, Grimm's *Beauty and the Beast* at least made a kind of sense, as did *Snow White* and *Rose Red*; and Anderson's splinter of ice in Kay's heart, and Gerda's search for her cold lover, seemed all too true, as parable rather than exercise in archetype, and as for *The Little Mermaid*, forget Disney, the story was all too masochistically, romantically accurate. Little girls should not be allowed to read *The Little Mermaid* or they'll be inclined to walk on knives all their lives, (or succumb to the cosmetic surgeon; much the same thing) in their hope that the Prince will eventually love them. The transformation from ugly duckling to swan fills the pre-pubertal child with unreasonable hope. After the wintry ice of rejection, the warmth of sun and acceptance will surely come. Well, perhaps, and Hi there, Mr Fox.

It was only when I stood in the Hans Christian Anderson Museum in a little town in Denmark in the early eighties, and listened to a tape of Laurence Olivier reading aloud the story of *The Little Red Hen* (who thought the sky would fall upon her any minute) that I realised how much of that particular style I'd brought to my early novels. The grabbing of the reader by the throat – the urgency of tale-telling, bubbling over narrative – 'Listen, reader!' 'Spit away, if that's what you feel like!' which I thought was all my own. No such luck: Hans Christian Anderson, that's all, as read by the child that was me, on the hot dry Canterbury plains of New Zealand in 1936, re-written by me in sombre Somerset in 1976, set in London's Carnaby Street, 1966. But what ever changed? Human nature stays the same: in old fairy tales or new ones. Even your writer turns willingly into Mrs Fox, protected by a ring. Transformation wins, okay.

Passing on an inheritance, in the winter of 1995.

Letter to an Unborn Grandchild

A fax came up on my machine the other day; inch by slow inch it revealed itself as an ultrasonic scan of you in the womb, six months on from conception, transmitted via your father's, my son's, computer. It went to all friends and family members sufficiently au fait with technological matters to receive it. 'Hi there!' you said, in effect, three months before your birth, 'Hi there, here I am, in this brand new world you have created for me. No sooner here, than recorded. Those that can see, let them see.'

This picture of your unborn self came as both blessing and shock: the sheer marvel of new life was sufficient to overcome its translation into the digital world and out again, and leave a smile of pleasure behind. The shock was the realisation of how little mystery we have left ourselves, yet how much mystery remains. There you were, all spirit, in grainy black and white: your temperament and disposition already clear in the foetal curl, the thumb in the mouth, a matter of body language; I read you as determined, cheerful, and very much in charge of the processes that formed you. You are no-one's bit part player, you play no minor role in someone else's drama; you are the drama itself, and you know it.

I already know you are a girl, that your name will be Ella. I know your antecedents. You take half your genetic material from your father, who has half of mine and half his father's: half from your mother's side, likewise, and back in exponential halvings to Mother Eve out of Africa some half a million years back. (If we are to believe Richard

Dawkins, geneticist and evolutionary theoretician, that is, who writes so brilliantly about the stream of developing life through the aeons, and not some creationist, who'd have us all in God's image and sprung ready made from Adam's rib. But all notions, all tales of creation mythology, tell of equal marvels: don't you worry about the origin of life for the time being. Enough just to *be*, and glow at us from the womb.) On your father's side you come from English stock out of the Viking invasion, a thousand years ago, and Jewish immigration out of Eastern Europe at the turn of the century: on your mother's side you are part English, part Italian. We are all world citizens, remember that: the liveliest people are the least likely to stay where they were born. So see no virtue in staying home: choose for your children a father most likely to startle your parents. This way you serve nature's plan for diversity, though it may not make for a tranquil existence. And what is tranquillity but boredom.

Wherever you look in your family history you will find the demimonde: musicians, painters, sculptors, writers, poets, film-makers, people often disgraced, sometimes notable. Add to those a handful of entrepreneurs, politicians. There is without a doubt a restless tendency in the family, especially in the women. My grandmother, born in 1878, would tell me of her grandmother, Mary Frances, born in 1841, a sculptress, who left her husband to earn her own living writing poems about the villainy of men.

Between us we have made a world for you in which it is more difficult for men to be villainous than it used to be. As a corollary, alas, you will be expected to earn your own living. I hope for your sake you will find an easy way of doing it: that you will have some special skill which will be recognised and well rewarded, so you have energy left over for love. I hope you are pretty because good-looking women have an easier time and can pick and choose in life: but not too pretty, so you don't bother to develop empathy with others. To this end my mother's generation never praised little girls for their looks, and made expressions of love dependent upon good behaviour: your mother's generation find it natural to say to their daughters, 'How pretty you look' and to demonstrate love even when, especially when, it is least deserved. Today's child is superbly confident; and I'm sure I wish it for you, even though wondering where it will lead. My generation spent its childhood waiting and preparing for adulthood: yours spends its living now with the adult world in servitude. Lucky old you.

I do not want you to be a feminist, if by feminist is meant a woman who derides and despises men, in the same way as it was once customary for men to deride and despise women. I want you to be a feminist in the sense that you see yourself as a person first and of a certain gender second: I want you to live in a world in which this is possible. I want you to have children and make me a great grandmother, no matter how much I know rationally that these days, in the professional classes, it's sheer folly for a girl to have babies. All expense, making-do, childcare and anxiety. I am glad your mother had sense enough to disregard all sensible advice, so now you lie sucking your thumb and feeding up on faxes all over the land, declaring your unborn presence amongst us.

Already, Ella, I feel you are capable of having orchestrated the whole technological world into existence, the better to make this ingenious and unforgettable entrance by fax into it. You take after your charismatic father in this. He was always one for an entrance.

I want you to have your cake and eat it too. I want you to like men but be able to be faithful and ask me to the wedding: I've never been to a white wedding, certainly not my own. Let me stagger on my decrepit legs to yours. My mother, your great grandmother, sees our function in the world as that of scavengers. God flew off leaving the debris of creation behind, and the task of the human race is to sort through the mess, salvaging what is good, waste-not-want-notting. We are, she declares, the salvage team of the universe. I hope you will leave the world a better place then when you entered it, but not to be too earnest about it. I hope you will be able to make others laugh: and that rooms light up when you come into them. I want you to be head-girl of your school, and get a first in Economics and be Miss

World as well, if you choose to. I want you to solve every paradox that ever puzzled me.

Over to you, Ella. I'm quite sure, from the way you suck your thumb, contemplate existence and conserve your energy for the great push into the bright, dangerous life of the world, that you'll live up to our expectations and be known through history as the solver of GUM, the Great Universal Mystery, and GUP, the Great Universal Paradox; why we are born in the first place, and why it's so difficult once we're here. May you be both High Priestess and Chief Scientist. Unto us a child is born. Welcome. May you grow up to create the fine, new, exultant Garden of Eden of our dreams. I'll swear we're nearly there.

Bibliographical Note

'Pity a Poor Government' *The Scotsman* Millennium Lecture, Edinburgh and published in *The Scotsman*, 1998; *Independent*, 1998

'Behind the Rural Myth' published in *The Daily Telegraph*, 1998

'Mothers, Who Needs 'Em?' published in *Mail on Sunday*, 1998

'The Feminisation of Politics' published in *Harpers Bazaar* (New York), 1998

'What This Country Needs Is:' published in *New Statesman*, 1997

'Take the Toys from the Boys' published in *The Observer*, 1999

'Girls on Top' published in *Mail on Sunday*, 1997

'The Fish and the Bicycle' published in *Good Housekeeping*, 1998

'Pity the Poor Men' published in *Vogue* (Germany), 1998

'Today's Mother – Bonded and Double-binded' published in *Independent on Sunday*, 1997

'Princesses and Other Myths' published in *Washington Post*, 1995

'Three Cheers for the Duchess of York!' published in *Allure* (New York), 1995

'Empress of Hearts' published in *Washington Post*, 1995

'Letter from London' published in *Washington Post*, 1995

'A Royal Divorce' published in *New York Times*, 1996

'An Open Letter to the Queen of England' published in *Die Zeit* (Germany), 1996

'Loving, Hating and Mourning – Diana, Princess of Wales' published in *Marie Claire* (Germany), 1997

'Money, Law and Madness, A Sample of One' Lecture at Birmingham's Literature and Psychiatry Conference, 1996

'Mind at the End of its Tether' published in *The Guardian*, 1997

'Mice in Mazes – Ourselves Confused' Lecture at The Royal Society of Medicine, 1995

'Kissing-and-Telling in Britain Today' published in *New York Times*, 1995

'Goodbye, John Major' published in *New Statesman*, 1997

'White Hope or Sell Out?' published in *Süddeutsche Zeitung* (Germany), 1996

'Over to You, Tony' published in *The Guardian*, 1997

'Protector Blair's Britain' published in *New York Times*, 1997

'Roseanne Dances' published in *The Daily Telegraph*, 1994

'Guess Who's Coming to Lunch' published in *Allure* (New York), 1996

'A Star is Reborn in 1997' published in *Mail on Sunday*, 1997

'Mindy in the Nashville Night with Fireflies' published in *The Daily Telegraph*, 1997

'Mindy over Tea with Minders' published in *The Express*, 1998

'But Has Dolly Got a Soul' published in *Mail on Sunday*, 1997

'Gaultier's Halo' published in *The Tatler*, 1995

'The London I Love' published in *Geo* (Germany), 1997

'My Thirty Years in Advertising' published in *Campaign*, 1998

'Joining the Writers' Introduction to *Writers' & Artists' Yearbook, 1999*, 1999

'Snip-snip' published in *Allure* (New York), 1995

'Yikes! The Frock in the Photograph' published in *Vogue* (New York), 1998

'The Journey to Mr Fox' published in *Into the Mirror: Anthology of Women on Fairytales*, 1997

'Letter to an Unborn Grandchild' published in *Letter to My Grandchild*, edited by Liv Ullmann, 1998